Clearing
Out

Clearing Out

A Novel

Helene Uri

Translated by Barbara Sjoholm

UNIVERSITY OF MINNESOTA PRESS
Minneapolis
London

This translation has been published with the financial support of NORLA.

Portions of *Clearing Out* were previously published in *Two Lines* and *Scandinavian Review*.

First published in Norwegian as *Rydde ut* by Gyldendal Norsk Forlag, 2013. Copyright 2013 by Gyldendal Norsk Forlag AS. All rights reserved.

Translation copyright 2019 by Barbara Sjoholm

Published by the University of Minnesota Press
111 Third Avenue South, Suite 290
Minneapolis, MN 55401-2520
http://www.upress.umn.edu

A Cataloging-in-Publication record for this book is available from the Library of Congress.
ISBN 978-1-5179-0652-8 (hc)
ISBN 978-1-5179-0894-2 (pb)

Printed in the United States of America on acid-free paper

The University of Minnesota is an equal-opportunity educator and employer.

30 29 28 27 26 25 24   10 9 8 7 6 5 4 3 2 1

To Helle and Ingvild

The heather on the tussocks is dry and crunches when she steps on it. In between the tussocks is wet moss, creeping rose, butterwort, and bog cotton. She moves from tussock to tussock, jumping if necessary. At each step the pack thumps against the small of her back, but that doesn't bother her. Anyway, the pack is light; it holds only a box of matches, wool socks, a plastic container with a bag of pancake mix, and an aluminum pan with a collapsible handle.

A bird, dark gray and medium sized, flutters up right in front of her. She doesn't manage to see what kind of bird it is, and she probably wouldn't have known its name anyway. She remains standing with one leg on a tussock and the other already planted on the next. Her eyes follow the bird a long time. There are no trees, no mountains it can disappear behind. The sky is bigger than any other place. Bigger and bluer.

She's certain that if she captured the air in a jam jar, a Mason jar, it would still continue to be blue. If she had anything like that in her pack she would have screwed off the lid, swung the jar a couple of times, stretching her arm high above her head and hurrying to put the lid on again. That way she could have had the full jar with her at home, on the desk, to the right of the computer, next to the ceramic pig, could have looked at it and enjoyed the blue color. And every time she needed it, she could have unscrewed the lid just a little, stuck her nose down inside, and breathed in the warm, moist air, so pure that it is full of smells.

A man's voice calls, "Ellinor!"

"I'm coming."

And she comes toward me. She's clear to me now. The features of her face, her hair, the pores on her nose. The pink, fresh weave of her lung cells. Her thoughts. I see everything. But she goes past me, toward the man who called, she doesn't notice me—or did she wave to me as she passed? In a crevice in the mountain lies the corpse of a *stallo*. *Stallo*s are evil creatures who appear to be people but are bigger and monstrously stronger. Fortunately, they are also rather easily fooled.

Perhaps I haven't been curious enough. Perhaps I should have been more persistent when I still had the chance.

My father was the silent type. Mama, on the other hand, has always talked incessantly about her family. Mama is from Oslo; her relatives are from the east and west of the country. They're named Uri and Østbye, Hovdenak and Alstad. They are people I have a general overview of, people I've seen pictures of, pictures that hang on the walls of my childhood home or in the rooms of the family farm in Romsdalen. Paintings in gilded wooden frames. Photographs in dark, glossy frames and in worn leather albums with heavy pages. Uri, Østbye, Hovdenak, Alstad, Friisvold, Linge, Mustad. On her side of the family you find a sheriff, a mayor, several engineers, teachers and dentists, the owner of an iron foundry. I know tons of stories about them, about Grandpa, who went to military academy before he began at the Norwegian Institute of Technology, about my great-grandparents, about a child who died at five while on a visit to her grandmother in the country, about the unusually clever horse Bjørke, who could climb stairs, about Grandma, who lost her hair in the influenza epidemic of 1919, about ration cards, blackout curtains, and Germans, about an earlier ancestor who walked all the way from Romsdalen to

Kristiania in the middle of the 1800s to learn midwifery at the Royal Hospital.

I know much less about Papa's side of the family. But some things I know. Papa grew up in Notodden, a town in Telemark. Kjell Nilsen, born in 1923. His mother, my grandmother, who just managed to see both my daughters before she died at almost a hundred years old. She spoke with the soft burr of southwest Norway, though she came from Sarpsborg in Eastern Norway. Sweet Grandmother Astrid, with narrow, sloping shoulders, so narrow and so sloping that she had to tie the straps of her undershirt together with a ribbon behind her back so it wouldn't slip off. I have shoulders like a wine bottle, she said. On her side of the family were shipowners and captains from the south of Norway, along with a rather well-known painter. Astrid's father was a postmaster. Grandmother herself was an engineer. Norway's first female engineer, it's said. I haven't investigated more deeply whether that's true or whether it's almost true. In any case, she was born in 1898, and there were certainly not many women born in that time who were educated as engineers. I'm proud of my father's mother, and I liked to visit her in Notodden and be given mutton-and-cabbage stew and to drink rosehip tea from thin white cups, among her old furniture, which she had inherited from her parents and grandparents.

My father's father, Nicolai Nilsen, was also an engineer. The family tree is thick with engineers. Nicolai and Astrid. My mother's father. Both my parents, and a long line of other relatives: uncles, granduncles, nephews, second cousins. Engineers on both sides, three generations back, in my generation and the generation after me.

You can claim this is a family myth, or in any case it's one of the family myths that's often repeated, this myth about every second relative being an engineer, and it's something I myself can bring up, flaunt, say something about it being an aberration that I, born into a family of technologists, ended up as a linguist and author. I know I've mentioned this in some interviews.

I know my father's father was educated somewhere or other in the United States. I know he comes from the north of Norway, but I haven't known much more.

Grandmother had a picture of him on the wall, in an oval, dark-stained wooden frame. Nicolai Nilsen must have been a handsome man. He has wrinkles between his brows and looks seriously into the camera, out into life; he looks right at the one who looks at him. I'm quite certain that Grandmother and Papa have looked a good deal at this photograph. Grandfather has a narrow face, blond hair, high cheekbones. Now it's me he looks at, his granddaughter, whom he will never meet. He resembles Papa. Grandpa died in 1937, when Papa was fourteen. My own father died in 1994. I've often thought about him in the years since. My thoughts have touched on Grandmother Astrid, too. I've thought about her with respect and admiration, and with subdued, resigned despair, not because she died—she departed in her ninety-ninth year and was of the opinion she had lived a full life—but because she was my link to Papa and Papa's part of the family. When she died, two years after her oldest son, the link was broken.

Since Papa died before Grandmother, our part of the inheritance went directly from her to my sister and me. In my dining room stands a black, old-fashioned secretary decorated with golden stripes. It comes from her relatives in Southern Norway, and Grandmother said, when I was small, that it was over two hundred years old. I was also the one who inherited her hot chocolate service, a white service for twelve, with a silver pot. I have many things from her, lamps, chairs, tablecloths. Grandmother generously distributed many of her things while she was still alive. You can't take anything with you when you die, she always said.

But some of the things I remember best from when I was small must have gone to others. There are three objects in particular that disappeared, yet when I think about them, they appear almost like magic. Each time we visited Grandmother Astrid in Notodden I had to look at them. One was a glass paperweight. It was the size and shape of half an apple and was transparent; red, yellow, blue canes rose from the bottom and ended in little flowers. This paperweight was one of the most beautiful things I knew. As an adult I've seen something similar in Italy, and when I now, as I write this, look online for images of "paperweight," right away I find something that reminds me of Grandmother's. Venetian, it appears to be.

On the fireplace mantel, next to the paperweight, Grandmother had a conch. A shell about as large as my child's hand. It was oval and smooth, white with brown flecks, and pink around the opening. And on its top *Fader vår* was carved, such that the letters were raised. If I turned it and held the crack to my ear, I heard the seven seas sigh. When I search for "carved cowrie," I see shells precisely like Grandmother's, except that the text on these snail shells is in English: "Our Father." You can even buy them on eBay for a few dollars. Just the word eBay destroys the magic.

The third miracle at Grandmother's was the puzzle cross. In one of the drawers she had a folder with some flat game pieces. I don't remember the number, but there couldn't have been more than seven or eight. These wooden pieces could be moved around to make a cross. It was just as difficult every time, and that was why it was called a *tankekors,* literally, a thought cross. When I search for *tankekors,* I encounter the word only in a figurative sense: puzzle, paradox, self-contradiction. I try other word combinations, cross puzzle

wood, but I don't hit on anything that resembles what Grand-
mother had, aside from an excerpt from my first novel, where
I mention a wooden-cross puzzle. Grandmother's, of course.
I try in English, but even a world language is not enough.
Perhaps I will find something similar one day. I must say, like
Mama: *Qui vivra verra.*

~~~

It was time that autumn to begin a new novel. The last one
was set in Oslo. Now I wanted another setting. Finnmark. The
thought appeared and wouldn't leave again. Finnmark. I had
often thought I would write something from Western Norway, where I'd spent a lot of time and where my mother's
side of the family originally came from. But no, it had to be
Finnmark. Did I think at that point that my father's father
came from Finnmark? I no longer know. I probably would
have remembered, if I'd thought about it, but for me there had
never been clear associations between Grandpa and Finnmark.
Grandfather was *from the North.* I don't believe it had ever been
more specific in my mind than that: from the North. Perhaps,
all the same, it was a desire to take hold of the connections
before they dissolved and disappeared completely.

I've been to all the Norwegian counties several times but
never to Finnmark. Yet I sat in our apartment in Oslo, looking
out at the wet, licorice-black sidewalk, and insisted on Finnmark. A woman from Oslo travels to Finnmark. What happens with that woman there? Who does she meet? Why does
she travel there? What is she traveling away from? I looked
at the city streets, at the small lawns in front of the entrances,
the neatly clipped, leafless hedges, the buildings from the past
century with their towers and spires and ornaments; at the end
of the street I can just barely see the hill of Grefsenkollen if I
tilt my head and lift myself up a bit from the chair. It's likely

the tops of the trees in the Palace Park I see if I turn my head to the right. I sat with a notebook, as I always do when I begin a new book project, glanced at the notes I'd taken earlier, tried to clarify the ideas, gather them, connect them. The cat curled up in a ball on the windowsill and stared, offended, at the rain. Could this main character of mine—whatever she's called—be a linguist? A philologist? I bit the tip of my pen; the plastic splintered between my teeth. The cat turned just slightly to cast a golden glance at me before it went back to concentrating on the street. The raindrops rolled down the windowpanes, thick, vertical trails of water. Between two wet trails, she popped up. Like a shadow without a face, without flesh or blood, but all the same it was her. Could she be called Ellinor? Yes, that was her name. Ellinor Smidt. She loves the smell of coffee, and she knows she could have been a good mother. Now she sits right next to me, in the chair by the desk, where the cat usually sleeps when it's not at one of its fixed lookout posts. She'll get cat hair on her slacks, not that she'd worry about that. She's quite careless of her appearance.

Ellinor snorts. The cat turned around again, but this time looked past me and at the chair alongside the desk. The pen was still in my mouth, between the molars on the right side. It crunched again, a splinter broke off and fell against my tongue. I took the pen from my mouth, removed the plastic splinter. Well, maybe not careless, but if Ellinor wants to sit in a chair, she won't let herself be stopped by cat hair. It can be brushed off. If she feels like it. If she feels like bothering.

Toward the end of the year, I made a clumsy attempt at a chapter about Ellinor. Ellinor Smidt is in her early forties. She is separated from Tom, who is probably a couple of years older. Ellinor has a PhD in linguistics. All the same, she is not strongly ambitious; she's not like some of her colleagues, will-

ing to sacrifice everything for an academic career. Ellinor herself believes she is a restrained, calm type who doesn't worry
about too much, whether it's an academic career, her clothes,
or seeing the right films. And to a certain degree, she's correct.
She sees the films she wants to, allows comfort to guide her,
not elegance. She takes a long time with her master's thesis,
starts with something that will never become anything, or at
least something that Ellinor believes is good enough, gives it
up, completes another. She has three or four rather close female friends, but loses contact with a study friend who has a
baby just a few weeks after the exam results are announced and
the oral exam is over.

After her master's degree Ellinor ekes out two years of
teaching at a community college while she quite often thinks
she should perhaps apply for a grant, that it would be nice to
have a doctorate. She is a frequent visitor to the local library.
One day she remains standing at the shelf with books on pregnancy, births, infant care. Instead of returning home she goes
over to her father's. He makes her coffee. "Are you worried
about something?" he asks. She shakes her head. Still, he holds
her hand, grasps her index and middle fingers and squeezes
them. She makes him dinner, they talk for a long time about
her mother, have one of the ritual conversations they've had so
many times, the same questions and answers, the same words
as always.

"When I was little . . ."

"Yes, my girl, when you were little."

"And Mama was alive . . ."

"Yes, when your mother was alive."

"Did Mama love me?"

"She loved you more than anyone. You were her troll
baby, her chicky girl . . ."

"Chick chicky. Did she sing to me?"

"Every evening."

"What did Mama sing to me?"

"She sang Mama's song."

One day Ellinor decides to apply for a fellowship. Now I'm doing it! Her on-and-off ex-boyfriend from the teachers' lounge, a historian with a short beard, encourages her. And in between mediocre sex with the bearded historian, corrections to Spanish exercises and Norwegian compositions, she writes a project description (about morphosyntactical structure and s-fugues) and sends it in along with letters of reference, a CV, and a publication list. Before summer she receives a notice that she is the third-in-line nominee to a single available fellowship at the university. She shrugs her shoulders, acknowledges that she *knew* it would end like this and it doesn't matter. She'll continue to live her teacher's life with lots of compositions, lots of special exams, and lots of elementary Spanish grammatical errors (shouldn't it be terribly easy to remember the difference between *ser* and *estar*?). She likes to teach. And what is this idea, really, about a doctorate? Other than vanity?

On the evening of December 20, I read through what I've written so far. I sit in bed in our bedroom at the Svea country house. Christmas is almost here. The document about Ellinor is helpless, dead. Like a catalog text. I know it must be this way. It takes time. And either Ellinor starts to materialize or I have to begin anew. It doesn't work to force it. Mama calls to me from below. She needs help going to the toilet. I head unwillingly down the stairs. She apologizes. I assure her it's no problem. When I come back up, I add to the paragraph about the two Spanish verbs, both meaning "to be," and close the laptop's screen. I won't get any further now.

During the night I dream of Ellinor. No, actually I didn't

do that. It happened in the morning, and I was almost awake, so perhaps I didn't dream, only thought, but the thoughts flew like dreams. Ellinor is indignant. She has never disguised the fact that she wants children. Not in front of others, not in front of herself. No, no, I say, raising my hands defensively, apologizing, that wasn't how I meant it. Of course Ellinor wants a family most of all, she admits that (*admits*, I think scornfully, know-it-all that I am). She just hasn't found the man she wants to make a family with. She has realistically assessed things but always comes to the same conclusion: she wants children, there's nothing she would rather have than that, but she doesn't want it with precisely the one she's with at the moment. Not with Pierre, not with the historian, not with any other man she's been in a relationship with. "It takes a long time to find the man who'll be the father to one's children," I say, because what else can I say? "For you it didn't take a long time." "That's true," I say.

I set the table, make tea. Coffee for Mama. She needs help in the bathroom. I say, I'm coming now. She says she doesn't like to ask me for help. She always says that. I never answer her, just do what I must do. The children come downstairs in a Christmasy mood, and both are clearly inclined to show their best side. In the afternoon Ingolv is arriving. The children will bake chocolate cookies. We've already made chocolate macaroons. Mama says she'll continue with the Danish mystery she began when she was last here. Mama's mouth has opened, soon she'll begin to snore. I go upstairs again and get settled with Ellinor.

In June the top person on the fellowship list receives a job offer from MIT, and the second decides he would rather have a lucrative consulting job in the private sector. When Ellinor is told the position as a university fellow is hers if she wants it, she's happy at first but almost immediately begins to worry. How will she manage to write an entire dissertation? And even supposing she manages it, how will she be able to stand in an auditorium and defend it? By this point, the historian, who has such a peripheral role in the novel that he doesn't need a name, has found another woman, so he no longer encourages Ellinor; yet when it comes down to it, she doesn't need encouragement. She knows that. I know that. In any case, she says a grateful yes to the position. And she'll surely manage both the dissertation and the defense.

"We don't have any more almonds," my youngest calls accusingly from downstairs.

"Yes we do, there are two bags on the shelf in the basement."

"What?"

I go out into the hall, lean over the railing. "Look in the basement!"

Ellinor Smidt is a fellow at the University of Oslo for four years. Like many others she doesn't finish her dissertation in the course of the stipulated time. She works as a substitute instructor and an adjunct and defends a few days before she turns thirty-seven.

Four years ago she'd met Tom. She has the immediate feeling this is different. Or is it only something she imagines? She comes to understand that Tom is the right one. Once having dared to think such a thought, she continues to call it forth, to relish it. Tom and Ellinor. Ellinor and Tom. They talk about getting married. Tom longs to be a father, he says. Preferably right away. Ellinor argues that it's probably best to wait until she's defended her dissertation. She has dreamed of children, she has wished for children so intensely—I *imagine* it, she says—but perhaps it's most sensible to wait until she's finished. Tom hints in a friendly way about her age, that, on the other hand, it could be sensible to . . . Ellinor doesn't answer, she shakes her head slightly. A memory rises up in her consciousness and vanishes again before she's really able to hold on to it. She stands by a wire fence and sees the rear lights of her father's car disappear. She doesn't make a doctor's appointment, and the IUD stays where it is.

But the day after her defense, early in the morning, she has a doctor's appointment. She's answered yes to the question of whether she needs to get in quickly and has been given an appointment with a different doctor at the clinic since her regular doctor is on vacation. Without embarrassment she puts a foot in each stirrup and scoots her bottom forward to the strange doctor's waiting hands. She takes a breath to say something about the defense, about children, and her age, but it's over before she's said a word. She's barely registered a sharp pain before it's gone.

She makes the bed with newly purchased sheets, sets a candle on Tom's bedside table and the biggest bouquet of all the flowers she received the day before on the chest of drawers. *Dear doctor! I am so proud of you. What a presentation! Papa.* But now is the moment when she wants to achieve something. She shoves her fear away and feels certain.

Yes, I moved things along with Ellinor Smidt that Christmas, but she's not in place yet. At the moment she's artificial. She irritates me. More strongly the more I write. All the same, I have to continue. She will not let me go. Ellinor holds me fast. She is newly separated, Tom has moved out of their shared apartment, which strictly speaking is Ellinor's, inherited from her father's unmarried aunt. She grows more and more depressed, less and less enterprising. She's stopped exercising,

constantly postpones beginning work on copyediting assign-
ments, which is what she makes most money doing. I allow
her to look for a research assistant position on a project about
language extermination and the Sami language. The position
would mean she has to move to Finnmark for a period of time.
Like Tom, I abandon her there, in the apartment. She barely
can stand to wash her hair, eats almost nothing but takeout
food and candy, but at least she has sent in a job application.
She doesn't believe she'll get the job, but I know better. Because I don't just know better. I'm all-knowing.

I celebrate Christmas with my husband, daughters, and my
mother, and the first chapter about Ellinor is, if nothing else, a
beginning to something that can perhaps be more.

It's a fine but snow-poor Christmas in Eastern Norway. We
are at Svea, our small farm on the Randsfjord, where we've
been every Christmas since we bought it. Ingolv, the children,
and me. Earlier, Mama spent every other year with my sister.
The last years she's been with us every year.

Mama, the children, and I have been here since December
20. We baked Christmas buns, and she looked on and tasted.
On the twenty-second we toasted almonds, and Mama says,
as she and Papa used to say every year in Swedish: *Dan före
dan doppar,* meaning it's the day to throw bread in the pot to
soften it.

The day before Christmas Eve we chopped down and
decorated the tree, and she insisted on more lights on one side.
On Christmas Eve we roasted pork ribs, made red cabbage
and fruit salad while she rested. For the first time she hasn't
asked to read what I'm writing. She hasn't even asked what
I'm working on. She hasn't had the strength to change clothes
while she's been at Svea, only put a jacket on over her pajamas.

But today my youngest has helped her grandmother dress herself in what has been her Christmas outfit the last years: black sweater, black skirt, which has become longer and longer on her, with a red patterned border on the hem.

She can't manage to circle the Christmas tree. She sits on one of the chairs by the Niels Møller dining table and looks at the four of us and at the top of the tree with its shiny stars. Our arms don't stretch around, we have miserable singing voices, we get the verses mixed up and don't remember the words. But we sing the same songs as every year. Everyone laughs. Mama laughs loudest, but when we sing the last stanza of "Oh Joyful Christmas," the one that goes

> My hand reaches out with gladness
> Hurry and give me your hand
> This is how we knit love's holy bonds
> And promise to love one another,

she cries.

I throw away chewed ribs, clean off the hardened rib fat with a paper towel before I put the platter in the dishwasher. Ingolv drives Mama back to Oslo late on Christmas Eve. She's tired, "not up to snuff," as she says, and is admitted to Ullevål Hospital the day after. We empty her mailbox and put the Christmas presents she received from us on her dining room table. She is moved to the rehab unit at Tåsenhjemmet nursing home; she's thin and weak, can't get out of the wheelchair, but she does well, drinks red wine for dinner, looks forward to coming home, is optimistic and happy. We drive back to Svea and spend the last week of the holiday there. With a guilty conscience. Go on, says Mama.

In January I continue to write, looking out at the slowed-down city streets and trying to bring Ellinor to life. I begin to have more confidence in her. Ellinor has no great confidence in herself. She's convinced that she's going to live just as she does now until she's old, scraping by as a freelancer, growing lazy and uglier, without exercising, without eating anything but prepared food in plastic pouches or candy chock-full of artificial colors and flavors. Not even managing to brush cat hair off her slacks. But she doesn't have a cat. And she insists that nothing matters, that she's quite fine, thanks.

One Saturday morning in the middle of January, I'm on my way to eat sushi with a girlfriend. The cell phone rings down inside my purse. I pull off my gloves, stand in an ice-cold wind on the sidewalk in front of the American Embassy, fish out the phone, and answer with my name. Mama is weak, and I'm uneasy getting calls from numbers I don't know. It's a woman speaking Northern Norwegian. She introduces herself, is called something I've forgotten a second later, says something I don't quite follow, because I'm certain that this is a librarian from Narvik or Mo i Rana who wants me to fly to Trondheim, change to a Widerøe jet, take a taxi to the library, speak to twenty-five people, spend the night at a mediocre hotel, get up at the crack of dawn, and fly back to Gardermoen airport, after which I'll fill out a reimbursement form from the Norwegian Writers' Center for two thousand kroner. I think about how I'll phrase it—that it's very nice to be asked but I unfortunately have no time now. I've in fact set aside time to write. I have plans for a novel from Finnmark, something about the Oslo woman Ellinor Smidt and her encounter with the Sami language. The last part I haven't planned to say at all, but this is the novel I'm going to write, so I must say no to the library visits for the time being. But the woman says something completely different. She says she is a relative. She's calling from Hammerfest, she says, and she is the granddaughter of one of my Grandfather Nicolai's siblings. Oh, I say, and my hand is completely numb with cold, my fingers change their grip, and I'm afraid I'll drop the phone. She is doing genealogical research and would like to have the birth dates for me and my silent sister, our spouses (she says "spouse," it sounds formal), and my children. Somebody else is trying to contact me, and I take the phone from my ear and see it's the friend I'm meeting. But I continue to talk with the Northern Norwegian woman, giving her the dates and ages. I say I'd love to see the family tree when it's finished, if she could send it to me by email. She doesn't have email, she says, but she can send it to me in the mail when it's finished. My friend, whom I should have met ten minutes ago, rings over and over. I hear it in the form of a short break in the conversation with the relative whose name I don't remember. I must hang up, I say. The hand holding the phone is frozen stiff. My friend must also be chilled to death. All the same I save the number on the phone before I call her back. *Relative,* I write.

Saturday lunchtime at a little sushi place near Frogner Park. I've never quite noticed this restaurant before, even though the name is in sunflower-yellow neon letters over the door. Eating

17

spots disappear, and new ones pop up. We're cold through and through, one of us from waiting for the other on the appointed corner and the other from standing on the sidewalk outside the American Embassy, talking on the telephone without gloves. We lean toward each other in the steamy warmth, drinking green tea, talking in low voices about our children, my two girls, her two boys, about our winter vacations, about a shared friend with a hopeless husband. The sushi is no more than average. At the neighboring table sits a Vietnamese family. At least I believe they are Vietnamese, but perhaps they're Chinese, perhaps even Japanese. At the table on the other side sits a couple in love, holding each other's hands tightly, his left, her right. They look as though they're afraid to let go. They hold on as if they're afraid the other will disappear if they let go. He bends over the table and with his right hand brushes away something from the corner of her mouth, perhaps a stray grain of rice. A tender, loving, and quite unnecessary gesture, probably with a touch of complacency, the smugness of ownership.

A woman in her early forties comes in and orders takeout. She looks as though she isn't bothered by how she appears, as if she doesn't know she has something about her. A radiance. A relaxed solidity. I don't know. She stares just a second too long at us, and I smile cautiously at her, in case she recognizes me and has even read some of my books.

I think about the relative. Hammerfest. I've never had any connection to Hammerfest (wasn't it there they got street lighting so early?), and now I have a relative there, probably several relatives. I have both the desire and no desire to tell this to my friend. Usually I say far too much, right away, so I don't understand why I hesitate. Perhaps I'm afraid that the meaning will be reduced when I dress the experience in words. It's so large inside me, perhaps I distrust that words will do it justice.

But of course I tell her. I can't let it be. That's how I am. I probably have it from Mama and her side of the family. And usually I have faith in words. My friend shakes her head as she listens. A new pot of tea appears on the table, but we don't touch either the tea or the food while I speak.

It's a sign, she says when I'm finished. A sign, clearly as a joke, but probably also to give voice to what is an unreal co-incidence. For once I don't say anything more, putting a bite of salmon and avocado in my mouth, chewing longer than is needed. I chew, shake my head. You can write yourself into the book, she says. No, I say. And me! says my friend. I don't write that way, I say, have never done it and will never do it. Oh yes you will, says my friend. I can promise you here and now that I'll never write a book with myself in it, I say irritably and pour more tea.

Afterward I go home. I sit in the kitchen, in one of the two easy chairs by the window. I take the cell phone, pull up *Relative* on the contact list, make certain that her number is still there. Then I go online and look for the name of my grand-father: Nicolai Nilsen. Several hundred thousand hits. Nicolai Nilsen is on Facebook. He has a courier service. He's done well in a ski competition. He lives in Drammen. Another lives in Oslo. One has posted pictures of a dog. None of the hits appear to have anything to do with my grandfather, who came from the North, who had high cheekbones, who died in 1937. In a flash I remember what I think is the name of the place he comes from: Bismervik. I search again. And I find him.

Nilssen it's written for some reason or other, with two *s*'s, that's not right, but it must be him. It's in a census from 1910, from Hammerfest Township. My father's father, born in 1896. In 1910 Nicolai isn't living at home in Bismervik on the island of Sørøya. Residence unknown, *probably Alten*. After his fa-ther's name, Ole Nilssen, are two letters: *lf.* His wife is *n*. After

all the children is the letter *b*. In the introduction to the registry I find the codes: *b* stands for blended, *n* for Norwegian,
lf for *lappisk fastboende,* settled Lapp. My great-grandfather was
Sami. Sami. No one ever told me that.

I know my father was born in 1923 in Kristiansand. I know
he is the eldest of three sons. I assume that Nicolai and Astrid married in 1922. In 1910 Nicolai's parents told the government census takers they weren't quite certain where their
son was, but that he was probably in Alta—or they must have
known that, the boy was only fourteen, perhaps it's a technical
detail. As long as he himself wasn't present, it had to be done
this way.

At some point in the period between 1910 and 1922, Nicolai Nilsen moved from Finnmark to the United States, where
he was educated, either at a university or more likely at a technical school, after which he must have chosen to move back
to Norway. He must have lived in Eastern Norway; in any
case, he met Astrid, and they fell in love. Perhaps it was spring
when they met, and they went walking together all summer,
kissing and unable to stop smiling at each other. Perhaps they
held each other's hands tightly, his big left hand around her
slender right hand, perhaps they looked like they were afraid
the other would disappear if they let go. Perhaps Nicolai bent
over and brushed a crumb from the corner of Astrid's mouth.
A tender, loving, and completely unnecessary gesture. Com-
placent ownership? The engagement must have been a large
leap upward for Nicolai. And maybe it was different. Maybe
they weren't in love at all. Perhaps they got engaged for completely different reasons. No, I can't go down those roads. I
knew my grandmother. I still recall what it was like to give her

a hug, remember the dry, carnation-like smell. I see before me the undersides of her arms, the one long earlobe, the permanent waves. If it had been Ellinor's grandmother, I could have gone into the darkness and perhaps found bruises, coercion, an unwanted pregnancy. Or I could have found a fraud who did more than he should have to get ahead. But now I won't do that. Astrid and Nicolai were in love, went on walks, and held hands tightly. When I don't know anything, when no one has told me about that time, it must be just as I imagine it. Love and summertime.

The first summer my mother's mother was in love with my mother's father, she picked a large bouquet with as many kinds of flowers as she could find, and around each stalk she tied a piece of sewing thread with a small paper that had the name of the flower written in elegantly looped script. Grandma believed Grandpa needed to learn the names of many wildflowers. This is what Mama told me. I've seen pictures. I know what kind of dress Grandma had, I know that Grandpa had on his uniform, a lieutenant's uniform, later to become a major's. But no one has said anything about the summer Nicolai and Astrid were engaged, or if they were engaged at all, but probably everyone was in those times. At any rate, they were married, the postmaster's daughter from Sarpsborg, with Southern Norwegian shipowners and, from what I hear, a rather well known painter in the family, and Nicolai Nilsen from Sørøya, son of a Sami.

I sit in an easy chair in the kitchen. There's no one else home this Saturday. Ingolv is in Germany. The girls are out. The oldest is with her boyfriend, the youngest with a friend. In my hand I still hold the phone, where I've searched my way to the electronic edition of the census for Hammerfest Township.

I've expanded the screen image so the name of my father's father covers the entire display. Then I begin to cry and can't manage to stop. Tears fall and fall, and I don't know why. The cat comes and rubs against my legs. Perhaps it's that I realize this book will turn out differently. Even if I don't want it to.

Ipmil he's called, the most powerful of all the gods, the all-knowing. He has grown weary of looking at the old world and decides to shape another. He calls to the most beautiful reindeer cow in the enormous herd, and from her Ipmil creates a new world. Her blood becomes the ocean, the lakes, rivers, and creeks. From her flesh he creates the earth. Her fur becomes the trees and plants. The shy brown eyes he places in the sky, one in the north, one in the south. They become the North Star and the South Star. Ipmil looks on all that he has created, and he sees something is lacking. And so people come to be. The sons and daughters of the Sun.

That's how simple it can be. A new world out of one's head with the raw material one has.

It's three days after Christmas. In Oslo the temperature is around freezing, and it's snowing heavily, wet snowflakes that slap silently against the windows. Ellinor sits scrunched up in a corner of the sofa in what was once her and Tom's living room. On the table in front of her is a round plastic container, half full of heart-shaped gingerbread cookies. Next to the red lid is greasy plastic packaging in which there had been sliced tongue. A vacuum pack with a quarter kilo of pickled pork loaf is still unopened. A bag of gummy bears is almost empty. On the TV screen blue-clad people are about to cut into a boy on the operating table—they nod seriously and speak with each other in confident American voices. Ellinor has seen five seasons of *Grey's Anatomy* in the course of the Christmas holidays, and she wonders if that's a Norwegian record.

This is her first Christmas alone. The first five Christmases it was her, her father and mother. She remembers nothing. She has two photo albums from those years, with pictures of Ellinor at the time. A young version of her father, like him, but all the same completely different, the same fleshy lower lip, the same vertical double wrinkle, just a bit less obvious, between the brows, but with life in her eyes, with clear thoughts behind the high forehead. Two full albums, fading color photos on both sides of the thin cardstock sheets. Some of the holes are torn, so the pages have loosened. Down at the bottom of the very last page in the more recent of these albums is a picture of herself in her mother's lap. This is Ellinor's favorite picture. In the background, the Christmas tree with tinsel, Norwegian flags, and candles. And at the top, a shining star. Coconut macaroons, syrup snaps, wafer cones filled with cream. Generation should follow generation. Christmas, 1976. Mama's last Christmas. Ellinor has crooked bangs and pigtails, white-ribbed, long stockings in folds around her ankles, black patent leather shoes, her mother's arms around her. And while Ellinor looks straight into the camera, her mother looks down at her. The following Christmas her mother wasn't there. From then on there was only her and her father, and every once in a while her father's thin, unmarried aunt, until she died of lung cancer in the middle of the 1980s. Ellinor and her father, that's how it had been except for three or four Christmases she celebrated abroad in the first years of her university studies, one of them with Pierre, the others with chance acquaintances she's no longer in contact with, is only friends with on Facebook. Thereafter, from the time she was thirty-three until last year: Tom. And Tom brought others with him; every other year members of Tom's large family came over. Loud and irritating. Ellinor envied Tom for his family. Ellinor's father was always there, of course he had no one else, though in the last years she hadn't been sure how much he took in. Last year he probably barely understood it was Christmas. But he celebrated with her and Tom, sat in a chair after dinner with a glass of Christmas soda and a bowl of dates. There must be red soda—*julebrus*—and dates, he insisted, when he could still insist.

This year she let him stay in the nursing home, only going in the morning with a bentwood box of dates and a pair of slippers wrapped in holiday paper. He sat with the dates and the gift in his lap when she left, looking down and not knowing what to make of them.

Who Tom was celebrating with this year she couldn't bear to think about. Cardboard boxes with Christmas decorations they'd bought together are in the locker stall in the basement. The only Christmas decoration Ellinor has this year is a hysterically smiling elf sitting on the windowsill. A newly hired, still naive and trusting university fellow had given such elves to everyone at the institute.

It's so early in the morning that it's still dark out. Ellinor has just woken, slipped on the robe she left on the floor by the bed the night before, gone to the bathroom, then to the kitchen to put on coffee before she sat down on the sofa and turned on the DVD player. She should take a shower, her hair is unappetizingly dirty. It smells rancid. Her scalp is scratchy. She knows everything will feel better if she cleans up the apartment, puts on some clothes she likes, goes out for a long walk and takes deep breaths of cold air. She knows she will feel better if she turns off the DVD player and does something else. But she can't bring herself to do it. On the screen the little boy has landed in a bed, around his head he wears a large bandage. Ellinor stretches out her right arm, observes her hand in the air above the gingerbread cookie container, knowing she's the one making the decision about her hand. There's still a lot she has control over. On the screen the little boy, in the air her arm. She drops her arm, allows her fingers to grab the cookies like a mechanical shovel; crumbs and bigger chunks fall down on the table. She chews the gingerbread cookies to a thick, crumbled mess, presses the clump up to the roof of her mouth before she lets her tongue dissolve it, and swallows.

At least I still know what I should do, thinks Ellinor. I still know what is necessary.

Outside, the day begins. She hears voices. A child's piercing voice. A man's deep voice answers. High voice, deep voice, alternating. She can't make out the words but hears how the two voices rise and fall. A car door slams. It's Monday, the day after Christmas, the first workday this holiday break. She should turn on her computer, begin on the nutrition book. It is almost four hundred pages, and she has agreed to finish the manuscript by the beginning of January. The first week, the editor had said. Ellinor had promised that, she had assured the agitated editor it wouldn't be a problem. We're already behind, repeated the editor. Ellinor said she would begin on the copyediting as soon as she put down the phone, I promise, immediately! Since then the document has remained unopened in her inbox. Four hundred pages on nutrition, calories, carbohydrates, lipids, written by a doctor who's had a certain success on TV programs but can't write or at least doesn't know the rules of comma placement. She has to get moving if she's going to finish it before the deadline. Ellinor presses the pause button on the remote. She slides down into the sofa and pulls the blanket over her head. Later, I'll start it later. I'll go get the computer then, no first I'll take a shower and straighten up a little in here, start the dishwasher and take out the garbage. Throw out the rest of the candy and that pathetic elf, pluck my eyebrows, and shave my legs. Water the flowers, pay the bills.

When Ellinor wakes again it's almost dark outside, the day has come and gone. The street lamps are on, the neon sign of the pizza place on the corner flashes. The three sunflower-yellow letters ZEN glow over the door into the new sushi restaurant. Ellinor shoves her body up into a sitting position. Her head aches. She's probably not had enough fluids, only crammed herself with vacuum-packed tongue with far too much salt, with store-bought gingerbread cookies sucking out all the water she'd drunk. One thigh is clinging to her robe.

She feels like she can smell the stink of her own unwashed body, sharp and nauseating. A wish to decompose, dissolve, to never pull herself together again rises in her, followed by the hope that the smell doesn't come from her but from the food leftovers all around the apartment and the row of tied-off garbage bags by the front door. As she sits all the way up, she discovers she's gotten her period. And even though she hasn't been with a man since Tom moved out earlier in the autumn, and so it's completely irrational, she's overwhelmed by the well-known sorrow: she hasn't been successful this month either. And then, in a small flash of something reminiscent of humor, the old Ellinor, the person she actually is deep inside, says: This is quite a good thing, because now I have to shower.

She showers, standing so long under the streams of water that the hot-water heater empties. She loads up the dishwasher, fills four more garbage bags, and feels she's ready to fire up the computer. She takes a minute to stop by the bookcase, where she's placed the ceramic pig, burnt red, unglazed clay, with white glazed stripes on the back and white dots for eyes. When she looks at it, she can't help but smile back. The pig has a wide grin under its snout, scored in by Ellinor's mother when the clay was soft and gray, once in a class in the sixties.

She needs food, she needs pads. She carries out the garbage, walks with a rather light step to the Joker shop on the corner, returns with pads and tampons, crispbread and toppings, a bag of green apples, crème fraîche, a tube of wasabi paste, tomatoes, buffalo mozzarella, and skin-and-bone-free salmon fillets. She unlocks the mailbox, collects the little that lies there. Up in the apartment she takes the bags to the kitchen, sits on the storage bench, and opens the mail. Free local paper, advertisement for a furniture chain, a belated Christmas letter from a childhood friend (her eldest son started high school in the fall, he had a part in the school play and is getting all As; the youngest son is playing advanced soccer, has had the chicken pox, and is still Mama's little boy). At the bottom of the pile is a letter with the logo of her institute, where she was first a student, then a fellow, and now clings on as an unsuccessful substitute instructor. She opens it, empty of expectation, without hope.

She's gotten a job. She's gotten a job. Ellinor Smidt has been hired as a research assistant on the SAMmin project through the summer. Endangered languages. Language death. Sami languages. She is going to Finnmark.

Ellinor has forced herself through forty manuscript pages, corrected a dozen comma errors on each page, suggested countless simplifications, weeded out some of the doctor's worst howlers. In between she searches for *Sami, Finnmark, language death, eradication* on the Internet. She browses Wikipedia, Nordlys, and other sites, and reads a pair of academic articles in English. Of the world's six thousand languages, around fifty die out every year. One language perishes each week. Linguicide. The most usual progression is that the language speakers become bilingual in one generation and then those in the next generations gradually become worse speakers; the language is downgraded "to the domain of traditional use, such as in poetry and song." Finally, everyone is monolingual in the new language. And it can go quickly, in the space of only a couple of generations. She indulges in a few more minutes of reading—to her surprise she's gripped by what she reads (perhaps this Finnmark project won't be so bad?)—before the pricks of guilt grow intolerable and she has to open the nutrition manuscript again.

She's come to a chapter about saturated and unsaturated fats. The doctor writes *saturatted* about as often as *saturated*. She inserts a note that it must be consistent; *saturated* is correct. She will be away five months, from February 1 to July 1. The apartment must be rented out. She must put in for a change of postal address. And she won't be able to visit her father for five months. The thought is unbearable, even though she knows that for her father it probably means nothing. She feels a sudden rage toward the stupid doctor writer who can't distinguish between *differ* and *differentiate,* and inserts a comment that is perhaps ruder than it has to be ("the two fats differ, but presumably it is essential for a doctor to be able to differentiate between the two").

Ellinor has had a little over two weeks to organize all the practical details. It will be good all the same to get away from here, from this apartment, hers and Tom's. Sápmi—here I come! Finnmark is the land of possibility! Where has she heard that expression before? The ceramic pig smiles at her from the bookshelf. Read one more page, just one more page. She corrects *neat* to *neatly.* Change of address. Cancel newspaper. Father. All she has to do runs through her head, paralyzes the fingers poised on the keyboard. Potted plants. Who will water them? She looks into the kitchen. On the counter she finds a limp basil plant and a pot of thriving parsley. On the windowsill in the living room is an orchid that has given up hope and dropped all its flowers and buds. Two living and one dead. She must get to page 60 today. What if she rents to someone who doesn't pay? Should she transfer her insurance from this apartment to—wherever she's going to live? Will the university take care of housing, or will she need to find a place herself? Shouldn't she be reading up on language death? She searches randomly, sees that Pite Sami is *critically endangered,* which means that the youngest speakers are the grandparent generation. Almost eradicated. South Sami, Lule Sami, Skolt Sami are listed as *severely endangered.* North Sami is only *definitely endangered.* Should she pack away the ceramic pig? What about the books? She must do what she has always done: write down everything that must be accomplished. Each time she can cross off a task, she is one step further from chaos. And the first task is to be finished with this copyediting assignment. She manages to finish half a page more, gets up, looks out the window. There are many people on the sidewalks outside, many returning from work, rushing home to family and dinner, some have to shop first. A woman pushes a stroller through the slush, the wheels have lumps of brown, half-melted snow. Half a page more. The digestion system. An outline illustration with arrows. She must find out what she has in the way of bags and suitcases in the apartment and in the locker stall in the basement. It's cold in the extra room that was supposed to be the nursery but that now serves as storage and for accumulated junk. The heater is turned off, the door always closed. She takes a bag and a small suitcase from the closet and hurries out, turns off the light, closes the door.

A turf hut, a *gamme?*

I look at him. I understand he may be correct, and I understand how little I know. I haven't thought about what kind of house my grandfather could have grown up in, but when Sigbjørn says the word *gamme,* I realize that I unconsciously have envisioned a large white house, a house recalling the farmhouse on the family farm in Western Norway, or like the main house in Svea. For me, my grandfather's childhood home has been long and narrow, with many small-paned windows, slates on the roof, a pair of chimneys. A bright, Hamsun-like merchant's house under the midnight sun up in Nordland. But of course it is not like that.

We sit across from each other on high barstools in Oslo's House of Literature. Sigbjørn had taken the podium at the annual meeting of the Authors' Union in March, two months after I was contacted by my unknown relative in Hammerfest, two months after I sat in the kitchen and saw my grandfather's name on the cell phone screen. Sigbjørn went up to the podium and called for a regular Sami-speaking member on the advisory Literary Council of the Authors' Union. He's someone I must meet, I thought. He can help me along, tell me whom I can speak with, where I should begin, what I should read. A couple of days later I send him a friend request on

Facebook, and he accepts. I write a message to him, not saying what it concerns, only that I need help from him. I don't know why I don't write what it's about, but I believe it's due to not knowing how I should express myself. It's also probably due to the fear he will reject me, say he has no idea how to help me. Do I think that just because he is Sami he will know everything about how I can find out more about my grandfather? For that reason I say as little as possible, but Sigbjørn agrees all the same to meet me when he comes to Oslo the next time.

On April 20–21 there's another annual literary meeting, this time in the Norwegian Writers' Center in Oslo. Sigbjørn has come from Tromsø, and we agreed to meet at the House of Literature. An hour before the meeting a nurse called and asked if we could come over and visit Mama. She had moved from the rehab unit of Tåsenhjemmet to St. Halvardshjemmet in Gamlebyen and was not doing well. Ingolv came home from work, and we drove as fast as we could to Gamlebyen.

~~~

A couple of weeks earlier we had a meeting with the health services office at the nursing home. We sat around a table in one of the meeting rooms at Tåsenhjemmet, Ingolv and I, a physical therapist, Mama's primary nurse, someone who is the head of the unit, and a woman from the health services office in the neighborhood. And Mama herself. Six women and one man. Everyone knows that Mama can't return home. Mama too. She is reasonable, she says she understands that she can't live at home again, and she cries, quiet tears that don't insist on anything, that don't attempt to persuade anyone. But all the same she wants to manage on her own, wants to continue on as before with visits from home health care two times a day. We go around the table. Mostly for appearance's sake, like a ritual we have to undertake. Mama looks down at the table. One crippled hand strokes the other. I could have extended one of mine, consoled her, patted her. She is wearing slippers, worn-out slippers of sheepskin, the only footwear she is able to get on. The physical therapist points out that she is no longer able to get up on her own; she hasn't walked more than a few steps since Christmas but sits in a wheelchair and propels herself forward with the help of her feet. Don't you think I can work to get stronger, asks Mama, but she doesn't ask with conviction. She keeps looking down, won't meet anyone's eyes. The physical therapist shakes her head. You don't actually want to try, she says. Mama doesn't answer that. We have also seen it. Mama has changed. She who, in spite of great pain, has always been an optimist, has always been light-hearted, has always looked forward. Her mantra through all the years has been, *It will pass. It will get better.* And then there are these sores, says the nurse, Mama's primary contact, Linda. She is large and gentle, and Mama loves her. Yes, says Mama. Mama's body is covered with sores, a side effect of many years on cortisone. Her skin is as thin and fragile as tissue paper and breaks open if you're not infinitely careful with her. Now, when she must be lifted and helped even more than before, her skin is covered with bruises where she doesn't already have bandages and Band-Aids. On her legs she has large sores that won't heal. It takes an hour to clean them, and it must be done every other day. The dead skin has to be scraped off. Mama seldom complains but she's said many times that this process is horribly painful.

The meeting ends with our filling out an application together for a permanent nursing home bed. Ingolv and I have already been to look at the available nursing homes. They look light and attractive and newly renovated. It will be fine, Ingolv says to me. It will be fine, I say to Mama. Mama requests the

Uranianborghjemmet nursing home first. It's near us, and the children can easily visit her. Nordberg nursing home, which is quite near where she lives and not far from her childhood home, is in second place. I fill out the form. She signs. The writing is almost unreadable. Mama's hands are unmanageable sticks after more than thirty years of arthritis; now, in addition, they shake. Ingolv takes the application to the office. Mama cries. Linda is there, bends over, and hugs her. It will be fine, Gerd. I'm afraid, says Mama.

Now she no longer has a home. Mama, who has lived many places in her life, in Norway and abroad, but who has always had a home, with furniture, silver service, paintings, and books. Now she's signed something that says she will no longer have that. She who was so happy to invite guests and who always lit candles in the evening. She who so enjoyed her view of the city and the bullfinches that sat in the birch trees outside. She's moving into a nursing home, a place she doesn't want to be, which is most likely the last place she'll live. In the car after the meeting I think about where she's lived, it's as if it's important to explain the homes she's had. I rattle off a long list for Ingolv, ten or twelve places including Trondheim twice, Stockholm, and several neighborhoods in Oslo. I wonder if I've forgotten any place, I say, but actually I don't wonder. I have the overview. Where Papa lived when he was young is, on the other hand, unclear. I know they lived at least in Kristiansand, in Ålvik, in Notodden—because Grandfather worked at Fiskaa Factory, later at Bjølvefosen, and afterward at Tinfos Ironworks. I must remember to ask Mama about it.

The day before we're going to travel to the United States on Easter vacation, someone calls from the rehab unit at Tåsenhjemmet to say there's a temporary bed at St. Halvardshjemmet. The woman from Tåsenhjemmet says Gerd has expressed that she absolutely doesn't want to move there. Oh dear, I say. Hmm, says the woman. Can't she stay quietly with you until she gets a place at Uranianborghjemmet? I ask. It's not possible. Those are not the rules. She's on the waiting list for Uranianborghjemmet, and according to the rules she can no longer stay in rehab. Oh, well, I say. But after all, it's Easter, and we're going away. When does she have to move? Tomorrow, answers the woman from Tåsenhjemmet. Tomorrow? I repeat. Must she? It's very abrupt, isn't it? Must she? Can't she continue to stay at Tåsenhjemmet until Easter vacation is over? No, answers the woman.

On the way to the airport we drive by St. Halvardshjemmet. She lies on the bed in a small room that hasn't been redecorated since the late eighties, with a portable toilet in the corner, plastic flowers in a vase on a low dresser, a direct view of the train tracks. St. Halvardshjemmet is in Gamlebyen, the oldest part of the city near the train station. Mama is an Oslo girl, but for her Gamlebyen is probably as strange as any other city. I imagine she's rarely been in this neighborhood before, but I don't ask her that. We have only some meaningless phrases to offer, but they're meant to be encouraging. We'll see you right after Easter, I say. I'll look forward to it, she says. The eldest hugs her, the youngest hugs her. It's not so many days, says Ingolv. They'll go quickly, I say. Mama nods. Ingolv and I wave, and then we leave for Miami. To the sun, swimming, a good exchange rate for us, ice cream, dinners. I have my laptop with me, as I plan to get further along with the story of Ellinor.

And today, precisely on the day I have a date to meet Sigbjørn at the House of Literature, they've called us to say she's gotten worse since we were there the day before, and wonder if I have time for a conversation. I don't have long before I'm supposed to meet Sigbjørn but there's still time. A friendly nurse is waiting for us. She's the head of the ward, she explains. Mama has grown much worse in the course of the short weeks she's been here. We nod. We saw it immediately when we came back from Easter vacation. She's been put on an IV drip. She is listless and dispirited. I'm afraid, she says. She is deeply unhappy. In her ward no one else is mentally sound. She mentions a lady across from her who at the dinner table takes out and then puts back in her dentures throughout the meal. That's not very entertaining, says Mama. It will be better once you get to Uranianborghjemmet, I say. But we've recognized that perhaps it won't be much better there. It's so difficult to find a bed at a nursing home in Oslo that those who get one are the very worst off. For some of them, it's only the body that's failing, as in Mama's case, but many have dementia. I say nothing about this to Mama; probably she knows it herself, and we still have hope that everything will get better. We're in Mama's room only for a short while. She's lying in bed today. Smiles when we enter, says it's nice to see us, complains about the pain, says she doesn't like to be here. She has eaten a little of the chocolate we brought from the United States. Someone has fetched her a book. It's a true women's romance novel with a gaudy cover. I can't remember ever having seen Mama read such books, so I hold it up and ask jokingly if this is the kind of literature she's taken up now. She doesn't appear to register what kind of book it is, merely nods and says that one of the sweet nurses brought it to her. I must run, I say. I have a meeting at the House of Literature. Usually she would have asked with whom, and I would have answered, but now she doesn't ask and I say nothing. I don't say I'm meeting Sigbjørn, an author who writes in Sami, and who can perhaps help me untangle the story about her father-in-law. I'll tell her everything about the book later. I pat her on the cheek and go.

I arrive almost ten minutes late, and I tell Sigbjørn my mother is doing poorly. But it's not critical, I say, and repeat what the nurse said. Sigbjørn and I have never spoken with each other, have only nodded at the annual meeting a month earlier and thereafter written some messages on Facebook and set up this meeting. But he is courteous and says the right things, asks how old Mama is and if she has been ill long. I answer him, feel the desire to say more, say everything, tell him about Mama's good qualities, but I content myself with some short answers. This wasn't what I wanted to speak with you about, I say. I suddenly don't know where I should start, feel remarkably stupid, clear my throat, wonder if I'm turning red, something I haven't done in many years. In a sense it does have to do with my family, I finally begin, but another part of the family. Sigbjørn nods, listens. I tell the little I know about my grandfather. He suggests the name of someone I can speak with. I make notes on my phone. It sounds like your grandfather was perhaps a Sea Sami, he says. Sea Sami, I repeat as if I've never heard the words before, and a confusing image of reindeer and mountain plateaus and oceans, boats, and fish pops up.

When I come home, I look up Sea Sami on the Internet. I read, in Wikipedia, in the Great Norwegian Encyclopedia, on a blog, on a couple of other websites. Sea Sami are Sami who live along the coasts. They earn a living mainly from fishing and farming, I read. Again I type in Bismervik and Nilssen (with two s's). Grandfather's father, Ole Nilssen, worked at "fishing and farming" and Grandfather's mother, Oline, with "animal husbandry and housework."

The Sea Sami, I continue reading, were more quickly assimilated because they lived in the same territory as the Norwegians. They lost more of their traditions than the other Sami. But it's a short article, and there's nothing about which traditions we're talking about. In the Wikipedia article it says: "There was more shame attached to being a Sea Sami than to being an inland, nomadic Sami." Was my grandfather ashamed? Is that why I've never heard anything about a Sami great-grandparent, only a hint of a Finnish Norwegian, a Kven, in my father's ancestry? My source is Papa, and I can't imagine him as a man ashamed to talk about his father's background. But Papa was born in 1923, and many attitudes have changed since then. And some are probably as they've always been. Perhaps Papa didn't know it? Papa was only fourteen when his father died, and by then Grandfather had been ill for several years. Grandfather was in a sanatorium a long time, and I know that Papa and his younger brothers weren't allowed to visit him. I continue to search, and I find a photo of a Sea Sami, taken in 1910. He's wearing a Sami tunic, a *kofte.* Did my great-grandfather wear a *kofte?* And my grandfather, when he was small? *Kofte* and *komager,* the heelless boots?

I type in the word *gamme,* and photos of earth mounds appear on my screen. *Gammes.* Most of them look like hillocks with a door. My father, who preferred Van Heusen shirts, wore a knotted tie in winter and ritually shifted to a bow tie in spring, had a father who possibly had grown up in an earthen *gamme,* a primitive hut without windows, with an open fire hearth and a smoke vent in the roof. Behind my eyes burn tears that want to flow. Am I moved? Perhaps, but most of all sad because I never asked. Or, yes, I did, but never enough. I never asked Papa what kind of house his father had grown up in. Papa must have sat on his father's knee and asked about his father's childhood. Tell about when you were little, Papa!

But maybe his father didn't answer, maybe he didn't want to talk about his childhood. Maybe he answered by talking about otter hunting and fishing, the midnight sun, and the winter darkness.

A *gamme*. The last time I was in Gjøvik, speaking at the library, I took a photo of the house where my mother's mother grew up. I pull it up on the cell phone. It looks like the apartment houses I see if I look out the window at home. Three stories (with an ugly, added fourth story), red-yellow tiles, red decorative border along the sides, multipaned windows, balconies in wrought iron. My great-grandfather on my mother's side, factory owner and mayor, built this apartment house with the imposing address Storgaten 1, and here Grandmother lived until the time she left for Kristiania to take her final exams. But this isn't about Mama's side of the family. It's about what I don't know. About Grandfather, who lived but about whom I know almost nothing. And about Ellinor, who won't live if I don't write about her.

She is, in all reality, happy not to have much time. It frees her to be active, and her thoughts have no chance to buzz along the usual pathways. It's been many nights since she's been awakened by nightmares about hospitals, exams, shots, disappointments. Last night she dreamed about the Sami. They were still flickering before her eyes when she woke, in their bright blue, belted tunics, with "Four Winds" caps and lassos, and with reindeer in the background. It looked like an illustration to a children's book. They pointed toward a *gamme*. That's where you'll live, they said. Or would you rather live in a *lavvo*, a tent? The dream made her smile, and she remembered that they had spoken Norwegian to her. The dream would have been more useful to her if they had taught her some phrases in Sami.

The copyedited manuscript has been delivered, the invoice sent. She's packed and sent ahead a box of books; the rest she can take with her on the airplane—and most of her reading she can download from the web. The institute has found her a house, for which they've paid rent in advance through July. It's a spacious house with three bedrooms, Wi-Fi, and "everything you need," as the project manager wrote in the last email. She's found a subtenant for her own apartment—a female physical therapist who appears tidy and thoroughly healthy.

42

Ellinor has visited her father almost every day, and every day she prepares him for the fact that she is moving to Finnmark for a while. Sometimes Jørgen Smidt is surprised ("What in the world will you be doing up there, my girl?"). Other times he's indifferent, staring at her and plainly struggling to recognize her again and comprehend what she wants from him. Ellinor doesn't give up, she continues to tell her father about the job and the project and at least prepares herself.

It's a cold Saturday in the middle of February, and she's leaving in just a few days. She cleans out her drawers and cupboards so the well-organized and healthy physical therapist will have room for her stuff. Ellinor puts things from her mother in a small cardboard box. MAMA she writes on the outside. The first times she came across what had belonged to Tom—the blue knit sweater, the squash racket, a deodorant stick left behind—they gave her a start, but after a while she grew immune, so to speak. She's kept at it all morning, sorting things into black garbage bags: to be given away, thrown out, stored. She sets the charity store bag outside the door, carries the garbage down to the backyard, takes the possessions for storage up to the attic. *A place for everything, everything in its place.* She is efficient and pleased. It's not just the physical therapist who can be tidy, no. She decides that she'll deserve a reward when she's finally gotten rid of the bag of clothes at that container for donations a couple of blocks away. She squeezes down the crammed bag so all the space is used. That's the way! Nothing is so satisfying as to create structure and order and get rid of ridiculous old stuff. That is research at its best. Clear out, make a clean slate, start afresh, with new theses, new angles of incidence. She's finished now with web surfing, endless DVD evenings, unhealthy food, zero exercise. She decides that her reward shouldn't be candy but sushi, and she

43

heads purposefully toward the new sushi place that she can see from her living room window. Once inside she glances at the people in the small restaurant (lots of Asians—that must be a good sign?), and there in the corner is someone she knows. She can't place the woman who sits leaning forward at a table with another woman who has short, dark hair. Ellinor begins to nod, then she remembers who the woman is, it's that author who's written a novel about the University of Oslo. The author smiles at Ellinor, who looks quickly away, goes over to the counter and orders. When Ellinor returns in fifteen minutes to pick up the sushi, the two women, the author and her friend, are fortunately gone.

Ellinor greets the woman who is always sitting on the sofa looking at the TV. Today it's MTV, with no sound. A young man, naked to the waist, bends over the microphone and roars noiselessly. The woman raises her eyes, smiles glowingly at Ellinor. How are you? asks Ellinor. Both socks and shoes, nods the woman, and Ellinor continues into the corridor. The first time Ellinor had seen her on the sofa she'd recognized her and automatically said hello before she realized who she was. Ten years ago the woman on the sofa was known for having one of the brightest legal minds and one of the sharpest tongues in the country. She always expressed herself to the press precisely and in a way that first surprised you and then made you nod approvingly. The next afternoon, just as Ellinor was again passing the sofa on her way to her father's room, a white-clad nurse came over to the woman.

"I *was* a lawyer once," Ellinor heard her say to the nurse.

"So you were," answered the nurse with the kind of voice you use to an overly imaginative child, overbearing and a little bit pitying—"but now we're going to go tinkle."

Farther along the corridor sits a man in a straight-backed chair, sleeping with his mouth open. On the table next to him is a Christmas begonia, almost leafless. Outside the laundry is a steel shelf unit on wheels, full of diapers and rolls of paper towels. A sweetly acrid scent of urine hangs in the air and mingles with the smells of fried hamburger from lunch and the perfume of the elderly ladies.

Inside her father's room it's cool, almost cold. Her father has always liked to keep it warm; when Ellinor went through an environmentalist phase in adolescence they had constantly argued about the indoor temperature. The wing chair, small pipe rack, and mahogany dresser have come from home, but the bed is institutional metal with elevation settings and a re-mote control attached to the frame. Her father sits in the mid-dle of the made-up bed. His shirt is buttoned askew. One of his slippers has fallen off. She takes his hand.

"Tomorrow I'm leaving, Papa."

"Leaving."

"Yes, to Finnmark."

"What will. Up there?"

She waits, but he doesn't repair the sentence.

"Papa," she begins, but her throat thickens, and the words don't flow.

"My girl," says Jørgen Smidt and squeezes her hand, takes hold of the middle and index finger and squeezes once more.

In the spring, I travel to Finnmark, not to find out more about my grandfather but to participate in Finnmark's international literature festival. When I go down the ramp to the tarmac at the airport in Kirkenes, I observe closely to see if I notice anything special. Do I? Grandfather's land. The airport looks like other miniscule Norwegian airports, a common arrival and departure hall, plain surroundings, patient passengers at the single baggage carousel. I don't quite know what I'd expected: a kind of déjà vu, an echo of memories and experiences that in some miraculous way have been transmitted to me through two generations? In any case, I'll use the experiences, observations, and details when I write about Ellinor's first encounter with Finnmark. It's not just my grandfather's land. It's also Ellinor's new land.

A cold gust comes from the door every time someone opens it. I take my wheeled suitcase and go out. A patch of ice hides under a thin layer of snow; I skid on high-heeled boots into the nearest taxi. I listen to the dialect of the taxi driver, ask myself if they speak very differently in Kirkenes and Hammerfest, don't know the answer, don't know either, in fact, if the taxi driver is local. Looking out the car window rather than at the driver's neck, something comes over me, the desire to write, now, immediately. What was it like to be a Sami child in this district during the most intense Norwegianization period, to be sent to a boarding school, to be prevented from speaking your own language? A serious boy sits on a spindle-back chair. He hasn't seen his parents for weeks. He's become friends with someone a year younger. They whisper to each other in their mother tongue before they fall asleep. Perhaps one hums a lullaby for the other, but mostly for himself. In my purse is a notebook, as always; it is reassuring to me. I *can* take it out, find a pen, a splintered pen, and scribble down some key words about the two boys as we drive. But I don't do that. The thought that it's possible is enough, and when I'm in my hotel room I'll sit down. I have some time before the reading.

According to the clock it's not late, but in March of course it's already dark. It's darker here than it ever is in Oslo with its streetlights, buses, cars, and streetcars, with ads that flash and draw the eye, with lit-up buildings that are always awake. All of this in a large city contaminates the darkness, makes the darkness less dark, and at the same time makes it more homogeneous than here. Here, in the taxi, on the way into Kirkenes on a March evening, I see all the nuances. I see that the darkness outside the car windows is violet and blue and quite tranquil.

11

Ellinor turns and looks out the plane window. Outside the sky is dark but not black; it has a tranquil blue-violet hue. The man who sits next to her has one of his long legs sticking out into the aisle. He reads the popular newspaper *VG,* glances at her, chuckles under his breath at something he reads. Ellinor ignores him. He was on the first flight, too, before they changed to this one.

Even though she has no desire for the flight to last longer, she's strangely disappointed when the FASTEN SEATBELT sign goes on. The captain says that they'll be landing in ten minutes, and the man next to her arranges his legs under the seat in front of him. The unexpectedly short trip destroys the impression that she, Ellinor Smidt, is on her way to the farthest outpost of human civilization, to Ultima Thule, which destroys the idea she's coddled that she, left by her husband, forgotten by her father, failed in her work life, has been driven up here to the wilderness.

She lands at three o'clock. The terminal is tiny, and it smells of new, untreated wood. The walls are paneled in pine, with dark marks left by knots. A ladder still leans against the wall, and something that looks like a pair of well-used overalls is draped over one of its rungs. An enormous window gapes at her, shiny and black, from the opposite wall. The baggage

49

carousel begins to move, and a woman with dark hair and glasses, in a practical winter coat and warm, low-heeled boots, pulls off the first suitcase. Ellinor's eyes follow her as she rolls her case out of the building. Surely a successful physical therapist. The other passengers disappear, one after the next. The carousel continues to go around, but there's nothing on it. Ellinor has gotten her bag and one of her suitcases, but not the other. The one she's retrieved is crammed with books. The other, containing her toothbrush, clothes, hairbrush, and the phone number of the man she has to call to get the key to the house, is most likely back at the Trondheim airport, where she changed planes. Her stomach rumbles; she hasn't eaten since she left Oslo. Hungry, abandoned, failed, luggageless. The carousel is still moving, and just as she, with a measure of satisfaction, has given up all hope, her suitcase glides out.

She maneuvers the two suitcases, a bag, a laptop case, and a purse out of the terminal, over a well-camouflaged ice patch, and into a waiting taxi.

She doesn't know what unleashes it, what it is that makes her think about her father the whole way into the city center. Perhaps it's the sight of the taxi driver's neck that causes it. Her father in the driver's seat, her mother in the passenger seat, and herself in the back seat. Her father's short cut with two stripes of hair down his neck, stripes she can run her index finger through, down and up, so the bristles tickle her skin. She's allowed to do that but not while Papa is driving. It can be dangerous, you know, Elli-mine! She hasn't seen her father from this angle since she was four. After her mother died, she always sat in the passenger seat, didn't she? In the beginning on a pillow until she was tall enough to manage without. How is he doing? Will he miss her if she doesn't visit? Is he able to do that? Can you miss something you don't remember? She thinks about him until her conscience hurts. She forces herself to think about something else, and she almost has to smile at herself with the first thought that pops up: Tom, who has left her, and who probably now, at this moment, is sitting hand in hand with a young, fertile woman, planning their future together. No, it would be better to think about the job she's going to carry out up here, the job she actually shouldn't have gotten that she's not qualified for and that she dreads getting started on. She soaks in self-pity, enjoying it. She takes off a glove to scratch an itch in one eye. The bright red nail polish she applied before she left, to compensate for the no-longer-svelte waistline and as an optimistic symbol of her new life, has begun to flake at the tip of the thumbnail. Of course! Ellinor smiles bitterly in the back seat. The driver catches a glimpse of the smile, half-turns and says conversationally that yes, now the lighter days are coming. Now it's not long until the dark time is over. Ellinor looks out the window. Yes, I see that, she says. The driver laughs and Ellinor laughs, and then they've arrived at the home of the man who will give her the key to the house where she'll live.

So, are you the one who's going to do all the Sami stuff? The landlord looks at her. Ellinor nods. You're not one of them, I see, he says, examining her up and down. You need to watch out for them. They're sly, bowlegged devils. Here's the key. You have to pay for a new one if you lose this.

After she's also received the password to the Wi-Fi network and admonitions to check that the window hasps are always properly fastened after she has opened them for fresh air, she asks the taxi driver to take her to the grocery store. She dashes in confusion through the aisles and grabs items at random, while the driver waits outside with the engine idling and the meter ticking.

Now she stands on the steps to her new dwelling, with two

suitcases, a grocery bag with miscellaneous food items, a bag, a laptop case, and a purse. It's pitch black. A pair of streetlamps creates circles of light. The sound of the taxi is completely gone. The house clearly lies some distance from the city center but is not remote. Many similar wooden houses are nearby, and light glows from the windows of some of them. Her house is ochre yellow. A square box, from the postwar years. She takes off one glove, digs out the bunch of keys from her purse. The metal of the key is cold against her fingers. A gust of wind makes the overhanging layer of snow on the roof whirl out horizontally before it mixes with the falling snowflakes. She sticks the key in the lock. Now I'm opening the door to my new life, she thinks, then sees the irony of the situation, and hears a soundless fanfare reverberate inside her head. Ta-ta-ta-tom! My new life!

In spite of the pervasive odor of burnt dust, the smell that comes when, after a long period of disuse, an electric radiator is turned up high, the house is cold. She feels it right away, even as she continues to stand there with her outdoor clothing on. It's so cold her breath comes out in a puff of frost. If there's something the landlord doesn't need to worry about, it's the window hasps. Who would need fresh air here! She brings the luggage inside in stages, closing the door between each load; after the last suitcase she thinks for a moment and turns the lock. In the countryside, in the old days, you didn't lock your door. But she's not quite in the countryside. In the ice-cold entryway is a chest of drawers with a low bench: a telephone table. A piece of furniture found in almost every Norwegian home some years ago, but you almost never see it nowadays. The telephone table is teak with a nubbly mustard-yellow seat cushion. It would have been perfectly retro if it weren't for the dreary surroundings: spotted beige wallpaper, linoleum on the floor. On the telephone table, next to a wooden bowl painted in the old-fashioned *rosemaling* style, is a tomato-red rotary phone, exactly like the one she and her father had when she was little. Above the telephone hangs a mirror. Ellinor turns away quickly. She's neglected her hair, and the cut has grown out. Her face looks doughy and unhealthy. At least she matches the style of the home's interior.

The house consists of a living room and kitchen in addition to the hallway and a bathroom and three small bedrooms with dormers on the second floor. Each room is colder than the last, and none of them appears to have been redecorated since the 1970s. All the bedrooms have the same wallpaper with large, stylized flowers in sunny yellow, orange, and brown. Up near the cornice molding and around the windows the wallpaper is bubbled and loose. The synthetic drapes have a geometric pattern, a little different from room to room. Diamonds, circles, octagons. Rag rugs lie on the floor.

She lugs the suitcase up the stairs and into the bedroom that seems the least cold and that makes her feel the least dizzy. Here the curtains have blue circles, and the rag rugs are composed of brown and gray. She shakes out the comforter and spreads it over the bed frame, opens the suitcase and puts her toothbrush and facial cleanser in the bathroom. The floor feels like a sheet of ice. Finnmark and no radiant heat in the bathroom floor.

She sits bundled up in a blanket in front of the old-fashioned TV. She's found an electric fan heater, turned it to high, and pulled it over the floor so the warm air blows on her. Blue sparks came from the heater when she turned it on, but she chose to ignore them; quite calmly she just turned the heat up a notch. She has the choice between freezing to death or burning up. She gambles on the latter.

To make dinner in a drafty, semidark kitchen is far from appealing—and she doesn't have the ingredients either. For dinner on the first day of her new life, Ellinor Smidt eats potato chips and candy for children made in the shapes of cars. With that she drinks a beer. She drinks right out of the bottle. There are grease marks on the cold glasses.

She should have begun to look at the outline of the questionnaire she was sent to use as a model. A long-forgotten Dutchman, a guy she's met at conferences a few times and who also has begun to work on language death, has taken pity on her after she asked for help on the LINGUIST list. The laptop case is in the hallway. She can see it from where she sits on the sofa.

The wind is rising. She's used to sounds from her apartment at home. A steady drone of cars from one of the traffic arteries. The squeal of the streetcar when it brakes by the cross streets. Neighbors below, above, and alongside her who live their lives. Steps, children's laughter, water faucets dripping, music, the muffled thump of sex, ill-natured quarreling. Here are other sounds. A loud and opinionated wind. Old wooden construction that creaks and groans. A sudden bang. A branch against the window. She gives a start. One time it's as if someone is walking across the floor on the second floor. Pull yourself together, Ellinor. The laptop case is in the hall. She looks at it and knows she can rely on her never-failing guilty conscience to swell and expel the fear. That helps. She has the TV sound on low, so she can follow the other sounds. Now and again she turns the TV completely off, sits still as a mouse, and listens. Dogs baying. Or perhaps it's a wolf? A car that starts, then spins its wheels in the snow before the sound grows gradually fainter. A resigned sigh in the house as the wind takes hold of the small roof over the porch.

It's of course the smell, the scent of newly washed cotton, the sense of cleanliness, the joy of soon being able to fold everything into neat squares and rectangles. The hand towels are still warm when I take them out of the dryer, warm and perhaps a little damp. They air out over the kitchen stools while I answer email. Then I fold, smell, smooth.

Terrycloth towels are of two types: new and still white or half-new and already grayish. I make quick work of them, take them to the cupboard in the bathroom, hang one up on the towel bar. The tea towels are what make me happy. Three generations of them. Some I bought: Marimekko flowers in pale blue, gray, and beige, one with a quote from Shakespeare in yellow on a white background; another has slang words written in boustrophedon, alternating lines left to right, right to left. Then there are those I've gotten from Mama's large collection. They're white with red stripes in a checked pattern. I see she sewed the hems herself with tape. Mama's tea towels have always been red-checked or white. I also have some that come from my grandmother. They're completely white, some with patterns woven in the material, some simpler, some coarser. They've certainly had different uses. On the family farm in Western Norway there was a towel rack with four hooks. Over each hook hung an enameled label in

Gothic-style lettering: Knife. Glass. I don't remember, Hands, perhaps? Spoons? All the hand towels from Grandma, those embroidered monograms, which survived being boiled in a stewpot, in a washing machine, and which now survive a dryer. The edges of several of the hand towels are beginning to fray, but the monograms in the corners are just as tight and smooth as they have always been.

Ellinor is going to meet a man up there in Finnmark. It's nearing the end of April, and I've just now pointed out the direction of Ellinor's love life. Or: I don't yet know how it will go, whether they'll fall in love and embark on a relationship, but at least I know that Ellinor will meet a man. She refuses. Yet she is going to meet a man. The last pile of hand towels is in place. I close the drawer. Time to write.

The investigation of my father's father stands still. He's on the desk beside me, but he's just as secretive. He hasn't come nearer. I must call the relative in Hammerfest, or compose a letter to her, but I'm reluctant, don't completely know what to ask, want to wait a bit. My behavior reminds me of Ellinor, who longs intensely for children and who constantly finds fault with her lovers, and who postpones removing her IUD when she finally meets Tom. A possibility is bright and new as long as it's untested. I look in the census and pull up another version, different from what I found the first time. Nicolai Nilsen is entered as being born April 2. That's one of the things I know. Papa was born April 2. His father was born April 2, and *his* father was born April 2. Papa was the eldest son, Grandfather was the eldest son, and Great-grandfather was the eldest son. And all three were born April 2. So it's said. Or? It's written here that Ole, my Sea Sami great-grandfather, was born April 22. Ah-ha. Either there's a family history that has been improved upon through the years or there's an inaccuracy in the census, a clerk who put in one number too many. An *s* too many in the last name, a number too many in the census.

There's more in the document than I found at first. Nicolai was a student at the district school in Alta in 1910. He was fourteen years old then. Fourteen years old and alone at school many miles from his parents, not an unusual situation and especially not a hundred years ago. I can't stop thinking about him. I see that he and a friend the same age were boarders, and both teenage boys are described as both students and fishermen. Was that how such an education was financed? Around ten years later he meets someone who will become my grandmother, Astrid. Her childhood must have been completely different from his.

In 1910 my father's mother, Astrid, was twelve years old and went to school in her hometown of Sarpsborg. Both her parents were from Southern Norway, and my grandmother's accent with its burr, something also inherited by Papa, originated from them. Her mother, born Tønnevold, was named Marie. My grandmother's postmaster father was named Abraham. I recall that Papa teased Grandmother about the biblical names of her parents: Abraham and Marie—it's not so strange you turned out so nice, Mother! I don't know how well-off the Jacobsen family was, how consequential a postmaster was around the turn of the century in a small town like Sarpsborg. There was perhaps no abundance, no extravagance, but I've always had the impression that there was a good deal of money in that family. In the census it's written down that Abraham Jacobsen was the owner of the farm where they and several other families lived.

I have quite a lot of silver with the initial *J* from Grandmother's childhood home. Abraham and Marie had six children, of whom Astrid was the youngest, a true afterthought.

So I suppose the original collection of silver was divided such that Grandmother received a sixth. Papa was one of three sons, so probably Grandmother's share was divided into three. And my sister and I have probably received half of Papa's third. If the math holds, one thirty-sixth of Abraham and Marie's silver lies in my drawers. I have quite a few forks and spoons marked *J*, along with a serving spoon for fish engraved *28/3 76 M & A J*, certainly a wedding gift to Marie and Abraham.

In the census from 1875 I find a postal agent Abraham Jacobsen lodging with the Tønnevold family in Grimstad. In the next census, from 1900, Abraham Jacobsen has become a postmaster and married the daughter from the house where he had lived twenty-five years earlier. Here's the answer to a question I haven't asked: how did Grandmother's parents meet each other? I wish I'd asked how Astrid and Nicolai met each other. While I still had the chance.

When I sit thinking of Grandmother, writing about her, the memories come back to me. The furniture, the lamp with the linen shade. Her voice. Her words of welcome. I remember the smell in the apartment in Notodden. The door to her bedroom was always closed, and inside it was ice-cold. The bed was a narrow Empire style in mahogany. Probably at one time there were two such beds. Grandmother believed it was the cold bedroom, along with the honey and the rosehip extract she ate every day, that kept her so spry. And spry she was, whether that was due to the cold, honey, or rosehips. She lived at home and took care of herself until she died, over ninety-eight years old. When she was well over ninety she told Papa that she and her friend Mrs. Berg sometimes visited the old people's home "to make waffles for the old people." I look for her name with no particular hope of finding anything, but up pops a photo of her on the web from Notodden's local paper, *Telen*. The picture was taken forty-six years before she died, and she's not much older than I am now. I put my index finger on her head and smile back at her on the screen. To me she looks like she always did, an old lady. Sweet, modest, a little stooped. Under the photo is written: *In 1950 it wasn't very usual that women had the chance to work in male-dominated fields. Astrid Nilsen led the way at Tinfos Ironworks laboratory. Her accurate methods of analyzing the elements of ferrosilicon were highly valued by the managers.* It's also written that Grandmother, "the widow of Senior Engineer Nilsen," was the first woman to graduate from Kristiania Technical School. And as I read the text one more time, my throat thickening, moved by the unexpected photograph, I recall Grandmother telling us she had, over and over, trained the newly hired young male engineers, who, as soon as they were qualified, received higher jobs and salaries than she had. She said this as if it were an unpleasant but natural phenomenon.

I remember the dinners she used to serve us when we visited, sturdy Norwegian dinners, fricassee or mutton-and-cabbage stew. I remember her dining room furniture, in light wood, with carvings in the form of little fruit bowls. They were made in Hardanger, in Ålvik, where Astrid and Nicolai lived for a time when Papa was small. I remember more and more of her stories. But I haven't heard them as often as I've heard Mama's, so I have problems with the details and relationships, and which people are involved, how they are related to her, to Papa, to me.

Once, I received some thin typed pages from her, copied from an article published in the *Grimstad Post* from Friday, October 27, 1916. They concerned Deacon Jacob, born in 1765, a "physically and mentally healthy man"—and my great-great-great-grandfather. In his third marriage a daughter came, Jacobine Kristine Molland, who was born the same year as Ibsen, 1828. She was Grandmother's grandmother, mother of Marie Tønnevold, who married Abraham. The article closes like this: "Most of this family's men and women have shown themselves to be both talented and industrious, some to a pronounced degree. It should therefore be said that Jacob's descendants in the course of their lives have honored their gifted founder's memory." Grandmother read this over the coffee table to Mama, Papa, and me, in her thin voice, accompanied by a little giggling. I still hear the burr in the words *talented, industrious, pronounced*. Inside the folder where I've kept the fragile papers is a sheet on which, in a considerably more childish version of my handwriting, I've drawn the beginnings of a rudimentary family tree. Papa's name is at the bottom, then two lines up to the names of his parents, Astrid and Nicolai. On Astrid's side, the names are filled out up to great-great-grandmother, while on Grandfather's side no lines go up. There is only his own name: Nicolai Nilsen.

Grandmother came to us on a long visit now and then and stayed for a couple of weeks. It was intrusive to have another person in the house, an extra person using the bathroom, but it was a fine thing to hear Papa call her Mother, a fine thing to see her sitting in the living room and drinking coffee from our cobalt blue ceramic cups, so different from her own thin white cups. I knew I should be polite, but I didn't always feel like talking to her when I came home from school and she shuffled around me. She was never pushy, that kind of thing wasn't part of her personality; all the same she radiated expectation. Or perhaps I, who have always suffered from a guilty conscience—it doesn't take much for me to get a queasy feeling in my stomach or other symptoms of being at fault—perhaps I interpreted her closeness as a mild, unspoken need. Perhaps I even took her presence in our house, in my life, as an expression of hope, a hope I couldn't fulfill. A hope that I would stop getting together with my friends, stop watching TV, stop lying around reading in my room, and sit and talk with her.

When I attempt to reconstruct her childhood and youth and marriage to find out more about Grandfather, I discover that in spite of everything, I do know some things. But it's only a small fraction of what I know about Mama's side, about her parents' relations.

My mother loves to talk about her relatives. She does it often and with a self-confidence that shows she takes for granted that this is something I want to hear about, something I want to know, something I should know. Most often Mama tells me about her mother, and I wonder if it isn't often that way, that mothers speak more about their childhood, their families, their relatives than fathers do, such that the strongest verbal transmission is always from mother to daughter and again to daughter. That's the way it is in my case at any rate. I see that now when I search through the census for all my grandparents, one after the next. I know the names, on my mother's side, of each and every one of Grandma's siblings, even though there were many. My Grandma Herborg, born in 1891, had seven siblings. I recite them, not because they have any meaning for my story, but because their names come most quickly to me. They simply roll out like nursery rhymes you never remember learning but know all the same: Aslaug, Marit, Gudbrand, Ole, Jorunn, Arnhild, and Herdis. In my mind all these names have the epithet *aunt* or *uncle* inextricably linked to them—Mama's designation. If I think about it, I also know all the names of my grandfather's siblings on my mother's side. Yet though I recognized almost all the names of Grandmother Astrid's siblings when I saw them, I probably could not have recalled them on my own. From the census I understand that

Grandfather Nicolai has four brothers and one sister, and several half-siblings who must be from his mother's first marriage. Johanna with the last name Kvelsig is born only a couple of years before Nicolai. Nicolai is the eldest of Ole's children, and the younger siblings are named Astrup, Trygve, Thora, Olaf, and Henry. My great-uncles and great-aunts. I say the names half-aloud. It doesn't help. They sound strange, like characters in a novel do on the first pages.

13

It's been almost a full day since she arrived. She awakens stiff and confused very late in the morning. Outside the world is night gray. Nasty taste in her mouth, the corner of it stiff with saliva close to the pillow, deep furrows of sleep on one cheek. Inside the bedroom the vinyl is ice-cold against her feet, and she can't bear the thought of taking a shower or brushing her teeth. Her skin is sticky with sweat and dirt from yesterday's travel, her hair should have been washed, but it can't be helped. Her wrists and hands stick out, bone-white, from the arms of her pajamas. Her whole body has goose bumps. Her head aches. She must have coffee. She has to go downstairs to the electric fan heater. Scrunched over, rolled up in the comforter, she begins to move down to the first floor. I'm shaking, she thinks, I'm inside, in my house, and I'm shaking with cold. Halfway down the stairs hangs an embroidered runner, the kind of runner that mothers and aunts and grandmothers embroidered by the dozens a generation ago. She doesn't stop to look; in any case, she knows it by heart. On a white background, in *kloster* stitch, three stylized people are placed under each other, a man, a woman, a child. An identical embroidery hung in the hallway of Ellinor's childhood home, with the same wrought iron decoration as a hanger. Embroidered by her shriveled-up great-aunt. Father, mother, child. Papa,

Mama, Ellinor. Now she's almost downstairs. She can see the tomato-red telephone. She must call her father, hear how he's doing. Down on the first floor it's light from the kitchen lamp she forgot to turn off yesterday. She boils water, which takes an eternity on the old-fashioned stove, mixes it with Nescafé in a cup, eats the rest of the chewy candy cars. The comforter like a tent around her body, a newly filled coffee cup in one hand. She swallows again, the muffler on the last chewy car breaks into fragments on the way down her throat; it nearly makes her retch. The candy is lodged like paste back in her upper palate, continuing to spray nauseating sweetness into her mouth.

In the living room she turns up the heater fan to high, no sparks or blue flashes this time. She makes an opening in her comforter, allowing the air to blow in and warm her body. Her cell phone is on the table. No one has called, no one has sent a text. She taps to call up her father's cell phone number. Jørgen Papa Smidt. The first time no one answers. She's used to that. In her mind's eye she sees his mystified look as he attempts to connect the sound of the cell phone ring with anything meaningful. She calls again, and this time he answers right away.

Afterward she puts her elbows on the table and her forehead rests on her hands. She remains sitting in this position awhile as she wonders if she should laugh or cry. She decides to cry, but against her will she smiles when she thinks through the conversation. First she had to explain who she was (Daughter? But isn't that nice!), then she had to explain where she was (Finnmark? What in heaven's name are you doing all the way up there?), finally, impatiently, she had to hear that he couldn't talk any longer now because he had to deal with an important client. He talked at length about this client and didn't allow himself in any way to be influenced by Ellinor's attempt to tell him that he was retired, that he no longer had clients, that she would love to talk longer with him. She noted to herself that when he spoke at such length his sentences grew awkward; they broke down far too often, dissolved into nothing. He searched for the words, occasionally choosing the wrong one so that the meaning grew hazy, and she had to guess at what he was trying to say. Quite without warning he thanked her for the conversation, wished her all the best for now, and hung up.

She allows her elbows to slide forward so that her torso is against the table, her head turned toward the living room window. It's just as dark. She sends her arm over to the left, hunts up a greasy potato chip, and puts it in her mouth. She chews, lying against the table; with every chew, her jaw muscles lift her cheek from the table's surface. Papa. She has to unpack, fold the clothes, put them in the drawers. She has to create the questionnaire.

She wakes when her hand begins to hurt. It's the same dream again. A dream without action, without sound. Just a picture, in red light, as if she sees everything through closed eyes in sharp sunlight. An infant in miniature with transparent skin. Veins pulse right under the skin. The viscera undulate. The thighbone looks like a white pipe cleaner. The child has grotesquely obvious eyebrows and eyelashes. It opens its mouth, flutters its all-too-short limbs. She wakes out of breath and with a physical pain she can't manage to localize until she understands she must have dropped off to sleep. The heater fan blasts; otherwise it's quiet. No sounds in the house, no sounds outside, only the monotonous droning and her breath.

The questionnaire, now she has to get going on that. After having discovered that only two of the four burners on the stove work, she's not particularly optimistic when she types in the password she's been given for the Wi-Fi network, but the laptop willingly starts up and is in every way at her complete disposal. She connects and opens her inbox. A couple of insignificant informational emails from the institute, an offer of scientific books from an American publisher. A "call for papers" for a conference she won't attend. She has to finish the questionnaire. She promised to send it to the project manager during the course of the day. But when she looks at the clock in the upper right of the screen she discovers that the workday is already over. Tomorrow I must send a draft early in the morning. She forces herself to work with the form. The first section is easy enough. Sex. Age. Birthplace. What language(s) do you speak? What language(s) do you write? What language(s) can you read? What do you consider your mother tongue? What language(s) does your mother speak? What language(s) does your father speak? But then it gets worse. It's supposed to deal with attitudes, to Sami, to Norwegian. The role of school. Parents and grandparents as transmitters of language. And this is not Ellinor's area of competence. She knows, the project manager knows, everyone knows that Ellinor Smidt got this job because she was the only applicant with a PhD. It wasn't so easy to deny her the job for that reason. But the doctorate doesn't help her at all now. And besides that, she's hungry.

She must begin to eat right again. She can't live on chewy candy cars, potato chips, and ready-to-bake pizza. She has a new life to tackle. A puff of optimism, of initiative, makes her stand up. It must be too far to walk to that grocery store she was in yesterday, and she's not certain of the direction either. But she should manage to find a store, and if she doesn't, she can probably ask someone. There must be some people living here? She pulls on her boots, throws a quick glance at the mirror. Her hair is lying flat on her head, her lips are pale and dry. She pulls on a ski cap, rolls a scarf around her neck, licks her lips, and goes out, in the certainty that she can't possibly meet anyone she knows. None of Tom's friends. Or Tom. She looks ghastly, but she won't have any witnesses. None of consequence, in any case.

She begins to walk without knowing whether she's getting closer to or farther away from her goal. She imagines that the city center lies below the hilltop she can see from here and that there must be a grocery store that's open. It's now six o'clock in the evening, and for the moment no other person is in sight. She feels like she's moving through a dream landscape, dark and still. Perhaps she's the only one around?

The streets are different from those in Oslo, and it takes a few seconds before she registers that, until she understands why: no sand has been spread. The snow lies pure and white on the sidewalks, and the street is also rather white. What a remarkable place, no people, no sounds, only her own muted steps in the snow. A Christmas tree losing its needles leans sadly against a picket fence. One home has four pairs of skis propped up outside the front door, two pairs of long, parental skis and two short pairs. She nears the top of the hill, and her intuition proves correct: below her lies what must be the city center, two or three lit streets, friendly shop windows, some cars in the midst of parking. She even sees people. The logo of a grocery store chain shines familiarly in glaring letters on one of the buildings. She hastens to it, dashing the last few steps, is childishly relieved to have found her way here. Right outside the store are three kick-sleds and a shiny snowmobile.

Of course there are going to be fewer choices than in the stores back home in Oslo. In the huge grocery and specialty stores around her street she can get all she wants, and if there's an Asian spice she needs she can always take the street-car eastward over to the Grünerløkka neighborhood. Her expectations about what will be for sale here haven't been great, but she must admit that almost everything seems to be here. They obviously don't eat only whale meat, dried cod, and reindeer. Norwegians in the far north also eat Indian, sushi, and Tex-Mex. She picks up bread, toppings, ingredients for at least two dinners, and she discovers, after a closer look and with a certain triumphant self-satisfaction, that the quality of the vegetables could be considerably better. On her way to the register she notices white and orange cans of rat poison. She shudders. Next to them hang rubber strips of insulation. She takes three or four packages. She's definitely sending the receipt to her project manager, who is sitting warm and snug in his well-insulated house with its atrium in an Oslo suburb. With a heated floor in his bathroom.

"Cold?"

She gives a start. He's standing a short distance from her. Gray-green anorak with fur trim around the hood. A little taller than she is, but not much, solidly built, around the same age. She wets her dry lips.

"Yes, it's a little cold, that house . . . my."

My comes after a pause, as if she doesn't quite know if it's correct to say that the house is hers or not. He has a three-day-old beard. *Of course* he has three days of stubble on his lower jaw.

"From the South?"

Ellinor nods. Isn't there something insistently masculine about him? Or is she in the midst of going mad from the northern lights, which she hasn't seen yet but she's sure they swept like angry floodlights over her bed the few hours she slept. She shoves the cart toward the register. He follows her with a red basket. She recognizes his scent: fresh sweat, ocean spray, open country, testosterone. Like a rutting reindeer buck. Pull yourself together, Ellinor. In his basket is just one thing, a package of sugar. A completely ordinary one-kilo package of refined sugar. Granulated. White package, blue lettering.

She finished placing the things on the belt, paid, and has put almost everything in bags when he sets his sugar on the belt. She wants to say something, something that will make him react, that will make an impression on him. Something that can bring him out of his Northern Norwegian, steady-as-a-mountain balance. She looks up, meets his glance, and looks away again. Then she pulls herself together.

"Hungry?" she says and nods at his sugar.

He smiles but doesn't answer, and she feels clumsy and embarrassed. Couldn't she have figured out a slightly better comment? *Hungry?* Was that really the best she could come up with, after six years of university and a doctorate on top of that, after having read novels and seen films and plays for several decades? The grocery door opens automatically, and she goes out sideways, like a crab, but she manages to catch what he says, the unknown man in the gray-green anorak.

"I could have answered that I like everything sweet. But you would probably have considered that pretty banal, wouldn't you, Ellinor Smidt?"

14

"Your mother has set off now."

"Yes," I said and handed the receiver to Ingolv.

It's rare that anyone calls the landline, but this man did. It was quite late, and we were eating Indian takeout while watching a film when the phone began to shriek. Mama died the evening of April 28, 2012.

The day after, the sky is china blue. As if everything is as it was before. Sun shines through all the windows. The herringbone parquet floor turns a beautiful, saturated color. The vase on the living room table throws transparent shadows. The leaves on the potted plants become lush green in the sunlight. *Aftenposten* lies on the front doormat as usual. Unruffled, the cat stretches, yawns, turns around, and lies down again. Ingolv and the children have gone to see Mama.

I walk from room to room in the apartment. Everywhere something reminds me of her. There's the blue-green Benny Motzfeldt vase—one year my sister and I each received one. There are the Tangen wine glasses I began to collect because my parents had them, and it was *so* practical that we could borrow each other's if we were going to invite a lot of guests, my mother claimed. By the fireplace are the low chairs she and Papa bought when we lived in Stockholm. Some of the chemistry books from the technology university, NTH, are in the bookshelves in our youngest's room; she's firmly decided she'll also become a chemist. *General and Inorganic Chemistry* from 1949. *Chemistry: Outline of Chemistry and Its Connection to Technology and Industry*. Written by Håkon Flood in 1951. On the title page it reads that he is a professor of inorganic chemistry at NTH; perhaps he was her teacher. An enameled bracelet lies on the nightstand of our eldest daughter: white squares with detailed miniature flowers, alternating red and blue. Red was Mama's favorite color. *Qui vivra verra,* she used to say. Now she doesn't do that any longer—live.

There's not a single room that doesn't show signs of her. I try the bathroom, first the big one where, by the sink, there's a perfume bottle she gave me once because she had far too many. She always got cologne for Christmas because, as she said, what else are you supposed to give an old lady but sherry and perfume? In the small bathroom is a balsam shampoo she wanted us to try. Schwarzkopf—so effective, and it smells so good, she insisted.

There shouldn't be enough space in the small bathroom for reminders. But there is. The mirror over the sink, which I bought at a secondhand sale at Ullevål School when I was nineteen and still lived at home. Both Mama and I went to Ullevål. It was our school. Neither Papa nor my sister had gone there. In my time, the school was mint green, in her time reddish pink, as it is now. The mirror isn't really a mirror but a picture frame. I brought the frame home, Mama helped me to soak it in lye, Papa and I set off for the glass repairman, who put in the mirror. Set off. The man who called yesterday also used that expression. Your mother has set off now. It's an unexpected and fine word choice. I like it. Mama set off. I don't know where, but she's no longer here.

I find I've continued to stand inside the tiny little room.

On the shelf above the built-in cistern I've created a still life of blue enamelware, bought at online auctions over the past few years. Norwegian-made Cathrineholm and Emalox, from the 1950s. And there's also a small ashtray I got from her just a few months ago. On the ashtray is worn gold lettering: *Union Carbide*. The American firm where Papa worked for many years. The sharp edges of the ashtray cut into my fingers.

I continue from room to room, open a kitchen drawer. A one-liter steel measuring cup. A grapefruit knife with a yellowed plastic handle: I remember the knife from when I was small. Half a grapefruit for Sunday breakfast, carefully cut so each section was loosened from the others, a mound of sugar, which spread out and blended with the fruit juices below. A cracked gratin dish from Figgjo. There's the cup she drank coffee from when she was here last. The sight of one object, the touch of another, the thought of yet another. One object after the next and tears squeeze out. I hadn't been able to control what I was searching for. Now I don't even search. I'm home alone, and my cheeks are already sore and stiff from the tears running down my jaw and throat.

And the sky. The unseemly clear sky. Mama was a person who to a greater degree than anyone I've ever known was enthusiastic about cloud formations, the colors of the sky, and sunsets. All the way back to when I was small I remember that she laughed at herself for always having to comment on the nuances of gray, on rain falling on water, on ruddy golden sunsets. The fireplace in the living room. I've never lit a fireplace or a stove when Mama was around without her saying that the wood crackling is the coziest thing she can imagine. I place both palms on the chilly marble mantelpiece; the next moment I'm standing with my head bent and my cheek on the mantel. The tears find routes from my eye sockets diagonally down my compressed cheek. Into the dining room again. The tall cast-iron stove we lit when she was last here for dinner. Listen, Helene! Such a crackling is the coziest thing I know!

I will never be able to light a fire without thinking of her.

Grieving resembles writing. When writing is at its most intense, I look at everything through the lens of the novel I'm working on. If I see an ice cream stick on the sidewalk I wonder for a moment how my protagonist eats ice cream. In big, greedy bites? Or does he wait until it's almost vanilla sauce and slurp it up? Does he like the cool sensation as it goes down? Does he detest everything that's sweet? If I hear a song on the radio, I envision how the main character might dance or ask myself if the scene I'm struggling with now can be solved if she dances with her lover. When I eavesdrop on conversations on the bus, I try to imagine them in my fictional character's voice. Yesterday morning, as Ingolv and I shopped for the weekend and I was still unaware that April 28, 2012, wasn't a completely normal Saturday, I stood standing for a moment with a loaf of bread in my hand before I put it in the cart. I understood it was the same kind of loaf Ellinor bought when she was out shopping and met the man who knew her name. Some people cut their bread in thin, even, perfect slices. Ellinor's loaves have a tendency to become lopsided, with the slices wider at the top than at the bottom. By the end of the loaf the slices are missing the crust on one side. That's what I thought yesterday. Now I see, hear, and smell Mama everywhere. When I open the bread drawer and see the rest of yesterday's bread, I think about her fingers, her poor, arthritic hands that weren't able to slice bread in the last years. The home health care assistant used to cut slices and freeze them, or we helped her when we came. When I was young, Mama was home. She sat at the kitchen table with the typewriter, dictionaries, carbon paper, onionskin paper, and normal paper and translated technical literature, but every day she called me into lunch. She had buttered nice, even slices for sandwiches with sausages or hot dogs and freshly ground pepper. Sometimes there were open-faced sandwiches with apple slices and a splash of jam in the space where the apple core had been. She drank coffee from a cobalt-blue ceramic cup. I drank milk from a cup I've used for my own children's milk. The one with a boy, a girl, and a lamb on it. We sat in the kitchen. Right outside, on the other side of the street, I could see the school I was going to go to. Our curtains had a pattern with green vegetables. The radio hummed in the background, with fishing announcements, stock market quotes, news in the Sami language. The radio was black and white. I *think* the radio was black and white.

Ingolv and the children come home. They are quiet. The youngest says it was good to see her. The eldest didn't like it. Ingolv says he has taken a photo with the cell phone. So if I want . . . ? I shake my head.

In the evening I fall asleep almost immediately. Just before I drop off, after I know I don't have to lie there sleepless, a wave of relief flows through me. I don't know what I dream, but I awake too early.

Both Monday and Tuesday, I wake without remembering that Mama is gone. Both mornings the pain comes after only a few seconds in the half dark.

Monday Ingolv and I are in the funeral home office. The woman who receives us speaks in a muted voice, wears discreetly attractive clothes, and smiles with professional compassion, not showing her teeth. I wonder whether they are sent to a course about how to act toward the bereaved or whether it comes naturally. We must decide on a day for the funeral, the menu for the memorial service, we must talk about the gravestone, flowers and wreaths, hymns and music. About the coffin, color, and molding. About the clothes she will wear in the coffin. I can't stop crying. There's a box of Kleenex on her desk. Ingolv keeps me supplied with fresh tissues. They become wet and black with mascara. I ball them up in my left hand as I use them.

Should she be cremated? Did she have a pacemaker? Should there be bouquets with the candelabras? Many feel it is simplest with just candles. You don't need to decide everything now, she says in a low voice, you can look at these in peace and quiet at home. We're given brochures with summaries of flowers and wreaths, customary words of remembrance, suggestions for hymns. We stand, nod, thank her. She shakes our hands. In my left hand I'm holding a clump of soaked tissues.

I slip on sunglasses; it's another insistently spring day. I decide to read the poem "Spring" by Olaf Bull as soon as we come home. In the flowerbed outside the funeral home office, at the corner of Kirkeveien and Blindernveien, bark has been strewn around the bushes. It gives off an intense scent, and I know Mama would have drunk up the smell and commented on it. But she will never again experience the fragrance of spring, and that's unbearable to know.

In the car on the way home Ingolv says he's spoken more with the nurse who found Mama. The man who called . . . Saturday? I ask. Yes, the Swede. The Swede? I repeat, and I understand in the same second that he, whom I just spoke to Saturday evening, hadn't said, "Your mother has set off now" but "Your mother has expired now."

Ingolv has driven back to work. I'm alone in the apartment. Our books are alphabetized, just like they were at home on Mama and Papa's bookshelves. Bull is under B, second bookshelf from the window, right on top, on the tenth shelf. To make room for all the books, an extra shelf has been placed above what should be the highest shelf. We've bought a white lacquered library ladder, and I'm balancing on it now: all the same, it's only by the skin of my teeth I can manage to fish out the Bull. The poem is about a young girl who dies, not an old woman. I know that. All the same I have to read it, remember precisely which words are used. I page forward to the poem, sit on the floor in the office, and read aloud the lines of verse I thought about when we passed the fragrant bark.

> *Up into all this bluing sky doesn't rise*
> *A single breath from her breast!*
> . . .
> *And my thoughts to those times go,*
> *When she was with me to call the swallows swallows*
> *And happily would call the air blue!*

When I read that "The joy of spring's growth doesn't reach her eyes," I understand this: I think I believed toward the end that it was I who meant a great deal to her, that I visited her, talked with her, stroked and soothed her for her own sake. But that's not how it was. She meant something to me until the end. I needed her as much as she needed me. I believed that, despite my grief, I would also feel relieved not to feel guilty on the days we couldn't visit her, that I'd feel relieved when I could let go of worrying about her, of organizing things for her, of seeing she was in pain. But I don't feel relief. I feel only grief that she is gone.

After Ellinor meets the man I already know is called Kåre Os, but whose name she doesn't know, the man she also doesn't know if she'll see again, she returns to the ochre-yellow house in a good mood. She's not worried in the least that he knows her name. She likes it. Nor is she irritated by him first acting like he didn't know who she was (are you from the South?). She also likes that. In the store she'd felt—and it had been a long, long time—a quick flash of movement in her lower abdomen, as if a fish lashed its tail somewhere inside below her navel. On the way home she's on the verge of humming, and she eats a dinner that for once doesn't give her gas and a guilty conscience.

That's as far as I've thought, and now I've written it down. I look at the seven sentences on the screen and realize they're completely meaningless. I italicize the pronoun *I* in the first line, then remove the italic because the word is more than emphatic as it is. In this way I set Ellinor aside. I could have put her aside gently, thinking I was happy on her behalf that her spirits have lifted a little, that the wireless is working, that she's purchased insulation to put around the doors and windows, that she's started on the questionnaire, that she has support from a man in a gray-green anorak. I could have been pleased to know she'll probably continue to work, think now

77

and again about the man, and basically manage just fine up there in Finnmark. But I toss her aside, don't think a moment more about Ellinor and her world for many weeks. I allow her to simply sail her own boat.

I don't think about my father's father either.

The reflex is still strong. Many times I'm about to call to tell her little things that I know she'll enjoy. Mama, you know what? The youngest got everything right on the math test. Tomorrow the eldest will have lunch in a tree; for taking that dare she'll be able to add a badge to her high school graduation cap! I want to call her when I need company as I empty the washing machine or as I carry watering can after watering can out to the thirsty window boxes on the veranda. Automatically I think we can visit her in the afternoon, stop by before dinner. Just behind my eyes the tears are ready. It doesn't take much before they begin to fall. I can't stand going to meetings; I cancel all appointments. The only thing I've written is a kind of journal. These lines. I continue to have great difficulties with the tenses. There's a painful reminder in every verb in the past tense. She liked. She resided. She used to. She was.

We have to tell people. What about the bridge club? What about her colleagues from earlier in life? Ingolv calls most of them. I don't want to, but I listen to Ingolv's words. Gerd died Saturday evening. Then I try to understand what they say from Ingolv's responses. Yes, she'd been frail for a while. Yes. Saturday evening at nine o'clock. Yes, all four of us were there just a few hours before. Yes, I'll do that.

On Christmas Eve Mama had worn what had become her holiday outfit in recent years: a black skirt with a red, orange, and blue pattern like a border at the bottom, a black sweater, and a scarf of the same material as the skirt. The children decided that she should be buried in these clothes. They have no doubts that Grandma should wear them when she's dressed for the last time. Ingolv fetches the clothes at the apartment and takes them to the funeral parlor office.

More and more bouquets arrive. I take the wrapping off. We don't have enough vases. One bouquet I put in a canning jar. Two go in the same vase. I place the cards in the secretaire.

Every day I turn on the computer and I write a few words, make some short notes, like the one about the clothes she should wear, about the flowers that are steadily delivered. I've also created a document called Memorialtalk.docx. I would so very much like to give a speech in the church, but I don't know if I'm up to it. For now I haven't even managed to write anything but a conclusion, the last two sentences. I, who write all the time. Books, speeches, articles, emails. I live to write. I've written many thousands of pages. Now I can't manage it. Except the two last sentences, a declaration of love to her that feels truer and more important than everything I've written. I envision standing, dressed in black, at the pulpit and saying the sentences so they ring out in the church, so everyone hears them. I visualize it the way I'm used to visualizing my fictional characters, a face whose features I can't quite grasp, seen from outside, in the third person: Helene went up the two steps to the pulpit. The white papers shone against the black dress. She placed the pages in front of her, looked out over the dark-clad gathering, and swallowed. But I don't know if my legs will carry me up there, if my voice will hold steady. One moment I know I'll be able to do it, for Mama's sake; the next I'm just as convinced I won't be able: not to walk, not to speak.

The obituary must also be written and quickly. I've postponed it for several days. Is it the black words on the white screen that frighten me? Will it become more real if I write it? Is it reluctance to face the impossible: to be forced to express deep emotions in four hundred characters? But of course that's not what I'm doing, I remind myself. The announcement is supposed to inform. People must be told. I write "Our . . . mother . . . mother-in-law . . . grandmother died today." What adjectives should I add?

When I give classes and teach creative writing, I often ask participants to choose adjectives when they start building the main characters. How is person A? Is he shy, self-confident, generous, curious? Arrogant, egocentric, hospitable, extravagant? I often start myself off with a similar adjective exercise. If I had opened the document in which I note ideas and everything I need to remember while writing, I'd see that before Christmas I'd noted that Ellinor should be *unambitious, resigned, self-ironic,* and that her father, Jørgen, should be *affectionate* and *concerned with traditions.* Now I sit struggling again with adjectives. How can I capture the essence of Mama in three adjectives?

A genre you don't try to bend is the obituary. I've never written one before. When Papa died it was Mama who took care of it, though I certainly was consulted. I've talked with Ingolv and the children. The youngest spontaneously suggested *happy,* and that also felt right to the eldest. There are many well-meant adjectives I don't want: *dear, kind, good.* Even though she was all those things.

It ends with "Our warm mother, brave mother-in-law, and always happy grandmother." I email the wording to the woman with the muted voice whose title is funeral consultant.

16

The funeral was yesterday. I sat in the front pew and looked at the coffin in front of me, just a few steps away, and I couldn't grasp she was there, in the coffin. My Mama had nothing to do with a shiny white coffin decorated with lilies the same color. My mind recoiled, refusing to take it in. When a little later I stood at the pulpit and saw the coffin below me and spoke about Mama's favorite color, I couldn't let go of thinking about what she was wearing. The black skirt with a red-patterned border. Then I knew she lay there, and my mind had no room for anything but that thought.

A heavy floral scent, stillness in the church filled with throat clearing, trembling breathing, and suppressed coughs. Speeches at the memorial service afterward: more crying, cathartic laughter. A catch in Ingolv's voice as he welcomed them. The piece of cake that remained on my plate, the fork sticking out from the chocolate-sprinkled marzipan curl, ready to scoop out a bite.

17

The project manager has given Ellinor a list of people who live in the district and who are registered as having Sami as one of their languages. The list contains twenty-three names, but in a follow-up email he had written that there were certainly more, "and as soon as you get into the social milieu, you'll certainly find additional informants." Typed at the top of the Excel spreadsheet is the name Anna Guttormsen. Next to the name the project manager has written: "Attention! Key person. Heavily engaged in Sami political issues. Has a lot of information. Should be contacted first! Important to establish a good relationship here."

She bites the tip of her pen, a cheap, transparent Bic pen. She likes the sensation when the plastic cracks. Ellinor's pens are always missing the blue cap and are splintered at the top end. She reads quickly through all the names. None of them says anything in particular to her, except that one is called Tom, and that gives her a painful twinge in her stomach that she chooses to ignore. It's probably best to begin with Anna Guttormsen. Should she call first, or should she just go there and knock? She finds both the phone number and the address on the Internet, looks at the number, reaches for the phone, but decides to go over to her house. In this part of the country people visit each other without advance notice. People are spontaneous, hospitable, and friendly. It's said. The last splash of coffee is bitter and lukewarm. Is that a bad omen?

Anna Guttormsen's house is all the way down by the fjord. Red clapboards outside, except for a short wall where unpainted logs are visible in a fashion that only an artistically inclined architect could have dreamed up. Large windows have been set into the wall, while the entrance door is probably the original; in any case, it is much lower than a modern door and is quite weathered. She seems to hear her father lecturing about the interplay between the traditional and the modern. It looks like a house whose owner has both taste and money. Along two sides of the house the snow has blown up in drifts that reach the windowsills. Outdoor lamps are lit on either side of the door, giving the entrance the appearance of a Christmas card. Ellinor isn't the type to think it's perfectly fine to approach strangers, but the house looks so welcoming that without hesitation she presses the doorbell above the brass plate where Anna Guttormsen's name is written in open, inviting capital letters.

The waves slam against the pier, and the wind rarely rests in this city. It's impossible to hear if there's a sound inside the house, if steps are coming, if anyone is taking hold of the doorknob from the inside. Suddenly the door opens.

"Yes?"

The woman in the door opening has milk-white hair pulled back from her face and enormous earrings in hammered silver. The weight of them pulls down her earlobes. Ellinor knows that the woman in front of her, if this is Anna Guttormsen, is close to eighty, but she looks astonishingly young. The skin of her face is pale brown and tight across the cheekbones, and her eyes are large and clear. She's wearing a woven tunic in shades of green and tight-fitting slacks of grass green. On her feet are felted slippers. She tilts her head questioningly and smiles at Ellinor. Ellinor smiles back. Is she only imagining it, or can she smell coffee?

"Anna Guttormsen?"

"Yes?"

"My name is Ellinor Smidt, and I'm employed on a project that . . ."

"So this is you. I've heard of you, Ellinor Smidt. You don't speak Sami then?" says Anna Guttormsen. Her mouth is narrow and closed.

It takes a few seconds before Ellinor understands what the woman, the key person with whom it is so important to establish a good relationship, is actually asking. Ellinor's right hand is moving forward to shake hands. Her hand stops midway and drops. Her smile falters. Anna Guttormsen's earrings gleam hostilely.

"Do you speak Sami?"

"No," answers Ellinor.

"Do you understand it?"

"No."

"Not even at the most basic level?"

"N-no, I . . ."

"Perhaps you know a few words?"

"I have picked up . . ."

"You understand the paradox in registering and documenting something you yourself don't have the possibility of understanding the meaning of?"

"Well, yes, but . . ."

"Do you know that none of our legends deal with where we come from? We have always been here."

The green-clad woman closes the door with a brief nod. Does Ellinor catch a glimpse of a smile as the door shuts?

In the middle of the Formica table in the ochre-yellow house sits an African violet in bloom. She went through the city center on the way home from Anna Guttormsen's, making purchases she knew would help. If for a brief moment she had imagined that her role in this project would be simple, she's lost that illusion by now. Her first impulse was to buy a bunch of candy, move the heater close to the sofa, and lie under the blanket and daydream about the man in the gray-green anorak (his glance, his intonation, the way he pronounced her name). The second was to fly back to Oslo. She had to remind herself that she'd started a new life. What she needed now was *good* coffee (a French press and a bag of ground beans) and a place she could write down her frustrations and problems and her good ideas for solutions (a notebook with a cheerfully patterned cover). Along with that she needed something pretty to look at (an African violet with flowers, lots of buds, and just the sort of furry leaves she recalled from her childhood home). She takes tiny, tiny sips of coffee, feels how her memory of Anna Guttormsen grows less frightening, more comical. This is something she can handle! She opens her Excel document. She only has to choose another name from the list. Kamilla and Aslak Hiberg. Ole Nilssen. Kåre Os. Hildur. This Tom. There are enough other people. Twenty-two names. She mustn't let herself be affected by this. Anna Guttormsen is clearly a difficult woman. She must find another way to approach her. She won't give up but will begin elsewhere, with one of the others. Who should she choose? She pulls out one of her mistreated Bic pens and opens the cheerfully patterned notebook to the first page.

Two days later Ellinor has slept four hours, visited five houses, and gotten seven questionnaires filled out. She has sat at dining room tables and kitchen tables, been served ordinary tea from Lipton bags. Lingonberry juice. Dynamite-strong boiled coffee and tasteless percolator coffee. At one place she was offered a glass of Russian vodka at three o'clock in the afternoon. She said no thank you, nicely. Almond tart and home-baked *lefse*. Chocolate cookies in a cut-glass bowl. She's been met with chuckling indifference, with politeness, with moderate interest, and in one place with something approaching enthusiasm—that was where she got the almond tart—and not one person has been unfriendly, the way that Anna Guttormsen was.

Ellinor's body isn't able to understand the endless darkness, and she sleeps only a few hours a day, is constantly tired. She's dizzy and has headaches, but she carries on with her interviews. Drinks coffee, eats almond tart, dry at the outer crust. She chats and coaxes out information, sits with the laptop on her knees, and fills in their answers in the correct columns of the questionnaire.

My parents spoke Sami to each other but Norwegian to me, my grandparents spoke Sami to me, I answered in Norwegian.

Mother spoke North Sami to me. Father is from around Trondheim, doesn't know Sami.

In my childhood home only Norwegian was spoken.

We spoke only Norwegian at home. Mama didn't want to inflict on us children the same disadvantages she herself had experienced.

———

Great-grandmother told Mother that she hadn't understood anything the first three years of school. The woman teacher was from the South and Great-grandmother had barely heard any Norwegian before she began school.

*My father spoke Sami at home with his parents, but in fact I didn't
know he could speak Sami until a couple of years ago. You
keep that background hidden. It was nothing you acknowledged.
Nothing you spoke of voluntarily.*

*You should honor your father and mother, and therefore it's a shame
we haven't honored their language.*

———

*You're powerless when you don't know a language properly, and the
language that counts is Norwegian.*

My sister and I had all our education in Sami the first years.

No, it wasn't necessary, my parents thought.

No, the language would only become a nuisance.

————

*Norwegian it was going to be. No, I didn't think and don't think
of it as a devaluing of Sami as a language, merely as a practical
decision. My children weren't going to have anything to do with
it. It was dead and buried. The past.*

*My grandmother became an island with her anecdotes and fairy tales
that nobody wanted to listen to.*

*It was as if the tie to the ancestors was cut. Mother, father,
grandparents, all the others could speak with each other in this
magic language, it was only we who didn't understand what
they laughed about, what made them serious.*

The ties to the past were cut. But that is how it has to be.

————

I remember that my father couldn't differentiate between p *and*
b *when he spoke Norwegian.* The briest breaches in the
church.

Finn-devils we were called. Our language was called crowtalk.

───

Stories from previous generations are some of the most valuable things we have here, but the language that is used to tell them doesn't matter.

Sami is the most beautiful.

The words—I lack words for so many things. Then I use Norwegian. It turns into an ugly, mixed language. A deceitful language. Hunting stories don't come across in Norwegian. Sami is richer.

Norwegian is a better language. That's just how it is. Just like English is better than Norwegian.

I like the sound of the Sami vowels.

Anna Guttormsen's name comes up several times during these days. It was Anna who started the classes that time, it was Anna who really has the knowledge. But she is a witch you should watch out for, says someone. Anna is a *noaidi,* a shaman. Anna is the world's nicest, says someone else. Anna Guttormsen can put you under a spell. It's said. Can she? says Ellinor, not knowing how to take in information of that kind. Anna was one of the first activists. Berit and Anna, like dog and cat, says someone and laughs. Oh? says Ellinor. It's ancient history, says another and blows on her coffee. History? asks Ellinor.

18

The fifth day, late in the afternoon, Ellinor has an appointment with the man named Tom. She's phoned in advance and asked if it's okay if she comes over, and he's answered that it is. The lack of questions from his end and the flat tone of his voice make her wonder whether he too has heard about her and her project. Her head is heavy. The winter darkness makes it so her body doesn't have the least idea of when it's day and when she should sleep. She doesn't sleep in the evenings, just lies there, tossing and turning, thinking about the new girlfriend *her* Tom has down in Oslo, about her father, about Anna Guttormsen. About the blue line on the pregnancy test. And when she finally gets to sleep, she can be awakened right afterward by a noise in the house, bolt awake and not be able to fall asleep again. It feels as though her whole self is in hibernation, and the only thing she longs for is a snug quiet hole where she can be left alone and just sleep.

It's been cold lately, twenty-five below zero with wind. Her fingertips are permanently numb, and her neck muscles are worn out from scrunching up in the blasting wind. Earlier today she had an email from her project manager that asked how it was going. She answered immediately, glad to be able to tell him it was going well without lying. She added a few lines about the dark and cold, but "Everything for science!"

He sent a new email, commenting neither about things going well nor on her attempt at a humorous ending. She had
been employed too many years at the University of Oslo to be
surprised, but she felt some support all the same. The project
manager wrote that he thought it might be a good idea to
make a separate case study of Anna Guttormsen. A popular
science article could come out of that as well, where Ellinor
could write about language death for a general public, based
on interviews with Anna Guttormsen. This would be a feather
in the cap for the project and the institute, he wrote. And for
him, thought Ellinor. What did Ellinor think about his idea?
How had the conversations with Anna Guttormsen gone? Ellinor closed the laptop again and put on water for coffee. She
looked at the African violet, stroked one of the furry leaves,
forced herself to breathe calmly. A cup of coffee, the patterned
notebook. She must plan a strategy for approaching Anna. But
this afternoon, thank heavens, there was only this Tom to be
visited. Apart from his name there was nothing to indicate
anything would be wrong with him.

She dresses layer upon layer, two hats on top of each other,
gloves inside leather mitts; she's freezing all the same. Her nostrils stick together, and the gum inside her mouth turns stiff
and unchewable. She walks as fast as she can toward the street
where Tom lives. As she sees what must be his house, she
notices that her speed slows, in spite of thinking it would be
good to get inside. Again she must reassure herself that there's
nothing special about this informant except for the fact he has
the same name as her ex-husband. He certainly won't look
like him. Why should he? The arbitrary connection between a
name and the named is elementary linguistics. There's nothing
about the word *cat* that makes it particularly suited to describ-
ing a four-legged, occasionally purring creature with paws and

a tail, nor is it likely that anything about the name *Tom* makes men with that name resemble each other. A friend has been so kind as to let her know that she's seen Tom, Ellinor's ex-husband Tom, at the cinema with a blond woman. But she's finished with him. She's begun a new life. She doesn't dwell any longer on her previous husband.

She's almost halfway through the list of people from her project manager, and she's also gotten the names of several more possible informants. In not too many weeks the registry work will be finished, and she can sit down and systematize the results. She'll look forward to that. It's always wonderful to be able to cross off the accomplishment of phase one. If only she were not so tired. She yawns and feels the veins pounding at the top of her head, just under the skull. Perhaps this Tom has a Tylenol. She rings his doorbell.

Tom is a plump, friendly guy around who seems her own age. He looks like a cherub that flits around a stone pedestal, and his appearance is as far from her Tom as it's possible to be. He has butter-yellow curls, ruddy cheeks, an unclear and quivering transition from chin to neck. Tom eats cookies, answers precisely and flatly all the questions while Ellinor fills in the questionnaire. She asks about further possible informants but only gets names she's heard before. The headache has returned, with renewed force. When Tom gets up to fetch more cookies, Ellinor asks if he by chance has a headache pill. He returns with a full plate of cookies, a glass of water, and an oval, dove-gray pill. She swallows the pill with a half glass of water and takes a cookie to be polite.

When she has come to the end of section three of the questionnaire, the effects of the pill kick in. She floats over the sofa. Everything sounds like it's packed in cotton. She fills out the last form, which she writes by hand, and she has trouble keeping the words within the lines of the columns. She asks what kind of tablet it was. The cherub says it was something he bought on the Internet, not dangerous at all, American, a completely ordinary *painkiller,* a word he pronounces with relish and a convincing American *r,* which remains in the air, grinding against her eardrums. Ellinor nods cautiously; her head feels like a solid helium balloon. She packs up her things, has to stop and think before she remembers that the papers should be put in a bundle in her briefcase, that the questionnaire should be placed in a plastic folder before going into the side pocket. She says no thanks to a last cup of coffee, says she must get back home, she's dog-tired, has hardly slept of late.

She stands swaying in the hallway as Tom brings her outdoor clothes. His red-marbled face comes right to up hers: Are you doing okay? Yes, she assures him and then remembers she forgot to ask him about Anna Guttormsen. She must find a clever, subtle way of formulating the question. Before she's finished the thought, she has asked. He looks at her, laughs with some embarrassment. Yes, I know Anna Guttormsen. Perhaps the oval pill has removed her filters, perhaps it's many days in a row of sleeping badly that is the cause. Ellinor hears herself ask what the story actually is about Anna Guttormsen, is she a shaman, *noaidi,* or a nice lady? Tom laughs again. His chin quivers. That's probably the problem with Anna Guttormsen, he finally answers, that she's both a witchy old granny and a nice lady. Depending on whose eyes see her or which mouth talks about her. Ellinor nods.

"Either you're on the side of Anna Guttormsen, or you're on the side of Berit Rist," he maintains.

"Berit Rist," repeats Ellinor. She tries in vain to focus on Tom's face, but then, without warning, from one second to the next, the fog lifts, and she feels rested and effective. The pain is gone. Totally gone. Her mind is razor sharp. Berit Rist and Anna Guttormsen were like cat and dog, wasn't that true? She's in great shape, she could run along the arm of the fjord or finish writing the SAMmin report. Preferably both at once. "I'm certain that name doesn't appear on my list."

"No, it wouldn't, because she died many years ago. Just after the Alta protests."

"Was she active in the demonstrations?"

Tom laughs. "No, absolutely not."

"But Anna Guttormsen was."

"Of course. And Berit's son is alive. Kåre. Are you feeling better? You look . . ."

"I feel completely fine," interrupts Ellinor. "Kåre Os? That's right. I have him on my list. I've tried to call him many times, but he never picks up the phone. Either he doesn't answer or I get the message that phone coverage is temporarily out of service in the area."

"Doesn't surprise me. Kåre fishes more than he watches TV, and he lives more in the tent than in the house. He doesn't always bother to pick up the phone," answers Tom. "Just a minute."

He raises his index finger and backs up halfway down the hall. Ellinor draws herself up, carefully shakes her head, the headache has truly vanished. Tom returns.

"He's home now."

"Did you call him?"

"No, I can see his house from the kitchen window. There's light and movement inside. It can't be anyone else but Kåre. How's the head?"

"Never been better. If you can point out his house, then I'll stop by, since I'm here."

"Are you cer . . ."

"And you?" interrupts Ellinor. "Whose side are you on? The Guttormsen family or the Rist family?"

93

Tom looks surprised, then he laughs, opens his mouth and laughs. The pale chin section wobbles.

"According to tradition I'm for Anna Guttormsen, but it's been so many years since all that happened. . . ."

"A family feud," Ellinor concludes. "What happened?"

"It's a long time ago. It just happened. No one wanted to cause anyone harm."

"But what happened?"

"To be honest, I don't completely know. I don't get into gossip."

Ellinor nods. It doesn't matter. She'll probably find out one way or another. She'll manage. She can sort out most things. Nothing is impossible. She's full of energy. She says goodbye, walks purposefully toward the home of Kåre Os with her outerwear, caps, scarves, in an untidy heap on one arm. Behind her Tom says something along the lines of her probably needing to go home and rest.

Kåre Os has no doorbell. She knocks. Three decided knocks. Self-confidence. Effectiveness. Vigor. Bang, bang, bang. She remains standing still with her hand against the wooden door as the world starts to spin and grow dim, and she suddenly discovers she's nauseated, she must throw up. One of her leather mitts falls to the ground.

"Hello, Ellinor Smidt," says the man in the door opening. It's the man from the grocery store. The man in the gray-green anorak. Aside from the fact that, of course, he's not wearing the anorak now.

Ellinor swallows, forcing back the urge to throw up. The first vowel in her name has another phonetic quality in his speech, more open than in the southeast of Norway; it makes her name sound exotic and beautiful. She tries to raise her head, look him confidently in the eye, but isn't equal to it.

Spots dance before her eyes. The outerwear falls down in front of her. She leans against the door frame, holds on to it with both arms.

"I'm not too well."

"I see that."

"I must go home."

"You must not go anywhere. You have to lie down."

When she wakes, she doesn't understand at first where she is. She's slept on a sofa in a strange room. She's dozed off on Kåre Os's sofa. She probably couldn't tolerate the combination of analgesic and sleep deprivation. Right next to her crackles a fire in a beautiful soapstone fireplace. On the wall behind her hangs what appears to be antique medical equipment, a cannula, a stethoscope, an anatomical wall chart. On the floor are many reindeer skins. On the table is a vase of dried heather, lit candles in pewter candlesticks. On one wall a collection of antlers is arranged. It is cabin-like, while at the same time it's modern. Masculine, but nice. Naturally he lives like this. In a cliché. On the sofa lies a coverlet with sheepskin on one side. She lies under it. In just a T-shirt and underpants. The rest of her clothing is a neatly folded pile on a chair next to the sofa. Outer clothing on another chair, the mitts on top of the pile. Her naked legs feel twice as naked next to the coarsely woven material. It smells pungently of sheep's wool. The T-shirt is worn thin. The coverlet has slipped halfway to the floor. She can see the shape of her breasts and the outline of her nipples under the shirt. Outside the window it's dark, but that doesn't give her any hint of what time of day it is. Kåre is in the kitchen. She hears him clattering glasses.

"How long have I been sleeping?"

"Well, good morning, Ellinor Smidt. Let's see, you've

slept approximately twelve hours. You arrived at seven o'clock in the evening yesterday, and now it's time for the morning news on the radio. And I've just begun to make breakfast."

Ellinor sits up on the sofa, pulls her thighs to her chest, wraps her arms around her knees. She smiles, rocks her body forward and back and smiles, can't stop smiling. Then she leans back against the sofa pillows, knowing she is rested.

19

We sit back to back, leaning into each other. Ellinor looks forward. I look backward. Every once in a while we turn our heads and glance over our shoulders, so I see the future and she, the past. My taciturn father grows clearer; he comes toward me, as Ellinor will finally come toward me with the pancake mix and the frying pan with the collapsible handle in her backpack. Mama slips away from me, further every day. Until they stand there together, my parents, at a distance, like two shadows next to each other. Grandfather likely chose to keep quiet. Anna Guttormsen chose to fight. I write. Too late for the truth, high time for fiction.

These days I reflect on what I thought when I discovered my grandfather was the son of a Sea Sami. The primary feelings aren't hard to recall, identify, and recognize: I was surprised and unprepared. It was something that had never struck me as a possibility, quite simply. I'd never thought along those lines. Was I ashamed? I've searched the depths of my heart, looking high and low for shame and disgrace, but I haven't found a trace of either of them. What I did discover was a hint of unease, yes, a sense that this couldn't be right. It just didn't fit together. With who I believed I was, with the stories I had heard, with the photos I had seen. The discovery was like a piece of furniture you didn't wish for, that you didn't order, that one day just appeared in the midst of your own well-ordered room. A room you'd lived in your whole life, that you were used to, as if it were the only possible room, where you'd scrubbed and polished some things in the room and shoved other things into dark corners. In the middle of this room, among the inherited pieces and newer purchases, stands this piece of furniture. I've begun to get used to it, yes. I know I even could have been proud of it, if I'd only had the chance, if this unexpected piece of furniture had been a part of my childhood's interior. It may never be completely mine now. I may always have a tendency to stub my toe on it, I may always notice how it creaks when I sit on it. For this is an old piece of furniture, yet all the same it's appeared without my parents having put their mark on it, having told their stories about it, having sat there together with me, making hollows in the cushions and scratching the varnish. As long as I haven't sat on it and kicked at it with my childish feet, taken command of it, spilled milk on it, it will always be different from the rest of the interior.

It suits me very well to have been born in Stockholm, to have grown up in Oslo. This is who I am. It suits me that a great-grandfather owned Norway's first car. It suits me that there's a good deal of blood from Western Norway flowing in my veins, along with that of Eastern Norway. It suited me to change my last name. It suits me that we alphabetize books, that every other relative is an engineer, that we say *A place for everything, everything in its place.* No, wait, it's in Ellinor's family they say that. In mine they say *Qui vivra verra,* and this is clearly more difficult to live up to.

If I dig deep into my vanity: maybe the truth is that I would have considered it finer to have a count in the family rather than a Sami? Would I have been less bewildered if the new sofa were covered in silk and had mahogany arms? Maybe I'm harder on myself than I deserve.

For I had been a proud child.

A cap rises to the surface, materializes in my consciousness. It looks like a bonnet, is made of reindeer skin and has red trimming and red strings. As a child I loved it. I pick it up, sniff it, and recognize the smell of fur, cocoa, and Oslo snow. It's called a Sami cap. I don't know where it came from, I probably inherited it from my big sister or maybe it was a present from friends of Mama and Papa. I'm certain it didn't come from relatives in Finnmark—they weren't around when I was small. I loved that cap, and I loved to pretend I was a Sami girl, the Sami girl Laila from the movie of the same name, because that was what Sami girls were called if they weren't called Ravna. And on TV there was a series about the Sami boy Ante, which everyone watched, if only because there was only one Norwegian channel. A Sami great-grandfather would have suited me very well. A becoming contrast. Suitably exotic, suitably distant.

20

Three women's bodies. Mama's, mine, Ellinor's. They hang together, one unthinkable without the preceding, first Mama's, then mine, then Ellinor's.

Often in her life, Ellinor has liked her body. It's slender, on the border of thin, with small breasts, narrow hips, long legs. Definitely a woman's body but without too many bells and whistles, as her father had said once when she was a teenager and needed to hear something like that. Since then it was exactly the functional, the almost severe, the lack of anything insistent she'd liked best about her body. But after many years of attempting to get pregnant, initially in a natural way, afterward with help from hormone shots and in vitro fertilization, she began to despise it. There was nothing physically wrong with her or with Tom, but the eggs just wouldn't attach themselves. They slipped out of her uterus, one after the next. And the one time she'd succeeded in becoming pregnant, the fetus wouldn't remain inside her. From the moment she'd stood hand in hand with Tom and looked disbelievingly at the blue stripes on the pregnancy test until she woke at the hospital, she could continue to feel that her breasts were tender, she could continue to imagine her child would be called Regine, she could continue to buy pregnancy books, she could continue to look at drawings and photographs of the stages of the fetus. A thirteen-week-old fetus is between twelve and fourteen centimeters long, and eyebrows and eyelashes have begun to grow. They could keep talking about it, she and Tom, saying that their child already had eyebrows and eyelashes. And the evening before, Tom put his lips on her stomach and whispered a good-night lullaby to his child, and Ellinor knew she'd never been so happy. He lifted his head and looked at her, half bashful: my mother always sang that to me.

After Tom moved out, she stopped exercising and began to shovel in gingerbread cookies and marshmallow candy. Ellinor is disgusted by her scrawny, unfit body, and she's more repulsed when it hits her that her thigh muscles are shrinking and her belly is spreading.

Mama's body became so small. Her height shrank, more than what was usual for older people; she lost more than ten centimeters because her skeleton was brittle and because her spine was more compromised than other people's. The grandchildren looked like giants alongside her. She weighed barely thirty kilos toward the end and was literally skin and bones.

Her body diminished year by year, but it asserted itself more and more. She had large, painful sores that wouldn't heal. Her gums wouldn't hold on to her teeth. Her stomach couldn't accept food. Her body dominated her existence. It was about pain in her limbs, about not being able to lift her arms, about not being able to hold a fork, about not being able to walk. The pains and torments ruled her daily life and dictated our conversations. Toward the end she spoke of vomit and diarrhea with great matter-of-factness, as if they were ordinary subjects for conversation and of general interest. The body took charge. Modesty disappeared.

In my childhood home, we spoke little of bodily matters.

You covered yourself when you came out of the bath. You didn't speak of menstruation, and where Mama hid her pads I have no idea. Papa said nothing about his tall, thin, and loose-limbed body when it sickened. He probably avoided going to the doctor for a long time. After he was diagnosed, his body was quickly eaten up from the inside. But bodies, infirmities, and death remained nonsubjects.

Mama didn't have the energy to go to the hairdresser she had visited since she began work at the University Press in the 1970s, and her hair grew long and tangled. At Tåsenhjemmet they cut it, finally, into a strange pageboy style, completely different from how she had ever worn it. Mama never used any other makeup besides lipstick (*libstick*, she said), apart from a gold powder case she had when I was small. Before Christmas the youngest painted Mama's nails fire-engine red. Mama found it funny, even though she said she got a shock whenever she glimpsed them. In January the nail polish began to flake off, and each time we visited her she asked us to bring polish remover, and each time we forgot. One day when we arrived, one of the nurses had removed the rest of the Christmas-red polish and applied a new layer of apricot-colored lacquer. She had a pageboy and apricot-rose nail polish with shimmer on the day she died.

She was different the last days of her life. I'm afraid, she said. It could have been she wanted to talk about what was coming. She was so restless. When lying down, she wanted to be helped up to a sitting position, and when sitting she wanted to lie down almost immediately. I recognized the restlessness from the times when I'd had a high fever: no position is comfortable, you twist and turn in the hope of finding peace and comfort, but it's not to be found. And her voice became that of a stranger. Only at times, in a few short sentences, did her voice sound the way it used to. My eldest was wearing clothes specially designed for her high school graduating class, and Mama said that in 1948, when she graduated, they'd gone on a class trip to Åsgård Beach. Then the restlessness set in again. She tried to rise. Do you want to sit? Ye-es! A despairing cry from someone who can't handle much more. Do you want to lie down now? Yes! The voice belongs to a child at the mercy of her parents, a child who tries to get them to understand but also knows that it's no use.

She was so little, so wizened. Like the Neolithic mummy Ötzi, which Ingolv and the youngest and I had seen in the Bolzano Museum in Italy just before Christmas. But in the middle of her yellow face, her eyes were large and a lighter blue than I can ever recall seeing them before. We were with her only a few hours before she died. We tried to get her to take some soup. She ate a couple of spoonfuls, both children fed her, just as she had once fed them. And me. But I didn't feed her, couldn't handle it, couldn't, wouldn't. There was too much body, too little Mama. The last time Mama was at Svea, at Christmas, I helped her to the toilet, supported her, stood her up, pulled up her pants. I did this with closed eyes. I feel shame about that now.

On her eightieth birthday, which we celebrated in a driving summer rain three years ago, one of her childhood friends gave a speech. They'd gone to elementary school together at Ullevål and later to Berg High School. The friend talked about how good Mama had been in sports, about how she became district champion in the high jump and was on the swim team. She came to the end of her speech and summarized it by saying: "Gerd had the most attractive body of all of us." I don't know what Mama thought, and I don't know what the other guests thought, whether they felt it was merely amusing and touching, whether anyone but me felt it was a little painful, too much body. Mama never despised her body, she was never ashamed of it. But I believe, down deep, she felt betrayed by it.

After her death, her body has again grown insignificant. It's not what I think about, that poor destroyed body of hers. It's her smile, voice, stories. Her words. The sound of her steps across the floor. The familiar scent of her.

My body. I don't think too much about it. My body has given birth, has nourished the children I wanted to have. It digests the food I put into it. It holds me up and transports me where I want to go. It still has a nice shape and can wear the clothes I put on it. It hasn't yet betrayed me. There are things I used to do with it that I doubt I could do now. It was quite good at pirouetting. I doubt I could do that now. It danced ballet for some years. I believe it has forgotten that. Before I could sleep on any old sofa or air mattress; I slept on the floor in the train through Germany on the way to Paris, my pack with the Norwegian flag was my pillow. Now my back begins to grumble ominously if the mattress in the hotel room is too soft. My body does what it's supposed to do, and I maintain it discreetly, like other adults who aren't yet old or dependent on others. In a private room I wash and shave myself, shampoo, groom, and rub oil into my skin, so my body will continue to be clean, odorless, and smooth. I can still allow myself modesty.

21

"Hey. I just . . . where is your bathroom?"

Kåre nods toward the hallway, and Ellinor slips into the bathroom, which is warm and light, with white tiles on the walls and with something that appears to be slate on the floor. She sits down on the toilet, with just one thigh on the seat, pressing halfway back and controlling the stream so it doesn't splash into the bowl. A tamed fountain, not a wild waterfall.

She turns on the shower, adjusting the faucet to find the right temperature. Scrubs her face, under the arms, in the crotch. Lifts up one and then the other foot and washes herself with Kåre's soap. She fills her mouth with water and spits, gargles and spits. She decides to steal a squirt of shampoo from him, too. After all the body smells are gone, she rubs herself dry. It's only when she's about to hang up the towel that she recognizes a faint smell of sweat, masculine sweat, and understands that he's used it before. She remains standing with the towel pressed against her nose. The fish with the short snout thrashes inside her; its fins wave repeatedly. Good God, Ellinor. There's mist on the mirror. She dries it off. The first thing she sees are her insistently obvious nipples, like an extra pair of eyes. She turns away from all four eyes, but turns back the next second. Her cheeks are red. Her hair is wet and dark and clinging to her throat, neck, and the top part of her breasts and back. Her breasts are small and round. She gazes shamelessly at herself, stands there with legs spread out, admiring herself. Then she gets dressed again, rolls the towel like a turban around her head, and goes out into the smell of bacon.

22

Thin, very thin.

Light hair, that is, the hair he has is light.

Blue eyes?

Nice smile.

Polite.

Can take some teasing.

Kind and helpful toward Gerd.

    At least.

Not downright industrious perhaps. Before.

Unbelievably charming.

Quite the sportsman.

Understands how to conduct himself.

Well groomed and likes nice clothes.

Many good friends.

Good at drinking and smoking. Sometimes too good.

Good at playing poker. Likes to

    play bridge.

Not exactly an opera singer.

Certainly a nice man to have.

~~Sweet~~ Engaged to a sweet girl.

I'd never seen this piece of paper before I found it today, along with Mama's and Papa's birth certificates, marriage certificate, school diplomas, and other papers that were put in a box for safekeeping. Mama treasured it for sixty years. Exactly what it is, I don't know, but I am certain it's a description of Papa. A yellowing page torn from a notepad, blue ink. Nice handwriting, neither especially masculine nor feminine, and I don't recognize it. The page must be from 1950 or 1951 since he and Mama are clearly engaged. Could it have been a guessing game, where you have to offer up one point after the next on the list? Is it written by a fellow student from NTH?

It could have been a first draft of a character in a novel and, in a way, that's exactly what it's become.

Papa always wore single-colored white or light-blue shirts. He wore a tie or bow tie with his suit or trousers and blazer. White handkerchief in his breast pocket. The inner jacket pocket held a dark blue Parker pen and a slide rule of white plastic. Calculators were for sissies. The last fifteen years of his life he worked at Sogn Vocational High School as a science teacher and changed his brand of whiskey from Ballantine's to Teachers.

After ten years abroad, ten secure years at Union Carbide, the latter years as manager of the Scandinavian division, he made a mess of things for himself and his family with his own businesses that failed, one after the next. Money problems, heavy drinking, trips to the pawnshop, quarreling while I lay in bed and tried to sleep. I could lie under the comforter with my fingers in my ears, but I couldn't escape those evenings, and I never will. Yet at the moment I do, for that is a story that will never be told. Besides, Papa pulled himself together, presumably giving up the dream of self-employment. He enrolled at the Teachers Academy, and in 1975 he was hired by Sogn Vocational High School and the quarreling stopped. From then on there was only Mama's irritated bark now and then about unimportant things, like a mess in the closet or forgotten food in the fridge. Papa was the personification of phlegmatic, nothing could destroy his composure. He was calmness itself.

He loved to read. When I ask Ingolv what he remembers best about my father, he answers the same as what I'm thinking: Kjell in a chair, with one leg crossed over the other, with a book or the newspapers, *Farmand* or *Aftenposten,* the old broadsheet *Aftenposten,* not the tabloid. It's likely I got it from him, my reading the same books over and over again. His favorite books were read until they fell apart, and he had gotten the bookbinding students at the vocational high school to restore some of them in attractive bindings with leather backs and corners, patterned endpapers, silk bookmarks. I come into the living room, ask about something; he looks up over his glasses, always obliging, but lost in a book. Light-blue eyes. Large. I've heard they were similar to mine, but mine are darker and have a muddier gray-blue color: multicolored, Mama called them. Hmm, did you need something, Helene? I see him before me, exactly in that posture. I hear his voice.

This was my city father, in a white or pale-blue Van Heusen shirt. The shirts of my vacation father were red-checked flannel. He wore khaki trousers. Shorts. Running shoes. Ski knickers and ski boots. But in the evening he liked to sit in a chair and read in the yard in Romsdalen, in the mountain cabin in Valdres. In the same way: crossed legs, book in his lap. He had a collection of bandit novels, as he called them, in both places. MacLean, Zane Grey, Dumas, Øvre Richter Frich, Wodehouse. At home in the city he read aloud to me a lot. When Mama's apartment is sold, when her things are divided between my mute sister and me, I hope I get Papa's books. Not all, I don't have room for them, but some. As many as possible.

When we were on vacation, Papa told fairy tales he made up himself instead of reading aloud. He told about the grouse couple who lived up in the mountains. I no longer remember what Papa called them, but they were something with *r*. *Rrr* in Papa's soft burr. Rupert and Rupertine, Rune and Rita. No, I can't recall it, but it was something in that phonetic direction. At least I remember that the male grouse in Papa's fairy tale had bright red eyebrows, and it's just now as I write this, while searching for "grouse" on the Internet, that I discover all grouse have bright red eyebrows, that it wasn't anything Papa made up to amuse me.

When I was little, I was convinced my father could do anything. He could build cabinets, lay tiles, mold a canoe, make stilts. He could draw horses, so lifelike that I heard them whinny. Wax skis, row boats, shoot thrushes and grouse, pick cloudberries and mushrooms. Papa had taken flying lessons, he could cut grass with a scythe—short handled and long handled. He could run with me in the wheelbarrow. He could light fires and make camp pancakes. The ingredients were in the backpack, and the recipe went like this: make the batter from a tiny bit of sugar and as many eggs as you have. Mix in the flour so it thickens and the milk so it's thin enough. Cook up in a ton of butter in a fry pan over the fire or a camp stove. Papa could set up a tent, whittle willow flutes, throw together a fish funnel trap, make boats with elastic-band motors that sailed over the water. He could answer everything I wondered about, and if he didn't have a ready answer he opened the *Encyclopedia Britannica,* which we had in twenty-four volumes on the lowest shelves. He could snap his thumb against his nicotine-brown index finger. He was a passionate fisherman, just as happy in salt water as fresh, with a fly-fishing rod, with a loop to hang the fish from. He could fillet a fish so the pieces were skinless and boneless. He had a gray backpack with maps in a plastic pouch. A compass with a shaving mirror in the lid. Camp stove, coffee kettle, and fry pan with a handle that folded in. Flies for the rod in a wax box. He smoked a pipe or blue Teddy cigarettes, filterless. He could eat cheese that smelled so disgusting the rest of us had to leave the room. He could eat the squishy stuff behind the eyes of a codfish. And his biographer from sixty years ago was completely correct in that he had no singing voice.

And I believe *I* am correct in suspecting that many of Papa's outdoor skills came from my grandfather. Papa went out fishing with his father. I know that. Didn't I hear that? The fourteen-year-old district school student was also listed in the census as a fisherman, so fishing should have been something he could do, my grandfather. I remember one of Papa's stories: When he was a boy, he and his companions caught some sculpins and fashioned bits of cork on the spikes of their back fins and threw the poor sculpins back into the sea. I recall imagining how they blew with the corks on the surface of the water, unable to dive. I thought this was horrible and hit him in the stomach. That's how it often is, my girl: you're moving on the surface and can never dive down to the depths. No, Papa would never say anything like that, that reply is far too pompous for him to have made.

Papa also told me he went hunting for hazel grouse when he was young. According to my father, hazel grouse are so slow-witted that if seven of them are perching on a branch, they'll remain sitting there until they are shot down, one after the next. I remember now that Grandmother had some silver bowls that were "Nicolai's shooting prizes." So Grandfather must have been quite a good marksman. I suspect Papa learned to shoot from his father, but I don't know that.

I have a photograph of Papa. He is perhaps ten years old and is standing with two other boys. They have Indian feathers in their sun-bleached hair. Once, Papa played Indians and shot arrows from his bow through the bedsheets hanging out to dry. It was winter, the sheets were frozen stiff, and the arrow disappeared straight through them. It seems to me that these sheets were hanging out to dry in the yard of their house in Notodden, that the house was white, that there were a great number of apple trees and berry bushes, that the house was quite high, with a view down toward Heddal's Lake. I have no idea whether that's true. It's a tendency I have, perhaps, to place relatives in large, white houses. But it fits, since the sheet episode must have happened while Papa was quite young and Grandfather was alive, and someone who was the chief engineer at Tinfos Ironworks in the 1930s probably had the money for a villa and apple trees. Later, money grew tighter.

Every time we went to visit Grandmother and we drove down over the hills to Notodden, I asked Papa if it was really true that he used to slide down the road when he was little. There weren't so many cars in the thirties, Papa always said. He and his companions pulled their sleds up to the top of the road at Meheia Station and sped down to the town.

For me, Papa's childhood was faraway and different, like one of the boys' novels from the Gyldendal series with red covers. They were books I never read. On the other hand, I have— they were moved to Svea—an entire shelf of girls' books, the series with worn blue covers. Some I inherited from my sister, twelve years older, and some Mama had when she was young. *Gerd Uri, Christmas, 1941. To the bookworm Gerd from Ellen, Christmas, 1943.* I've read them all. I read many of them aloud to my girls when they were small. There are many good morals, language history, and memories in old books for young girls.

~~~

Papa was born six years before Mama. In 1940, Mama was only eleven. Papa was seventeen. Mama told me time after time about the blackout curtains, about standing in lines, about ration cards, about the potatoes grown in the garden in Ullevål Hageby, about the Germans who dug trenches between the currant bushes on the farm at Romsdalen. The table from the farmer's cottage ended up with a photographer in Åndalsnes. Loyal Norwegians held their jackets together with paper clips. On Mama's report card *English* is crossed out and *German, written and oral* is written by hand. The school was used as a hospital, and Mama's class had afternoon courses at the university campus at Blindern. Grandma fried slices of rutabaga in cod-liver oil and made "cream" from skim milk and potato flour. She and Grandpa had a large wheel of goat cheese in the attic that lasted a long time, and it was a stroke of sheer good luck they had managed to lay hands on it.

Mama wouldn't have been Mama if I hadn't known the tons of stories from the war that she told me. I have an envelope with the ration cards she saved. I have her club book, where she and a girlfriend wrote their meeting notes, preferably in verse: "Of poetry I know nothing because I'm just a little patriot."

I know the stories of the clothes she managed to sew, of the lines at the fish shop, of which teachers were Nazis. But I know one story about Papa, too. Papa was in the Resistance, one of the boys in the woods. He became responsible for an illegal newspaper when the teacher who was its editor was sent up to Kirkenes. I wrote a paper about that in middle school and got an A on it. What Papa told me was like an especially exciting boys' book from the series. The light-footed boys, they were called. They shot moose. The British parachuted supplies down to them. They had weapon caches in the forest and code names for each other. He had been given a medal. The group was supposed to make sure that the industrial areas in Telemark weren't destroyed in the early phases of the war. So it was said. When I was writing my paper, Mama showed me the certificate he got, which I now have in a drawer in the secretaire: "Kjell Nilsen served in the Resistance in North Telemark, 1941–1945. Norway thanks you for your contribution to the liberation." *Olav* is written at the bottom. I remember I asked Mama, is it really the king who signed his name? Yes, answered Mama, but he wasn't the king then, just the crown prince and the head of defense.

Only a few years ago I read the report Papa wrote in 1946, typed on paper that was falling apart, with many errors, delivered in free and easy boys' book style. The war was over. They had won. He was one of the boys in the woods, and now he was going to report on it. A boys' book. And then, a few pages in, the lively tone changes, and then comes this. Someone was shot. One froze to death. Juster. He died "in our arms," Papa writes. "No one could enjoy the mood in the woods or mountains as much as he could; no one could fall completely to pieces seeing an idyllic *seter* farm building as he could, our future architect. Alongside his mental abilities, he was incontestably the most practical of us all. He made food like a trained cook, sharpened axes, built huts, fireplaces, hiding places for weapons, all with the same calm matter-of-factness. I know my report should have been short, but I hope you will excuse me. Juster was one of my best friends. I learned to value him more and more as I came to know him, and it's difficult for me to write briefly about him."

Papa never said anything to me about Juster or the others who died. To me it was all about English chocolate in the parachute drops and about moose hunting. It seems that years passed before he said anything to Mama either.

When the war started, Grandfather had been dead for three years. Papa didn't say what it was like to lose his father. Nor did I ask. At any rate I didn't insist. I could have asked about it instead of always asking if it was really true that they rode their sleds down the hills on the road, which in the seventies and eighties was a highway with lots of traffic. What did you do the day you learned of his death, Papa? You were fourteen. Did you cling to Grandmother, or did you tear yourself loose? Did you have a close friend? Did you already know Juster?

Grandmother wasn't yet forty when her husband died and she was left responsible for three boys: Kjell at fourteen was the eldest. Before Grandfather died he had been—for a long time, I have the impression—at a sanatorium. His sons weren't allowed to visit him there. Those are the facts as Papa told them to me. Or maybe Mama told me? Yes, the more I think about it, the more certain I am that it was Mama. Sickness, sanatorium, no permission to visit, death. That's how it was then. Nothing could be done about it.

Grandfather died of silicosis. I read about silicosis on the Internet and in old medical books. The disease is called "stone-dust lungs" because it attacks people who work in mines or industry. Grandfather worked in the smelting industry. To produce ferrosilicon you need quartz. In the 1920s and 1930s the smelting ovens were open and the air in the oven halls swirled with quartz dust.

The jaw is wide open, a glowing red interior, a puffing animal that never ceases to demand more. Muscles and machines work together. An undulating motion, one effort, one organism, with hundreds of limbs that know their place, that look after their task. The metal sings, the ore thunders as it is emptied into large containers, and the noise reverberates through the space. The air is thick with dust. Close to the ovens the heat shimmers. The workers have blue overalls, strong footwear. Their faces stream with sweat. One of them has a dirty stripe across his brow where he's dried it with his forearm. The engineers have lab coats to protect their clothing. Underneath they wear suits. They have a pen in their breast pocket, a notebook in hand. Outside spring has just begun to make itself known. Yellow-gray clay can be seen between the snow drifts. There are small, choppy waves on the fjords. Fresh new leaves on the birch trees. At home the housewives prepare dinner: the workers' wives and management's ladies. The white-collar wives have household help, but they set the table themselves. Cloth napkins in napkin rings, every family member has his or her own, in silver, with name and date of baptism. A coltsfoot flower in an eggcup in the middle of the table. Children clinging to their mother's aprons. Soon the fathers will come home. The warm potatoes will be peeled, fish placed on the serving platter, the stuffed cabbage rolls browned up. He could arrive any minute. Is the table set? Is my hair nice and neat? Are your hands clean? Let's see.

Inhaling small stone dust particulates can lead to fibrosis, scar tissue on the lungs, which then makes it hard to breathe. It is a work-related illness, quite widespread in Norway before attention was paid to it and people began to use protective clothing. It's so simple. If Grandfather had worn a mask over his mouth and nose, he wouldn't have become sick.

Silicosis can develop into tuberculosis. Perhaps Grandfather got that, too. Perhaps that was shameful. I seem to recall that Grandfather emphasized that he didn't have tuberculosis. And perhaps the plain story is that he didn't die of tuberculosis, perhaps *that's* the truth. Sometimes people stick to that.

I sit here thinking about Grandmother, pulling up the picture of her from the newspaper. She peers at me from my computer screen, not unlike the look Papa gave me over the top of the newspaper or book. Yes, Helene, what can I do for you? It strikes me that she and Papa always carried on a conversation about whether Tinfos had failed its workers. Papa and Grandmother were similarly undramatic, similarly low voiced, but their exchanges could accurately hit their target, and they did in these conversations. Mama was less talkative than usual, and I, I listened disengaged while I tried to move around the pieces of the puzzle cross or slid my palm over the raised letters of the conch shell. I barely paid attention, so now I must merely guess, trying to recreate the mood from the conversation that inevitably repeated from visit to visit, that trickled forth like a stubborn brook, something you couldn't do anything about but that all the same you had to comment on because it was so important, so impossible to ignore. I'm certain that the conversation had to do with a time when the gender of the worker was more important to the salary than her knowledge and work skills. Grandmother was resigned, never bitter. Perhaps it also had to do with a miserable widow's pension, or a lack of compensation. Silicosis, which caused Grandfather's death, is an occupational injury, after all. I'm only guessing, don't know anything. I do a simple search for *silicosis tinfos ironworks*. The government and national archives come up among the first hits. Alongside restricted reports. Dust lungs, silicosis research on Norwegian industries, index files of those affected, all with restrictions or conditions. So I resign myself as well, along with Grandmother, many years too late.

And I'm really only guessing. I don't remember the content of the repeated conversations, only the mood: the necessity of speaking about the same things. Grandmother's mild but insistent voice, shifting over to other conversation topics. The weather. Grandmother's neighbors, how school was going for me, how my sister was. The almost magical effects of rosehip extract and honey, the advantage of an ice-cold room. The dinner that was almost ready. Mutton-and-cabbage stew, again.

23

She still has the taste of bacon in her mouth, a salt and fat smoky taste. The hand towel she'd wrapped around her hair lies on the floor. The sheepskin rug chafes with unbearable heat against her ankles, but she can't manage to kick it away. She only wants to enjoy herself now. She shoves all thoughts away to give pleasure all the room it demands. He's supporting himself on his forearms at the same time he holds her around the shoulders. She has both palms against the small of his back and feels how his muscles are working. A drop of sweat falls from his forehead and down his left cheek, lies there quietly before finding a path down her face, over the jawbone to her throat.

For a few seconds he rests heavily on her before rolling over to the side. Ellinor doesn't see his face, but she hears that he's smiling.

"I'm not interested in a relationship," she informs him.

"Is that so," he answers, right in her ear, still out of breath. "What kind of postcoital conversation is this, Ellinor Smidt? Can't you say anything nice instead? That I'm an outstanding lover?"

"I just thought . . ."

"Don't think."

Kåre places his mouth against her throat and blows. She laughs, wriggles away, but he holds her fast, moving his lips to her breasts.

Afterward they sit on the kitchen stools, each with a coffee mug and a bottle of aquavit on the table between them.

"I just meant . . . ," Ellinor begins.

"I understand what you meant. It's completely fine."

She is strangely disappointed that he's so understanding.

Outside it's even quieter, and it seems even more desolate than before. He offered to walk her home, but she refused, laughing the suggestion away. That would be so intimate, she explained, and meant it. Uh-huh, he said.

It feels like cornstarch under her feet, and her boots make an even track in the snow. She walks in the middle of the street. It's the first time in many years she's had sex without thinking about hormones, fertile periods, sperm quantity, favorable positions, cycles. Ha! She slept with a man she doesn't know, without even thinking about preventive measures. Well, anyway, she's incapable of getting pregnant. It's promiscuity, full steam ahead. This is her new life. She sticks out her tongue and catches one of the featherlight snowflakes, just like when she was a child with no worries. Or like a childless, worry-free woman.

Up until now she's worked steadily, but with no passion, on her project. So far she hasn't been fired up in the way she was with her doctoral dissertation at the end, when the knots were untying, when suddenly the pattern danced before her eyes and she knew she'd discovered a new corner of the world, a connection no one else had ever seen. Even if it did concern only a grammatical fugue formation and its function in compound words. She'd thought of the SAMmin project as something to put food on the table. She hadn't expected at all to be pulled into it in the same way. But she notices she's beginning to like what she's doing. She inserts the results of the questionnaires into a database, as she's supposed to, as is expected of her, but it's not sufficient. She wants to learn more. She doesn't know enough about threatened languages and language extinction. What she knows has to do with the technical. She knows that language extinction can arise when entire populations are cleared out, something that happened with certain Indian tribes. She knows it's generally less bloody, that smaller languages get crowded out by larger ones, and that the speakers more or less voluntarily stop speaking the mother tongue because the majority language gives more power and prestige and opens more possibilities. She knows this, she learned it at Blindern and from books. She has a guilty conscience because she doesn't know enough about the emotions. Yes, she's read about wing clipping, about heart language, about language and identity, but she has no experience. She is and remains an unconscious native speaker of her own majority language, a language with five million speakers and a bright and secure future. She's just a Southern Norwegian with a provokingly well-meant project, directed by a professor in Oslo. Two thousand kilometers south. *From the South.* Anna Guttormsen had it shamefully right that Ellinor knew nothing. But she is learning.

She asked Kåre about Anna Guttormsen, but he just kissed her naked shoulder and said that one day he could maybe tell her what happened between the two families many, many years ago. It's not important, he said. But it is, she said. For me. Can't you tell me now? she begged. One day, he said, but not today. And I've heard the story from my father, who heard it from his father. Maybe it was completely different.

The project manager has sent yet another email and excitedly asked about Ellinor's meeting with Anna Guttormsen.

It's probably best to be discreet? Kåre nods, but shrugs his shoulders. Yes, of course it's best, but it's no use. In this place everyone knows everything about everyone. All the same Ellinor sneaks to and from Kåre's. She does it several times a week—day, evening, nighttime. It's almost as dark no matter what time it is. The nights are black, but the days are blue, occasionally violet. The third night she sees the northern lights. They appear without warning. She stands there with her mouth open. She feels what she's seeing all through her body. Large, blue-green flashes over the sky that transform into a belt that twists, turning on its own axis before finally dispersing and disappearing. Other, yellower waves come instead, from nowhere, appearing and moving around, high overhead. Soundless, strange, and beautiful. She's stopped, bent her head back, and remains standing a long time. *That* is a sign. It flickers and waves to her. Before she's thought about it she waves back. You should never mimic the northern lights, that means bad luck. It's said. But she doesn't wave only to the heavenly waves but to her mother's soul, which lives up there in the sky. When she was small, she believed her mother saw her, and just now, when she's standing with her head bent so far back that her throat is naked in the cold, she believes that again.

She has taken to humming often as she sits in front of the computer. She sleeps better, too, though perhaps she doesn't; she's only stopped thinking that she has problems sleeping. She's no longer afraid of sounds in the empty house. She's not in love with him, far from it. They sleep with each other. They eat together. Kåre himself believes he's possibly a better cook than lover. They shared an occasional bottle of wine or drink a glass of aquavit. And when the time is right, Kåre promises, you'll get a taste of my homemade cloudberry liqueur. She showers in his bathroom, with its heated floor and soft bath towels. Ellinor sneaks home. She hummed some more. She has a perfect relationship. No feelings other than the sexual are involved. Everything has been made clear, cleanly and satisfactorily. No expectations, misunderstandings, or unexpressed hopes. No past or future. Just the present. Food, sex, and a bathroom like she's used to. As mentioned: perfect.

In the top cupboard of her kitchen she found a calendar from the Society for the Blind, with a request for a donation and a return envelope. She throws the envelope away with a guilty conscience. On the calendar she writes down the day the sun is supposed to return, and then she numbers the days backward to the current day. Sixteen days left. Fifteen. Two weeks. Thirteen. Twelve, eleven, ten. Nine days. Just a week now! And one day the dark time is over. The sun moved above the horizon a few weeks ago, but a hill blocked it off to the south. Today the sun's rays will light the houses for the first time in almost three months. The school and kindergarten are off, the school band will play. The commercial businesses hang *Closed* signs on their doors. No one appears to be doing anything but waiting for the sun. Ellinor is touched by what she sees. Once again she's an observer who doesn't understand, a tourist in the Kingdom of the Dark Time. She's merely experienced half of the dark months and won't go through any more.

How did Grandfather celebrate the end of the winter dark? When he was a boy on Sørøya, toward the end of the nineteenth century and the beginning of the twentieth, how did he celebrate the return of the sun? Perhaps one of his younger brothers pulled him impatiently by the arm: Nicolai, when is the sun coming? Is it coming soon? But he stood there unaffected, calmness itself, the personification of phlegmatic, like the firstborn son he'd later have, the boy who would become my father. He barely listens to his surroundings, stands there with his face turned up to the sky, closes his eyes—and there. The first glimmer, a long shaft of sunlight over the surface of the sea. Nicolai allows the first pale sunbeams to become visible through his eyelids; he sees the whole world turn red and bright.

She wakes with a familiar ache in her lower back, sits up in bed, and discovers a reddish-brown, spreading stain on the sheets. The disappointment washing through her is so strong it's useless to ignore it. She must immediately give up the idea that she hasn't had any hope. She's been full of hope. To believe anything else has been unforgivably naive.

She scrunches down, remains lying on her back under the comforter. What should she do now? What she most feels is a desire to tell Kåre everything, lie close to him and tell him how she has longed, hoped, been disappointed time after time. Should she call him? Ask him to come over now? Her cell phone is on the night table. She reaches for it, feeling how the movement unlooses a thick, flowing stream down onto the sheets, which she absolutely must put into cold water right away. She pulls up his number, is going to call, changes her mind, starts to write a text instead. How should she put it? What, actually, should she say? She writes *Feeling down, come over,* but erases it. *Come!* No, that just seems desperate. So she writes that she has a lot to do, that he can't expect to see her for a while. She looks at the message. Yes, that looks fine. She needs to know that she'll be saved. He'll ask why, beg to see her now, right away, he can't stand it without her. He answers almost immediately. *Ok. See you.* What? That's all? She lifts the phone up close to her eyes, as if there were some letters, some words, some affectionate explanations that had hidden lower down on the screen. It's humiliating, but she must admit with shame she'd been hoping for more than what seems so cruelly apparent this morning. *Ok. See you.* What a cynical dirtbag of a man. That's how they are, all of them, whether they're called Tom or not.

Today the cheerfully patterned notebook isn't enough, nor is the fuzzy-leaved African violet, which has been neglected lately and is beginning to wither and show dead spots on its leaves. But good coffee always helps. She sits on the sofa with a full French press carafe within reach and *Language Death* by David Crystal on her lap. It's almost 11:30 in the morning, and with a little goodwill you could maintain it was daylight outside.

She takes a walk before she goes to bed. It's mild and damp. The snow is sticky, and if she'd been in a different mood she might have stooped, made a snowball, and thrown it. Now she just walks, her mittened hands deep in her pockets, her chin buried in her scarf. She avoids the neighborhood where Kåre lives. Instead she walks toward the sea, and she doesn't stop until she stands a few meters from Anna Guttormsen's house. A welcome light glows from the outdoor lamps and from what are probably the living room windows. Perhaps she should just knock. She walks a few steps nearer but naturally turns back.

For once she sleeps as soon as she lies down. She puts on a T-shirt and ragg-wool socks, changes to a bulky night pad, refuses to think of Kåre. She wakes to a pulsing blue light in the bedroom. Like the northern lights she saw one night, not long ago but it already seems distant. It takes a few seconds before she recognizes it's the cell phone, on mute but flashing blue light in time with the soundless ringtone. *Jørgen Papa*

Smidt reads the display. Immediately her heart speeds up and bangs painfully against her ribs. She picks up the phone with one hand and turns the nightstand lamp on with the other, as if the lamplight could chase away the fears. Yes, Papa? What is it? First, silence, and then her father's voice right in her ear. Elli-mine, is it you? Yes, Papa. What is it? Her father says something, but his voice is weepy and his pronunciation unexpectedly unclear. What are you saying, Papa?

Finally she grasps that he's asking her to come. Now. But, Papa. I can't just now. Don't you remember that I'm in Finnmark? Fli-lim-r, he says. What are you doing up dere? Sounding like a little child. Ellinor skips the explanation this time and asks to speak with someone. Isn't there anyone with you, Papa? Can't you pull on the cord so a nurse will come? Nah, no, answers Papa, no one here, only my cl-cli-clients, now I'm going to go see them. Hang up, Papa, so I can call the night shift. Don't move!

She's put the number of the unit in her cell phone, and now she cuts her father off in the midst of an incomprehensible word he's carefully trying to set on its feet, and calls her father's unit at the nursing home. A woman answers on the first ring: Third floor, how can I help you? She has a low voice and speaks broken Norwegian. Ellinor introduces herself, explains the situation, and the woman promises to investigate and call her back. Ellinor goes into the bathroom. In spite of the wool socks she shivers as her feet cross the vinyl floor. She pees, changes pads, avoids the unpleasant mirror. Remains standing with the comforter around her, looking out at the foggy night through the window of the bedroom. Finally the phone rings. The warm, broken voice: Your father has been sent to the hospital. The on-call doctor believes it may be a stroke, but we won't know for sure until morning. Try to sleep. There's nothing more you can do now. Ellinor thanks her. Sleep well,

127

says the unknown woman. You too, says Ellinor. The woman laughs quietly. I shouldn't be sleeping. Ellinor also laughs a little. That's true. They wish each other good night again and hang up.

She sleeps restlessly, kicks off the comforter, wakes up because she's cold.

26

I lie on my stomach, squeezed over next to the wall. I've kicked the damp sheets as far from me as I can; all the same I can feel that the fabric is getting colder. On the closet door is Bambi, with her long, thin legs, white spots on her back, and a butterfly at her throat. But I don't see Bambi. It's dark in my room; the door is framed in light from the hall. I've slept and awakened. For the grown-ups it's not yet nighttime. I have one ear pushed down into the pillow and a finger in the other. But I can hear anyway. Angry, loud voices that force themselves into my ears no matter what I do to avoid them. They're always saying the same things. Money, the rent, bills to pay. Too much wine and whiskey. Business failures. Bills. Debt collectors. Obligations, you have obligations. I'm perhaps seven years old, and I'm afraid of air-raid warnings and that the Soviet Union will come and take over Norway. But I'm even more afraid we will be thrown out of our apartment. The paintings disappear from the living room walls, leaving behind lighter rectangles on the wallpaper. The picture of a low house with snow on it and a girl making tracks, painted by a quite well known artist, which has always hung over the desk, is gone and will never come back. On the top shelf of the bookcase was a space where a leather-bound collection of

129

Bjørnson once stood. Are there any other girls in class who know the word *pawnbroker?* I feel again the bad pain in my stomach, so many years later, when I write the word. Papa comes home one afternoon with a doll's bassinet for me. It's made of white, waxed canvas, and you can fill it with water and bathe the dolls properly. I see from Mama's face that Papa shouldn't have bought it. One day the car is gone, the white station wagon; an old, much smaller car appears a few days later.

The year I turn eleven, Papa gets a steady job again, and as if by magic the angry voices in the night go silent. Neither of them said anything about those years. Nor did I. Perhaps they don't even know that I lay awake.

~~~

Even now there isn't a day that goes by when I don't cry. I'm growing tired of the part of my body that's beyond my control, that drips and leaks at all hours. This summer is a wet summer. We've been at home in the rain, in the Svea farm-house in the rain, in Copenhagen in the rain, in Berlin in the rain. I've written about Ellinor and Kåre, have let them sleep with each other. Jørgen Smidt has called his daughter. Now he's been taken to the hospital, and he, Ellinor, and I wait for the diagnosis. I've written a lot throughout the summer. I've written a whole chapter about my father. Some sentences I toiled over a long time. And if I couldn't manage to write more on the manuscript every day, then I made a few notes in a notebook that doesn't have quite the cheerful pattern of Ellinor's but otherwise resembles it a fair bit. All these words and sentences that must be written down, not just thought, that don't feel thought before they're written. I can't stop. I can't not do it.

June 5

Silverware, a cupboard from Grandmother's Southern Norwegian family. A shimmery green Benny Motzfeldt vase. A grapefruit knife with a golden handle. Words and expressions. *Qui vivra verra.* "Nine pulls the ace" when playing cards. I've also inherited nearsightedness, oval fingernails, a miserable singing voice but an accurate eye. For good measure I also received a huge, unsorted pile of traditions, customs, habits, and attitudes: ribs, ground pork patties, homemade sauerkraut on Christmas Eve, a freshly ironed white damask tablecloth. Christmas dinner must begin precisely at five o'clock in the evening when Christmas is rung in. Lamb at Easter. Open-faced sandwiches with hard-boiled eggs and caviar on the weekends. A dislike for the glitter on the Christmas tree, for oilcloth on the table, vanilla sauce, ketchup—for people who pull grapes off one by one (if you don't have grape scissors handy, you should break off a small bunch from the main bunch). Disgust for people who wear life jackets in small boats (this disgust for people wearing life jackets was immediately revoked when our children went out in a boat for the first time); a conviction that red and pink don't work together (this conviction began to waver several years ago and is now gone). A love for all things French, for salted *seter* butter, for the Norwegian mountains. Lit candles and crackling fires. Currants with sugar. Wildflowers. Mossy lawns. Chanterelles and sweet tooth mushrooms in the autumn.

In addition, I have what I believe are my own independent habits and attitudes—but they aren't that at all.

A few years ago I was contacted by a journalist from *Aftenposten* who wanted to know what were Oslo's finest and ugliest buildings. I was trying to get somewhere, dashing down the sidewalk, and answered breathlessly but with confidence. The finest building, in my opinion, was Børsen, the Stock Exchange. I still hold to that. And the ugliest, I felt, was the Harbor Warehouse. "A hideous block in a very ugly color," as it's written in the newspaper article, which I found again on the Internet while typing my notes into the computer from the little notebook without an attractively patterned cover. When the afternoon edition of the paper came out the next day, the front page had an enormous photograph of the Oslo Harbor Warehouse, referring to the article. I looked at the photo a long time; actually it was quite a fine building. Handsome. And strictly speaking, wasn't the color quite fresh? It shouldn't have been, at any rate, difficult to find a building in Oslo that was considerably ghastlier than Oslo's Harbor Warehouse. While I was perusing the front page, Mama called. She'd read the newspaper. I completely agree with you, she said with pleasure, it's an awful building. Big and ugly, she said. Revolting color, she said. Fruit juice pink. I've never liked Oslo's Harbor Warehouse, she said.

June 16

Today I walked from the house at Svea down to the dock. Ingolv has cut a path in the meadow, two passes of the lawnmower wide. The meadow is at its most beautiful now, with lots of flowers that willow herb hasn't completely taken over, as it will do late this summer. Mama loved wildflowers. She and Papa were married on December 28, just like her mother and father, and Mama had roses in her bridal bouquet, but she always said that if she had been a summer bride she would have wanted wildflowers. For the cover of the funeral service program I chose a photo of her sitting with a bouquet of wildflowers that I picked on the way down to the lake, almost a year ago.

I walk on the path and notice cow parsley and willow herb, dandelions, crane's bill, steadfast, violas, campanula, daisies, bird's-foot trefoil, forget-me-nots, veronica, hawkweed, vetch, wild mustard, sticky catchfly. Ingolv maintains that he can't learn any flower names, and he always suggests blue campanula, regardless of the color of the flower, when I, in a futile attempt to teach him, wave a flowering plant in front of his face. My father was like that. He knew the names of trees, of edible mushrooms; he knew the names of the fish he caught and the birds he shot, but not the names of flowers. Mama knew many, and it's from her I learned the names I know. At Svea we have a new flower guide in a plastic cover, as well as *Flora in Color,* which we had at home when I was small. Occasionally I look something up, but if I manage to identify a flower I always forget the name until the next time I encounter it. But the flower names from childhood remain.

I walk down toward the lake and enjoy the beauty of the flowers, and I swallow hard because I'll never again pick wildflowers for Mama, who valued them so much, and because I know I'll never find anyone to be as happy about a bouquet of wildflowers picked by me as she always was, whether I was six or forty-six. And I think about the fact that the flower names I know are the same ones Mama knew, and she probably learned them from *her* mother. Because it was, after all, my newly engaged Grandma who in the summer of 1916 picked a bouquet of wildflowers and knotted a piece of paper with the flower name around each stalk.

My daughters aren't too bad with the names of flowers either.

June 19

My editor is going to eat a summer lunch with me. The youngest has the day off from school and helps me set the table on the balcony. We'll have cheese, fruit, three kinds of bread. I've set out a bowl with salted *seter* butter and put chocolate squares on a little enameled plate. On the secretaire in the dining room is the box from the funeral home. I wasn't aware we would get something like that. There are cards with condolences from the ribbons on the wreaths and bouquets in the church, there are business cards people left, the remaining copies of the program. The obituary. Photographs of the coffin with flowers around it. I've added the letters that have arrived and the cards from the bouquets delivered to our house. I also placed there the page of my memorial talk and the talk given by my eldest.

I should have written thank-you notes to everyone who sent flowers. I should have answered the letters I've gotten. But at the moment I can't manage that. Now I put the box in one of the cabinets in my office. The doorbell rings. Should I open it? asks the youngest. Yes, do, I say, and pull myself together, dabbing a hand towel dipped in cold water against my cheeks.

We eat cheese, cherries, and dark chocolate. Drink tea and water. How is the writing going? asks my editor. Of course she asks that. I haven't written as much as I should, I answer. But it's going better now, I add. I'm making notes almost every day. She nods. Good!

June 28

I've always had a tendency to shift between present and past tense when I write. *Kåre himself believes he's possibly a better cook than lover. They shared an occasional bottle of wine or drink a glass of aquavit. She showers in his bathroom, with its heated floor and soft bath towels. Ellinor sneaks home. She hummed some more.* Present and preterit in an eternal muddle. Often the two tenses are completely interchangeable in my fiction.

For Mama it's only the preterit now. I no longer forget that she's not alive. Two months have passed today since she died.

July 3

At our house, when I was little, no one drank tea. The children and I drink liters of it, black, white, rooibos, and, above all, green. Even Ingolv has a cup of green tea from time to time. I've made a pot of genmaicha and sit on the balcony under a quilt reading *Language Death* by David Crystal. It pays to keep ahead of your novel characters, but I'm afraid Ellinor has finished her copy of the book a long time ago; she's become so energetic lately. On the other hand, it's still winter in her universe, so it's hard to know. Soon she and Anna Guttormsen will meet again. I have to figure out how I'll get them to talk together. And what's happened between the two families in the past? I know Anna's grandmother was named Ravna. I know Ravna had a son. He might be called Juhán, the Sami form of Johannes.

Later in the day I sit leafing through old papers. I'm home alone. Ingolv has accompanied the youngest to a language course in Germany and has stayed on in Frankfurt a couple of days. The eldest and her boyfriend are in Western Norway with Ingolv's parents. The papers are in a small, gray cardboard box, and they've probably been there for many years. Layer upon layer of papers have built up, which Mama and Papa once thought necessary to have or simply nice to save for later.

I carefully turn the box upside down. The first thing I find, which has lain on the bottom, is the sheet of paper with the description of Papa, he who is light haired, not quite an opera singer, and engaged to a sweet girl. Here are their passports, a whole pile of hole-punched passports, large and bright red as Norwegian passports once were, full of stamps and visas. Here are vaccination cards, certificates, and school reports no one will ever ask for. Papa had a summer job in Tinfos in 1949 and earned two kroner, twenty-one øre an hour. Mama spent the summer of 1949 in London and the summer of 1950 in Amsterdam. A certificate that says *During the entire occupation Nilsen has shown a wholly patriotic attitude*. First place in the slalom race for men, Tuddal mountain hotel, 1947. Then he went for a year to the Oslo Business School and raced for its team at the Holmenkollen relay race. From 1949 a certificate from his student days in Trondheim: *Downhill racing, a complete mess; Ski-jumping competition, fell over; Cross-country, too drunk.*

And here's a report card from Ullevål School: "Gerd is very kind and clever," signed by the homeroom teacher, Magnhild Hoel, who Mama once said was the writer Sigurd Hoel's sister. In December 1937 she received grades for the first time: M for *meget godt,* very good in Norwegian class and the same in arithmetic, neatness, and conduct. Mama was eight years old and certainly happy and proud. At the same point in time, Papa had just lost his father. In the box there's a folder full of war reminders: ration cards and travel permissions that Mama kept. In 1955 the civil engineer Kjell Nilsen was offered a job from the smelting factory in Sauda, 19,875 kroner a year and an apartment for 54 kroner a month. *Ausländerausweis* resident permits from the years they lived in Geneva; pictures of them are stapled to the third page. Papa works at Union Carbide and is an *ingénieur*. Mama is *sans occupation*—this is how gracelessly it was expressed in Switzerland in the 1950s—and she and my older sister live *auprès du chef de famille*. I guess that they laughed at this wording and that Papa may have asked for respect from his ladies; after all, he had it in black and white that he was head of the family. Letters, documents, certificates in Swedish from the six years in Stockholm. This is where I was born, though I can't find any trace of it in this mound of paper. Mama's employment contract with the University Press from 1978, with a yearly salary of 102,178 kroner.

Some old newspaper clippings. One about Norway's first car, which could run at a top speed of twenty kilometers an hour. It was owned by my great-grandfather on Mama's maternal side, Anders Østbye, purchased from Karl Benz in Mannheim, delivered to Norway in 1896. It cost five thousand kroner. Today it is in the Museum of Technology. I was allowed to sit in it when I was small, because it had been Great-grandfather's. A copy of *Ullern Avis Akersposten* from 1976. It's stiff and brittle, as if it had gotten wet and dried again. A smiling Mama, editor at a publishing company, Gerd Uri Nilsen, was interviewed about the choice of goods available in the shops of the residential area Ullevål Hageby. They don't have much in the way of fresh vegetables, she says, but the clerks are very cheerful. A clipping from *Åndalsnes Avis* about the Oslo family that spends Easter break on the mountain *seter* belonging to the ancestral farm.

Nothing about Grandfather Nicolai. I hadn't expected it either.

July 8

Mama's birthday.

The last of the flowers we received have faded. The bouquets have long been gone, but a friend I studied Norwegian with sent me a potted orchid, and today the last white flower fell. I've always searched for such things. A sign. Four crows in a particular formation. A candle that went out the same second the tsunami struck in Thailand. Northern lights across the sky when you're in love but don't want to admit it. But I've never seen the northern lights. My girlfriend saw a sign and mentioned it, half-jokingly, the time we ate sushi together after the relative from Hammerfest called.

I throw away the orchid, clean out the decorative pot, and put it in a kitchen cupboard, not knowing if it's a sign, not knowing if it means anything for me. It probably doesn't.

July 10–12

It bothers me that I can't remember how it looked, the radio we had at home when I was small.

You can't take things with you, said Grandmother. Objects are a connection to the past, connections you can see, touch, smell. What is this, this slightly reverent obsession with things? I have never been especially preoccupied with possessions before, have I? But when I think about it, Mama and I did talk a good deal about them. Yes, we did. There were many topics we never touched on. There are topics reserved for girlfriends, topics reserved for a husband. But furniture, silverware, paintings, and photographs were easy to talk about. Not the things that just disappeared, that left behind pale patches on the wallpaper, empty spaces in the house. Those things you didn't talk about. But other things were easy: So, was it Uncle Gudbrand, the colonel, who originally owned the secretaire? Individual bowls for pickled cucumbers—not too shabby! Who owned all these padded plate dividers? And did she also embroider the long tablecloth?

The radio continues to pop up in my thoughts. I visualize the row of knobs, white and rounded. Otherwise, wasn't it black? It was often on, as a comforting background hum, beginning in the morning with the entertainment show at nine o'clock, and onward through Request Concert and the stock market tips. If the weather forecast came on, you had to stop talking. The high point was Children's Hour on Saturday evenings at five o'clock. I was given a bowl with raisins and baking chocolate and sometimes some wonderful cookies, tiny and round, with a tall swirl of pink, yellow, or pastel blue rock-hard icing. Apple juice in my own mug, the one with the girl, boy, and lamb on it.

I think about the cookie tin we had. Square, metal, with Disney figures along the four sides. Snow White and Prince Charming on the lid. Mama always baked syrup snaps and coconut macaroons before Christmas. Papa pressed dough into the tartlet tins to make shortbread cookies and claimed it made his thumbs go flat. Every year.

I think about what kinds of flowers we used to have. Cut tulips in one of the Benny Motzfeldt vases when we were going to have guests. African violets, with furry leaves that water wasn't supposed to touch, and with blue flowers, the same blue as our coffee cups. I believe there is only one of the coffee cups left, and Mama took it to Svea to put her dentures in at night. I don't know what I'll use it for now; it's definitely never going to be a coffee cup again. We used to have azaleas in clay pots for Christmas. And hyacinths, always hyacinths before Christmas. Intensely scented hyacinths. Small, red, Christmas tulips. She placed the tulip bulbs in a black ceramic bowl with reindeer moss that we'd collected from one of the mushroom-hunting expeditions in the autumn. The ceramic bowl with red miniature tulips, moist moss, some Christmas elves, and decorative spotted mushrooms sat out on the dining room table during the Christmas holidays.

These plants came and went, dried up and died, the decorative pots were cleared away, the windowsills were empty for a while, and then eventually new potted plants were bought.

But there was one plant we always had in my childhood home, a green plant with delicate, oblong leaves, semitransparent with a visible line down the middle, pointed at the tip. Vigorous stems. Pale green in color. Rarely did the plant bloom, and the flowers were white and insignificant. Hardy, asking little, most of them survived. At our house it was called the eternal Jew. I've also heard it called the wandering Jew. *Tradescantia.* Mama's sisters had the same type. They probably all came from the same mother plant. If you wanted another plant, you just clipped a runner and stuck it in a pot with some dirt. I don't believe Mama and Papa had one after they moved from Ullevål Hageby in 1987, and I never spent a moment thinking about it in my life. Yet last December I saw one in a flower shop, immediately recognized it, and bought it on the spot. Now it sits on the fireplace mantel. It's grown large, reaching all the way to the floor. I wash it in the shower, fertilize it, and remove the dead leaves. Every once in a while I talk to it. I thought several times I should tell Mama that I'd found an eternal Jew, but I had other things on my mind. It irritated me after we'd had a phone conversation, after we'd left the nursing home, that once again I'd forgotten to tell her that.

When Ingolv, in May, began to talk about summer vacation, I thought for half a second that I couldn't go on vacation, that I had to stay home and water the plant. It was extra important now, I thought. I came to my senses before I said anything. And the day we left, I made sure to wash and dust the plant extra well, and then set it in a basin with a tiny bit of water in the bottom.

Fifteen minutes before we had to leave—we had a dinner engagement in Copenhagen and it was necessary to get going —I remembered I needed to take pictures of our silver service. Mama had nagged about that every year. You must photograph the silver, so if it's stolen you'll have something to show the insurance company. I blew it off, forgot it every time, went on vacation and didn't think a second about the silver. But this time, just before we absolutely have to leave, I assemble all the silver we own on the dining room table and take pictures of it with my cell phone. Ingolv carries the luggage out to the car, asks if I'm coming soon. Yes, I'm coming soon, I answer. I realize that someone can also steal a cell phone or I can lose it, and so Ingolv also has to photograph the silver. Patiently he follows my instructions and takes pictures of the silver from various angles. And then, when I'm going to return everything back to the drawers, I can't manage to put back anything but the new silver, just the spoons, knives, forks, serving spoons we received at our wedding. The old things I put in a bag. All the forks and spoons with Ø for Østbye, U for Uri, J for Jacobsen. The slotted fish spade, the large heavy serving spoon, the grape scissors. Mama's christening spoon. The lobster forks, even if they are just silver-plated. A cake server from Ingolv's family. I look at its back side for dates and initials, must not miss anything, sort in two piles: back in the drawer or else in the plastic grocery bag. And then I see a spoon with an engraving I never noticed before. *A and N N 5.10.21.* Astrid and Nicolai Nilsen. Grandmother and Grandfather. They married a year earlier than I'd believed. I say to Ingolv, Grandmother and Grandfather married in 1921, not 1922. Uh-huh, says Ingolv. What else is he going to say? I put the spoon carefully in the plastic bag, look around. Ingolv is standing by the door: Now we *have* to leave, otherwise we won't get there in time. I check out the fireplace in the TV room, but end up cramming the bag in a closet, behind the winter clothes. I race down the stairs after Ingolv, embarrassed, almost laughing, but relieved I've saved the ancestral silver. Mama smiles in pleasure: It was about time, Helene.

July 13

Papa. In a month, August 15, it will be eighteen years since Papa died. A wound that in the beginning hurt all the time but that after a while was painful only if anyone bumped into it, or if I purposely picked at the scab. This summer there has been a lot of picking. And the bumps come more frequently.

Last week I stood at the ICA checkout. An older man pays for his food with a credit card. I see in front of me Papa's coin purse. It was dark-brown leather, shaped in a half circle, like half a slice of bread from a round loaf. And when you opened it, it became a whole slice, and when you tipped it to one side, the money ran down into the open half. It was for coins, not bills. The bills were in his wallet or just in his pocket. When Mama found loose bills in his pocket, she scolded him.

The second day in Berlin I awake and have two thoughts in my head. I remember what Papa's grouse was called: Reidar. The grouse cock with the red eyebrows was called Reidar. And I know that Ellinor likes rain. She can of course maintain that she doesn't, that she becomes depressed by it, but in reality she likes it. She likes to sit inside, listening to the raindrops pounding against the windowpanes or watching them glide down the glass. She likes rain puddles on the sidewalks, dams in the street that cars unsuspectingly turn into fountains. And she likes to go out in the rain. Feeling her neck get cold, feeling a single droplet that has sneaked past her collar and down her back. I lie in bed, listening to Ingolv run a bath; I look out at the gray German rain slip down the windowpanes; and there she is. I see her in front of me. I don't quite know what color her hair is, probably medium blond. It's not important, but I see that her hair is dark with water. Maybe she's thinking about Kåre? I can make Ellinor happy. Her life is in my hands.

We take a walk on Unter den Linden in pouring rain. Ingolv asks, Were your parents ever in Berlin? I can't answer. They traveled a lot in Europe, but Berlin? I don't know. It's east of most travel routes. Does it matter whether they were here or not? No, it doesn't. All the same, it seems to me enormously sad that I can't ask, that I no longer have the choice.

Before we left, I discovered that the dining room table at Svea had warped. It's the old table from the farm in Western Norway, the one that survived the war in the house of a photographer in Åndalsnes. But it hasn't tolerated being moved from the damp climate of Western Norway to the dry, inland climate of Eastern Norway. What do you do with a very old wooden table that has a warp in it? In such matters she was my answer book, my reference, my almanac.

July 16, in the morning

On the ferry from Kiel, sailing up the Oslo Fjord. Cabins and small houses on summer-green steep slopes and islands. Pleasure boats out in the fjord. Nothing dramatic and spectacular, but calm and appealing, in the Eastern Norwegian way. We eat breakfast, sail past Oscarsborg and hear a waiter, in English with a pronounced Norwegian accent, tell the story of the sinking of the *Blücher*, April 9, 1940, the day Norway was invaded by Germany. We imagine the listeners, an older, married couple three tables away from us, are British. But perhaps they are Germans, otherwise wouldn't it have been impolite of the waiter to entertain them in such a way over their orange juice, smoked salmon, and scrambled eggs?

We're back in the Norwegian cellular network. Ingolv reads the newspapers on his phone. I sit with my notebook. I suspect that the census report from 1910 about my grandfather's ethnicity is correct. Grandfather's father was Sami, and

143

that information was gone before it reached me. Did Grand-father keep it hidden from his wife? Was it so shameful to be half Sami that he didn't say anything about it, just mumbled something about a Finnish Kven in the family? It could have been completely different. Maybe Nicolai Nilsen was proud of his origin, but Astrid refused to allow him to speak of it. I don't know, but I have difficulty imagining that Papa was the cork. It must have happened before he came along. Papa and his brothers probably knew nothing about it.

Both speech and silence can control. A talkative woman and a man of few words. They both have power over their stories.

I know that the Sami were looked down upon. I know that even non-Sami Norwegians didn't find it easy to be from the North in Southern Norway. I heard it alleged that far into the 1960s—the decade I was born—there were classified ads about rooms for rent that said "North Norwegians Not Wanted." Grandfather was born at the end of the 1800s when tolerance for the Sami wasn't exactly high. I've read Hamsun. Probably Grandfather said nothing, and perhaps Grandmother didn't ask.

July 18

I've been to the library and borrowed books about the Sami. I read, so disbelieving I could almost laugh and then depressed. Shaking my head I stick yellow Post-its on the most attention-grabbing pages. Amund Helland was a professor of geology and geography at the university. He is most known for his work—in many, many volumes—about Norway's land and people. In 1906 the volume on Finnmark was published, and here the Sami, or "Finns," as Helland calls them, were de-scribed. They are short in height, many to the point where they could almost be considered dwarves. They are filthy, every single one of them. They read the Bible from time to time but nothing else. Compared with Norwegians, they're considered "weakly developed both intellectually and physically." In their appearance, there's not much to praise either. They have "a small, flat nose, which is often turned up. Also, the mouth is almost always very large and not attractive with thin lips. The ear opening is usually exceedingly large." But they have nice teeth, writes Helland. The eyes are blue or gray: "their eyes can seldom be considered beautiful." In 1906, Grandfather was ten years old. He probably didn't read Helland, but the professorial pronouncements say much about general attitudes.

The politics of Norwegianization were brutal. The Norwegian government has admitted that—and issued a formal apology. You might well ask if the state deserves to be pardoned. Sami language and culture were suppressed in favor of Norwegian. From 1889 all education was supposed to be in Norwegian: "Teaching shall take place in the Norwegian language" but "Lappish and Kvenish can be used to help with learning." At the beginning of the twentieth century church services in Sami were also forbidden. In 1922, the year after Grandfather and Grandmother married, a suggestion was raised that Sami-speaking schoolchildren might be taught in Sami, at least for the first three years. This was rejected by the Board of Education because, among other things, "the Sami are less gifted," and because there is no such thing as Sami culture. The Sami children were herded into boarding schools, where it was forbidden to speak anything but Norwegian.

Just Qvigstad, rector of the Teachers College in Tromsø, a philologist, theologian, enthusiastic scholar of Sami language and culture, wrote in 1938, the year after Grandfather died of silicosis, that the Lapps lag behind the Norwegians in all areas: "in childcare, cleanliness, food preparation, dairy work, farming, rational exploitation of the forest." He also emphasizes

145

that the coastal Sami pass their summers in idleness, that they squander their earnings, and that poverty is consequently "often self-inflicted."

When the people of Finnmark were forcibly evacuated the winter of 1944–45, the Nazi and minister of police, Jonas Lie, believed that the Sami didn't need to travel to the South; the Sea Sami in particular were a "totally degenerate mixed population . . . which neither physically nor psychologically has any great worth as workers or a population source." I don't know if my great-grandparents evacuated, probably they did, both the Sea Sami and his wife from Sunnmøre.

While brushing my teeth (nice teeth at least!) that evening, I study my face in the mirror, one-eighth Sami, as I've newly become. Small, flat nose? Very large and not very attractive mouth? Exceedingly large opening to my ears? I arrange my hair over my ears and go to bed.

July 27

I've baked a honey cake. In the handwritten book from my mother's mother's mother, Ellen Anna Østbye, born in 1855, there is a recipe for it.

Mama also had a handwritten recipe book with the same recipe for honey cake. If I turn the book upside down and begin to flip through the pages starting at the other end, I find notes for Papa's thesis from NTH: notes on vitrification, ore, charges, calcium and heating. Six hundred and fifty degrees. In Mama's recipe section of the book, dated 1952, are words like granulated sugar, sifted white flour, and baking soda, about the oven temperatures and salted leg of lamb. And the recipe for honey cake.

I am alone in the apartment, eating warm honey cake and drinking Pernod and writing this, thinking about asking the girls to bake a honey cake. Then there will be five generations of women in our family who have baked it.

This summer I do stupid things that I keep secret from Ingolv and the children. I call her cell phone number to hear her voice on voicemail. I wash my hair with her Schwarzkopf shampoo and breathe in the familiar smell of it and cry in the shower. When the eldest was a newborn, I stopped wearing perfume. The artificial fragrance felt wrong around an infant, and in fact I never started up with it again. But *now* I begin, dabbing on a drop of the perfume she wore the last years, Trésor, on my wrists. There's an old lady's perfume smell on you, says the youngest one day.

The first year after Papa died, I took care of one of his sweaters; I stored it in a plastic bag, opened it, and, also in secret, breathed in the smell of him. I continued doing this until I must have sniffed up all the particles of scent. The sweater lost its efficacy, and I threw it away.

The weeping has subsided, but I feel Ingolv has cried too little. I've even told him that, in anger, in desperation, I don't know. He hasn't grieved enough, it seems to me. It's stupid, petty. And unjust. I can't imagine a more tender son-in-law than he was. I've also said that to him. In spite of everything. My unreasonableness, even to my nearest and dearest, has limits.

Today Ingolv said he had stood at her bedside, in the room at the hospital. He was alone with her dead body, and he looked at her and cried with gratitude for what she had been for the children. Ingolv is a rather quiet man, but he told me this. Fortunately he didn't say it as a direct response to one of my outbursts.

Mama's sisters say they recall Mama and Papa talking many times of going up north to try to find some relatives. Nothing came of it, in spite of so many travels and the long car trips they took. I don't believe either of them ever got farther north than Trondheim. Didn't he want to? Or was it because of chance occurrences, laziness, other more tempting travel destinations that they never made the trip?

I've decided to call the woman who called me in January. She who on my cell phone is listed as Relative. I must go up to Hammerfest, Sørøya, Bismervik. I must see it, hear the stories in the air.

Along with that I decide to look up the children of Papa's middle brother. I have a male cousin and two female cousins on that side. They are all three pragmatists, and at least two of them are engineers, of course. I haven't seen them often. The last time was at Grandmother's funeral in fall of 1996.

The day after, a doctor calls from the stroke unit at Ullevål Hospital to say it's true that Jørgen Smidt has had a small stroke. Her voice is friendly but matter-of-fact. Ellinor slides down to the floor, her back against the wall; she remains sitting with her thighs hugged into her chest, the cell phone still against her ear. I see, she says, and she has no one to pass the phone to. It's not critical, says the doctor. It sounds critical, says Ellinor, and her voice is so weak that she doesn't know if it can be heard down there in Oslo. She has to force herself not to end the conversation with the matter-of-fact doctor, not to get under the blanket on the sofa and curl up, feeling the warmth return. Ellinor whispers into the phone that she is temporarily in Finnmark, working, but she must definitely come south, to be with her father in case something happens.

The doctor patiently explains that her father is doing well, but they want to keep him in for observation. There is always the danger of a new stroke, but as far as they can assess, there's no reason Ellinor should abandon everything she's doing. They will take care of him in the best way. She can naturally not promise anything, but there is nothing to indicate that anything is going to happen to Jørgen Smidt anytime soon. D-do you think he will die? asks Ellinor. Most of us do, in the end, says the doctor, and Ellinor can hear that she's smiling and that she's said these exact words many times before. Yes? says Ellinor. But it can take years, continues the doctor. He is tough, your father. It will be fine. It's not critical. All you have to do is call this number if you have questions. Ellinor nods several times. Yes, she finally says, but by then the doctor has hung up.

She sits with her back pushed into the wall and her legs at a sharp angle up against her chest. The phone lies on the floor. It's cold leaning against an outer wall. She feels the cold in the gap between the waistband of her pants and her sweater, which has slid high up on her back. All the same, she remains sitting. In some ways, she's already lost her father. It's been a long time since his brain began to fail him. And her. But she still has him. She must go south, see him, hold his hand. She wants to go home to Oslo, to daylight, to crowds of people and neon advertising. To her girlfriends. To bars, cafés, and restaurants. To prize-winning baristas in hip espresso bars with the world's best coffee. Coffee! Theaters, galleries, and the cinema. Oslo, her city. Tom's city. Her parents' city. She has to book her ticket immediately. Just as she's made this decision, but before she's managed to get up, her cell beeps twice. The signal for a text. Kåre. *Miss you. Are you coming soon? Pun intended.*

From Oslo you can fly to Berlin, London, Copenhagen, for a few hundred kroner. To fly from Finnmark to Oslo costs several thousand. She changes her mind about going not because Kåre has sent her a text but because she doubts she has enough in her bank account. Not critical, the doctor has said. No reason to abandon everything she's doing. Perhaps it's not necessary to travel? Perhaps it's hysterical of her to consider it? She can, in any case, try to call. Finally, on the third try, she reaches him: Architect Office of Smidt & Son, how can I help you? The ache in her stomach arises immediately: his voice is unclear and much fainter than usual. The vowels are mixed up. It is only because she has heard him answer in this way hundreds of times, though it's many years ago now, that she understands what he is saying. When Ellinor asks how he is doing, he answers something she doesn't catch. She asks again, and this time he responds that he's fine. That's so good, says Ellinor. Yes, says her father. Is it going okay at the hospital? Yes, he answers. Is the food good? No. No? repeats Ellinor. Yes, says her father. Is the food good? Invoice, says her father.

She calls the main reception at Ullevål Hospital and asks to be transferred to the stroke unit. It rings a long time before a breathless voice answers. Ellinor introduces herself, says she's worried, asks how it's actually going with her father. The breathless one flips through papers, mumbles, says that she . . . She goes away, and then a new voice comes on the telephone. She says she is Jørgen Smidt's primary nurse and that he is well. Considering the circumstances, she adds. Should I come? asks Ellinor. It's not critical, answers the nurse.

Ellinor decides to stay, or to travel down south in a few weeks when there may be a chance to combine a visit to her father with a meeting at Blindern and in this way have the trip expenses covered. In a couple of weeks she'll also get her salary again, if the institute won't pay for the travel. Yes, best to wait.

But the past few years her father has, more and more often, asked her to hold his hand. A little condescendingly and shyly she's allowed him to do that. She should be there for him; the guilty conscience turns into a hard clump, taking up all the space in her stomach. She must go to him. On the other hand, he barely knows the difference between her and a nurse who holds his hand. That is the truth. Often he doesn't recognize her, and his condition has probably not improved. She will wait. It's the only reasonable thing to do.

She seldom wears makeup, but today she does. Smooths on the foundation, puts on gray eyeshadow and black eyeliner, closes her eyes and brushes mascara on her lashes. She needs some groceries, she should pick up the lamb steak she ordered. And maybe she should stop by Kåre's on the way home from the store. He wrote he missed her. She adds a layer of mascara. You don't fool even yourself, Ellinor.

She stands with her back to Ellinor, the white hair up in a knot. Even though Ellinor doesn't see her face, she understands that Anna Guttormsen is angry. And now Ellinor hears her voice. It's no accident, says Anna Guttormsen. Then a stream of quiet Sami words that even someone who doesn't speak Sami understands must be swear words.

"This has nothing to do with old history," says the man behind the meat counter. He has a plastic hat on his head and wears a blood-spattered white jacket.

"You have Rist blood in your veins, you can't behave any other way," says Anna.

"All you have to do is order your meat beforehand, like anyone else," says the man. Then he turns to Ellinor, who has come to a halt a few meters away. "Smidt, isn't it? Your lamb steak is in the back. One minute."

Ellinor gets her Easter lamb, picks up some dish soap, a rosemary plant, a head of lettuce, mushrooms; she weighs some smooth eggplants but decides against them. Outside the window she sees Anna Guttormsen draw her kick-sled into position, hanging a grocery bag from each handlebar. Ellinor pays, throws her groceries in a bag, and runs out of the store.

"Wait!"

Anna Guttormsen stops and turns. Ellinor approaches, out of breath.

"Here, you can have my lamb."

Anna Guttormsen looks at the white paper-wrapped package, then she looks at Ellinor.

"Thanks," she says, takes the package, puts it in one of the bags, kicks onward.

The grocery bag lies in the entryway, right by the front door. A brown paper bag is open, and some mushrooms have rolled out onto the floor. One of the mushrooms, a rather small one with a few flecks of dirt on its cap, lies only a few centimeters from her nose. She thinks she can recognize a scent of forest floor and dampness from it and from the gaping paper bag. She lies there as if someone has released her from a great height, just allowed her to drop straight down. Her limbs are slack. Her breasts fall to each side, the circles of her nipples stretched to ovals. Panties in a crumpled figure eight around one ankle. She smiles at the mushroom, is touched by how helpless and sweet and round it is. She hears him approaching, but she doesn't move, stays comfortably lying in precisely the same position. Kåre's feet come into her field of vision. One of his feet kicks her caressingly in the side. Her breasts shiver. She raises her eyes and begins to laugh: Do you realize how funny you . . . it . . . looks from this angle?

The mushrooms, including the tiny one, now properly washed, are sautéed in butter, along with some chanterelles that Kåre had picked the previous autumn. Wolffish fillets, also from the freezer, caught in a net by Kåre. Green salad from her shopping bag. Wine from his refrigerator. You *are* a divine cook. Yes, aren't I though?

They sit next to each other on the sofa, under the reindeer pelt. He has lit a well-made pile of wood and kindling in the large soapstone fireplace; it has a friendly rumble. Ellinor always calms down inside at the sound, perhaps because her father invariably said, anytime they had a fire in the fireplace, that Ellinor's mother loved the sound of the flames. Your mother always said that the crackling of an open fire was the best sound she knew. At that point in the conversation Ellinor used to sit completely still and just listen, to the flames, to her father. And I believe I agree, her father always said, a few seconds later. Me too, said Ellinor then, and with that she used to press more tightly against her father. Now she moves even closer to Kåre. He glances at her, chews, and smiles with a closed mouth. He understands, without her having said anything, that she's been through a difficult time, that her father is ill, that her divorce from Tom was hellish. The lullaby she didn't get to sing. She's been in Kåre's home at least a dozen times now, but they have never really told each other much. Some breathless instructions of the erotic kind, comments on the food, wishes for a good night. Nothing more. Now it is time. Here in front of the fireplace. Now.

He has been divorced six years. He has a part-time job as a teacher, he doesn't want to work full-time, manages fine on his salary. He has two children, a son and a daughter. The daughter is in her second year of community college and at the moment is in an exchange program in the Netherlands, in the Frisian-speaking region. Ellinor raises her eyebrows. Yes, she *wanted* to go there. She's broken with family tradition and is engaged with minority languages and that kind of thing. Ellinor smiles. His son has just begun his second semester of medical school in Tromsø. My grandfather was also a doctor, says Kåre. Ellinor nods. He was one of the first Sami doctors, he continues. Impressive, says Ellinor politely. One of the very first, or maybe the first, says Kåre. Mmm, says Ellinor. But he didn't know Sami, continues Kåre. Ellinor doesn't answer. I have a sister, says Kåre. Ellinor nods. My mother is dead, but my father is still living. He is an economist. Neither he nor my mother was ever interested in their Sami roots. The opposite, more likely.

After a quarter of an hour she's more or less given up. Yes, she's gotten a good bit of factual information, and that's all fine and well. She values knowing his marital status, number of children, ages, education, the birthplace of the man she frequently sleeps with, but besides giving her this information and half-heartedly asking her the same things, he says nothing. Nothing of interest, nothing that he might not have said to anyone. Is that what she is to him? An anyone?

And shouldn't he have asked more about her project?

"I must get Anna Guttormsen to talk to me," she says after a pause of a few moments, a pause charged with irritation, which completely bounces off him.

"So then just go over to Anna's. She can't do anything worse than eat you. If she doesn't cast a spell on you, of course."

She looks at him until he's finished laughing.

"What is it with Anna Guttormsen? Can't you help me, so it's easier for me to understand how I can approach her?"

"It has nothing to do with you and her. I could imagine actually putting all this behind us and getting to know her. Do you know that, from olden times, Sami has never had a word for war?"

She doesn't answer, doesn't know what she should say, only knows she's wounded in some way. There's silence between them.

"I fucking gave her my lamb steak."

"What are you talking about?"

"It doesn't matter."

Then Kåre says something about a school job. She looks at him.

"A job that someone in your family should have gotten?"

"Yes, something along those lines," answers Kåre.

"When was that?"

"Last year."

"Last year? Isn't this an old quarrel?"

"Well, yes."

Ellinor sighs demonstratively. Kåre smiles at her, takes a sip from his wine glass, clearly doesn't notice that this is an uphill conversation, is unaware he'll soon appear just as idiotic as her ex-husband Tom. She moves slightly away from him.

"What happened? Who was involved?"

"Me."

"You? Why didn't you say that?"

"I'm saying it."

"I'm just trying to do my job," says Ellinor, and to her astonishment she feels on the verge of tears.

Kåre gets up, goes to the kitchen, and returns with a small, potbellied flask.

Ellinor sits scrunched, rolled up like a ball on the sofa, but ready to leave. No matter what he says now, it will be wrong. As a conversational partner he's hopeless, or else she's the one who's hopeless, unable to find subjects to engage him, powerless to get him to open up. Now she wants to go home. She can't stand being around him, much less close to him. It was good she got rid of the steak.

"*Bures!* Maybe you should learn some Sami words?" says Kåre and holds out the flask containing a straw-yellow, viscous liquid. "I've managed to learn some. And what about a taste of my cloudberry liqueur?"

"No thanks," answers Ellinor. "And we'll talk together just as badly in all languages."

Kåre smiles, still offering the flask to her. She gets up, puts on her outerwear, and leaves, knowing she's childish, knowing she is a terrible person for having delivered a cutting reply. *We'll talk together just as badly in all languages.* She is ashamed. So dumb, so painfully awful. *Hungry?* She understands she's irrational and unstable, even understands why, but can't act any other way. Bye, calls Kåre from inside. What an asshole!

She walks quickly through streets and paths, growing sweaty and agitated. She's cold, but isn't there all the same a promise of spring warmth in the wind from the sea? No, she's probably imagining it. This too. *She could be anyone.* Anyone with makeup on. A naive clown.

29

She leaves Kåre and goes home that springlike winter evening knowing she's acted stupidly. She could run back and ask forgiveness, but doesn't do that. If her father had been here—back when Jørgen Smidt was Jørgen Smidt and the world was more predictable—he would have taken hold of two of her fingers and, in some magic way, she would have felt better. She walks quickly, in part because she continues to be angry, in part because she thinks better that way.

There are certain things she has always known. Ellinor is a family name; she was named after her grandmother. Her mother's name was Regine, and if Ellinor were to follow the pattern, her daughter would be named Regine. Her father's side of the family teems with architects. Jørgen Smidt often spoke about his years of study in Trondheim at NTH, and Jørgen's father also went there. If she were to do as tradition required, she would take over the firm.

Her father has told her about his own relatives and almost as much about her mother's. He's told her stories about fishing trips with his father, about Ellinor's mother, who learned to crochet pot holders when she was only five years old and couldn't yet speak properly. He taught Ellinor some of her mother's favorite words, pet names, *chicky and chicky mama,* and some of the sayings she threw around: *A place for*

158

everything, everything in its place. He's told her that her mother had a beautiful singing voice but that his was nothing to brag about. Well, you can hear that on a daily basis, Elli-mine. He drew Ellinor's family tree. Both he and her mother came from families with few twigs, both were only children. Nor did they manage to produce any more offspring than a single child. For that reason family and stories are even more important, her father believed. You belong to an endangered species.

When your mother and I met each other, he said, we immediately saw that the other one didn't have siblings. A particular searching look, a loneliness, but also a strength. Hmm, said Ellinor, I don't feel lonely. No, that wasn't what I meant, but I believe it does something to you to be the only one, not to have siblings. It makes you strong but also more vulnerable because you have to carry everything yourself. The whole past. And the future, said Ellinor, who at that point didn't know yet how difficult it would be to become pregnant and stay pregnant. Relatives and family are important, repeated her father, especially in small families. The stories must be told. Ellinor nods, listens to the stories politely and with a certain interest but without being persuaded that what her father is saying will ever come to mean anything to her.

Everything directly having to do with her mother, however, she listens to greedily, repeatedly asking questions. She scrutinizes every picture they have of her. When she is eight she creates a kind of altar in her room. On a white crocheted tablecloth made by her mother, she places a studio portrait. Black and white, taken by a photographer in the sixties. Her mother has medium-long hair curled up in a flip at the ends, a pearl necklace at her throat. Her lips are closed in a half smile, but it's a true smile, because her eyes smile, too. The photographer has succeeded in capturing her gaze, so it actually appears as if she's looking right at Ellinor. In front of the portrait, which is framed and standing on the table, Ellinor has placed small objects that belonged to her mother or that her mother gave her as gifts—an unglazed red ceramic pig with white stripes, an enameled bracelet her mother had gotten from her mother. Foremost is a birthday card with kittens. On the back of the card is written, in a beautiful cursive that she had just learned to read: *Dear Ellinor, dear Elli-mine! Happy 4th birthday. Love, Mama.*

It remained that way for many years, eventually the only neat spot in a chaotic teenager's room. When she moved into a place of her own, the things went with her, but they were spread out around the room, and then later in her and Tom's apartment. The pig was a somewhat successful bookend, though being hollow it lacked the weight a bookend should have. The card in a drawer of the desk, the photograph on a small sideboard by the sofa, the crocheted tablecloth on the nightstand, the bracelet in her jewelry box. Now everything is back together again, in a box in the basement storage locker at home in Oslo. And now, leaving Kåre, she longs madly for the pig, regrets not taking it with her from Oslo.

Ellinor often thinks about her mother. When she does, her thoughts travel along the same tracks, the same well-trodden paths of memory. She doesn't know any longer what she truly remembers and what she merely imagines she remembers, what are impressions of memories formed by her father's stories or created from photographs. The memories of her mother are like double exposures where she only dimly sees the underlying image; the figures on the surface confuse and distort.

Some things she feels are true memories: the back of Mama's head, the sight of her, half in profile as she looks out the car window. Her hand, white and slender with raised blue veins like a map on the back. Other things she's more uncertain about: the last Christmas. Surely she remembers something from it? The dates, the Christmas soda, and decorations. But they buy dates and Christmas soda every single year, and the decorations always come up from the basement on December 23.

Yet: her soft stomach, a glimpse of her stomach between two buttons of her blouse. Several hikes in the forest, which blend into each other. Dry pine needles on a path between dark trees, an enormous anthill, much taller than herself. Soft haircap moss. Blueberries in her hands, under the nails. Lilac-blue soap bubbles on the white porcelain basin in the bathroom at home. Mama bending over her in bed and saying good night. The smell of the hospital that stole Mama's smell. The lullaby. It was called Mama's song. That was what Papa always called it, because Mama sang it. When the troll mother had put her eleven little trolls to bed and tied them fast to her tail. Mama sang every night. Then it was Papa who continued the ritual of singing, kissing, sending a kiss from the doorway. The same song, and Mama's voice sang along inside Ellinor's head. At some point she no longer heard Mama's voice singing, only Papa's, and the memory of Mama's voice no longer existed except as the certainty that her mother always sang Mama's song to her. She loved you more than anyone. You were her troll baby. Her chicky. Did she sing to me? Every night. What did she sing to me? She sang Mama's song.

Without warning, in the middle of a silent street, in a small city in Finnmark, she recalls a sweater her mother had. A gray ski sweater. She suddenly sees it in front of her. Perhaps it was the thought of the ceramic pig, perhaps the sight of snow shoveled up against a picket fence, perhaps it was the sense of being alone. A forgotten memory of a winter that felt endless. She doesn't know why, but something calls forth the picture of the sweater. Something that has been stored and forgotten in her mind and that has released again the memory of the sweater. A spark that ignites something lying next to it. Now it appears before her in all its details. Raglan sleeves, white-and-red pattern up near the neck. She is certain it is her mother's sweater, and she is certain she hasn't seen it in a photograph. She has looked so many times at the pictures that are left and knows she hasn't seen such a sweater there. She must remember it from the time her mother used it.

Tears overwhelm her. It's just the way it feels when an outside force determines things for her, sweeps her off her feet, knocks her to her knees, makes her body do things she can't control. Her whole body shakes with weeping. She lets the tears flow. It's good, it's as if something melts in her, something rushes out of her, like an avalanche. In a strange way it reminds her of the orgasm Kåre just gave her, there on the floor of the entryway, face-to-face with the round, poignant little mushroom. She smiles at herself. The tears disappear as abruptly as they appeared. She's alone in a snow-covered street of single houses, far north in Norway, is angry about an uncommunicative man and a lamb steak, has cried over a sweater, longed for a pig, laughed over a mushroom. The thoughts fly around in her brain like weightless snowflakes, moving here and there before drifting peacefully down. She is thoroughly limp and faint. She remains sitting like that, on her knees, in the middle of the street, until the warmth of her body melts the snow under her knees and the wet seeps through her trousers and long johns. She is about to get on her feet again, and that's when she hears it: a weak shout. At first she's convinced it's something she's imagining, but then the shouts become clearer. Help. Help! She runs in the direction of the shouts, comes to a side street, and there, in the middle of the road, lies an overturned kick-sled, and in the ditch is a person. Ellinor starts toward the person but stops when she recognizes who it is. Anna Guttormsen. Anna Guttormsen with a reindeer-fur jacket and large fur gloves. On her head, over her hair knot, she has a cucumber-green ski cap and around her neck a silk kerchief that can't be anything else but French and very expensive.

"Hi," says Ellinor (because what else can she say?) and then, after a few seconds, "Have you hurt yourself?"

It appears that Anna Guttormsen thinks about this and makes a quick decision to answer politely, that doing anything else would be quite stupid.

"Yes, I think I must have sprained my ankle."

Ellinor reaches out a hand and takes a large reindeer-fur glove, but it slips from her grasp. They try again, and this time Ellinor manages to pull her up. She rights the kick-sled, and then she manages to maneuver Anna onto the seat. This foot? Anna Guttormsen nods. Ellinor loosens the colorful shoestrings on one of the reindeer-skin boots. Anna Guttormsen smiles when her foot, swollen and painful, is exposed to the winter air, and Ellinor stares at it, surprised. A sockless, bare foot.

"It's actually best with dried sennegrass and no socks in the *skalle*," says Anna Guttormsen. Then she smiles, in the midst of a grimace of pain. "I sound like I'm the program manager of a radio documentary. *Indigenous footwear. Today: the Sami.*"

Ellinor laughs, partly from pure relief, partly because the situation is so absurd. "I'll wrap it up in my scarf for the time being," says Ellinor. "The foot has swollen up. You won't be able to get the . . . shoe . . . back on."

"The *skalle*."

"The *skalle*. And then I'll get you home on the sled. Maybe you . . . we . . . should call the doctor, too?"

Ellinor steers the kick-sled carefully through the streets

163

with Anna Guttormsen on the seat. The night is black, without the northern lights, but with bright stars, and the Milky Way like a pale band across the sky.

"What are you doing out so late?" asks Ellinor, mostly to fill the silence.

"I was just out for a stroll. And you?"

A natural question to follow up with, of course. Ellinor should have anticipated it, and now she doesn't know what to say. Before she has a chance to think further, Anna Guttormsen says:

"You've probably been with Kåre Os."

"Maybe."

From Anna Guttormsen comes a sound, a snort perhaps? At any rate Ellinor interprets it as an expression of disapproval. She doesn't plan to say more, and luckily they are nearing Anna Guttormsen's house.

"Kåre Os . . . ," begins Anna Guttormsen.

"Whatever was between me and Kåre is over," says Ellinor brusquely.

"I see."

"Yes."

"You can park the sled here," says Anna Guttormsen. "Can you help me to the door?"

Ellinor supports her while she finds her key, holds her arm until she is safely inside the door, and hangs up her outerwear. Anna Guttormsen leans against the wall and observes her. Her face is like a clenched fist, but Ellinor believes she sees a glimpse of something in her eyes. Irony? Expectation? Laughter? Ellinor doesn't know and doesn't dare look too closely. And then she starts blurting, rapidly, and once she's begun she can't seem to stop. She says she really gets it, that she's clueless, that she understands far too little, that she gets why Anna

Guttormsen reacted the way she did the first time Ellinor came to the door, and that Anna Guttormsen had good reason to react that way. Ellinor can understand that Anna Guttormsen wouldn't want to just let her inside.

Anna Guttormsen extends her right hand.

"Now that will do. I can manage on my own now. But another day, come by for coffee."

The front door closes, and Ellinor again stands outside, with her right-hand glove stuck under her left armpit. She still feels the pressure of Anna Guttormsen's warm hand. Stop by for coffee another day? She slowly begins to walk home. She puts on her glove again, though her hand is so warm it hardly requires it.

Perhaps it's true that Jørgen Smidt can no longer feel the difference between her hand and that of one of the nurses. But, and this is not insignificant either, Ellinor knows it's her father's hand and no one else's that she holds. Maybe her father can't squeeze her fingers. But all the same her father can locate them. All the same she can go to him, bend over his bed, take his face in her hands, stroke his cheeks. The warmth of his skin exists. His voice exists. His hand in hers. Maybe she can no longer have a conversation with him, maybe she can no longer ask about the sweater or whether he and her mother were ever in Berlin together. Jørgen Smidt is no longer master of the same language his daughter uses. Maybe he'll still understand what she says to him, even though his words no longer behave as they used to. They don't allow themselves to be governed; they lead their own lives, in spite of him. Maybe the time is completely past for him to say anything sensible. But she recalls much of what he has said and told her. An only child has a particular strength. Family is important. Stories. Expressions repeated so many times that you notice them only when they are no longer said. Pet names. The fixed objections, the loving criticism. You have always been engrossed in language and words, he used to say when he was discouraged with her. An occupational hazard. I'm a linguist, she would answer. And after that response, the dialogue had two possible outcomes. Most often he laughed, and the conversation ended there. But if he was really irritated, he said she needed to watch out for her morbid urge to verbalize everything, to describe everything. There will be instances, he said, where you will search in vain for the right word, because it's not to be found. The words confuse you, he said; instead, recognize what you feel. *Enough talk, Ellinor, feel it instead.* You're right, Papa, she says aloud. Her words are white clouds in the cold. You're always right in all things, Papa. And this is actually very simple.

She opens the door to the ochre-yellow house.

~~~

Oslo is noisier than she remembered. Empty cabs in a long line outside Oslo Central. Passengers on the way into and out of the train station. Suits and briefcases. Laptop cases over the shoulder. Dresses with short spring coats. Rolling suitcases in tow like reluctant lapdogs. A few passengers with ski equipment, struggling, red faced. Some daring skateboarders defying the remains of ice and a slippery surface. A crowd of windblown people with creaking knees. The roofs are dripping, and there's a thin layer of slush in the roads. But it's her own ugly-beautiful city. She drinks two cortados in a row at her favorite coffee bar at St. Hanshaugen before she takes the bus onward to Ullevål Hospital. The sun hangs low but with the greatest matter-of-factness on the horizon and casts a pale light over the rooftops. She pauses a moment when she gets off the bus and allows the sun to shine in her face, closes her eyes, and lets everything redden.

He doesn't recognize her. His eyes don't meet hers. His mouth moves, but even though she puts her ear down next to it, she doesn't hear a sound. The comforter lies flat over his body, which must have become much thinner. He's worn out, the nurse pipes up. Come back in an hour, when he's rested. When she returns, he speaks. He turns his face toward her, and it is so changed that it jolts her. Pale, thinner. Trembling. The nose looks sharp. He speaks. Disconnectedly, almost incoherently, and with a far too high-pitched voice. She takes his hand, and his hand is the same: dry, large, and warm. He manages to locate her middle and index finger, squeezes hard, much harder than she expected, he doesn't want to let go, holds on until she can't handle being there any longer and has to go. I'll come by tomorrow too, she whispers, stroking him again on the shrunken cheek, putting her lips against his forehead.

She lets herself into her father's apartment, not so far from her own apartment now occupied by a physical therapist. It is Ellinor's childhood home, she knows the apartment inside and out. It smells as it always has, only more concentrated because the air is stale, unmoving. The drapes are pulled closed, no lamps are lit. The sun outside makes the room dim. A dust-white cone of light shoots into the dining room from a gap in the drapes. She hears her own breath, she hears a rubbing sound where the stiff fabric of her sleeves touches the body of her jacket. She doesn't hear his voice. Or his neighing laugh. His steps on the parquet floor.

The fireplace, which her father himself has designed and built, is black and empty. A sheet covers the velvet sofa that architect Jørgen Fredrik Smidt Sr. had in *his* first office, and that he gave to his son when Jørgen had finished his degree in civil architecture. As a child she loved this sofa; it was so soft and welcoming compared with the other pieces of furniture in the apartment: rigid Danish icons. Panton, Wegner, Arne Jacobsen. On the walls hang graphic posters, some charcoal drawings her father made during his studies, a photograph of Grandfather's first building. A ski certificate from NTH: *Downhill racing, a complete mess; Ski-jumping competition, fell over; Cross-country, too drunk.* Family pictures from both her father's and mother's side.

She doesn't open the door into her old bedroom, just heaves her suitcase into the guest room, slams the front door, and turns the security lock. Outside on the sidewalk she calls a friend. What a nice surprise. Yes, she'd love to see Ellinor. Can they meet up at the new tapas place everyone's talking about?

They sit at a table by the window, looking right out on Karl Johan Street. She says nothing about her father, other than he's been taken to Ullevål Hospital. It's not critical is all she says. Finnmark is now far away, has become a strange adventure, nothing like the ordinary life she'd experienced over the past two months. She tells her friend what she expects to hear. The dark, the cold. The absence of sun, sushi restaurants, and coffee bars. Kåre, an outdoorsman and a skillful lover. A *real* Sami? Oh yes, answers Ellinor. So exotic, says the friend, is he . . . hot? Does he have one of those Four Winds hats? Does he own a lot of reindeer? Fantastic pheasant, by the way. Delicious, says Ellinor. Yes, *of course* I've gotten over the breakup with Tom. As she says this, she wonders if maybe it's true. At times, in the most surprising situations, people tell the truth.

She manages more coffee and a visit to the hospital before the return flight the next afternoon. She chats with him. His eyes follow the movements of her lips, and when she asks him a question, he opens and closes his own mouth. But no sound comes out. Like a fish gasping on land. He's getting tired now, says the nurse. She rocks back and forth on her white comfort sandals. I'll be going soon, says Ellinor. The last thing she does is bend over her father and sing, *When the troll mother had put her eleven little trolls to bed . . .*

. . . *and tied them fast to her tail,* murmurs her father. His speech is unclear, the melody falters, but the words are recognizable. It's not unusual that they remember songs long after all other language has disappeared, says the nurse impatiently. Now I really think you must go, so I can take care of him.

In the same way as before, Anna Guttormsen stands at the outer door and blocks the view into the house, broad in her slenderness. It smells temptingly of coffee all the way down to the front steps. Ellinor greets her politely, apologizes for disturbing her again, asks how it's going with the foot.

"Come on in," interrupts Anna Guttormsen, and she opens the door all the way, taking a step to the side. Now Ellinor can see that Anna Guttormsen can't quite help holding back a smile, not a triumphant smile, but an amused one. Ellinor follows her into the house, kicking off her boots, unwinding her scarf, hanging up her jacket, putting her gloves in the jacket pocket.

Anna Guttormsen's house is fantastic. That's the word that Ellinor uses anyway when she's shown into the living room. What a fantastic house, she says, standing there and looking around. The living room has a low ceiling with a loft above it, but the room opens out to two-story height on the section facing the sea; here the windows are almost floor to ceiling. Outside the day is gray-lilac and misty, but it's not difficult to imagine an expansive view of sea and sky. The wooden walls are unfinished, heavy rough logs that show the ax cuts. Only one of the walls is smoothly wallpapered, in a pattern of gray with red touches. In front of the modern wall is a spinning wheel, and on the floor next to it is a flat, shallow bowl filled with brightly colored balls of yarn. In the middle of the room is a deep sectional sofa, piled with more pillows than there is actually space for. Colorful, soft. Some from an earlier time, with elaborately embroidered flowers, others in printed material, alphabets and numbers; one signal yellow in velvet, another covered in sparkling silver sequins. On a low table in front of the sofa is a group of tea lights, each placed in different colored glasses. They cast a flickering light over the table surface: cobalt blue, grass green, red, yellow, turquoise. As far as Ellinor can judge, they're the cheap tea lights you can buy in any interior furnishing store, but the arrangement of candles on the table gives the room a fairy-tale feeling, a special blend of *One Thousand and One Nights* and the Norwegian folktales of Asbjørnsen and Moe. From hidden speakers, quiet music flows into the room, something classical she doesn't recognize. On the walls are woven tapestries, political posters. An old banner with "Let the River Live." A collage of newspaper articles from the demonstrations to stop the building of the Alta Dam in the 1970s. Over by the dining room table hang two large black-and-white photographs in narrow frames. Kåre Kivijärvi, explains Anna Guttormsen, who has been openly following Ellinor's gaze. He was from Hammerfest. A Kven. Ellinor nods.

In a dark corner of the living room is an old-fashioned secretaire, painted black, with golden decorations on the drawers and the extended leaf. Objects are arranged close together on the leaf, bathed in golden light from a lamp with a parchment shade. They stand there like a collection of various characters on the lit stage of a theater. Some are tall and thin, others short and plump, some four times as large as the others—like towering giants; some teeny, some dark, some light. They stand in groups, in intimate pairs, some set up in several rows like a class photograph. Ellinor gets closer, she *must* get closer, and the figures step out of enchantment, becoming things, some highly ordinary, some unfamiliar and remarkable. They become candleholders, vases, ornaments. An old iron, a paperweight made of glass. A dozen small bone-white human figures. *Tupilaks,* says Anna Guttormsen softly. They are Greenlandic spirit figures, made from walrus teeth. And this, she says, nodding in the direction of a heavy-bottomed drum away from the rest, is a Sami runic drum. How does it work? asks Ellinor. Anna Guttormsen looks at her. It has an on-off button on the back. Does it . . . , begins Ellinor before she sees Anna Guttormsen's expression, and both begin to laugh. You believed that for a few seconds? Yes, admits Ellinor.

In the middle of the secretaire, next to the ten Russian dolls in step formation and a single tarnished silver creamer, lies a shell, a little conch shell, smooth brown and white with spots. On top of the shell the whole Lord's Prayer is etched in. Done by a patient and skillful seaman sometime during the 1800s, says Anna Guttormsen. If you hold it to your ear, you can hear the ocean sigh. Ellinor smiles and takes the shell carefully in her hand; she feels the letters under her fingertips and has to run her index finger over them a couple of times before she lifts it up to one ear.

And this? asks Ellinor, pointing at a pink china cat. The cat looks up at them with large glass eyes; between its ears dangles a dirty bow tie. The cat stands out from all the others, with its strong colors, with its insistent mass-produced shape. It belonged to my daughter, says Anna Guttormsen shortly and turns away. Where is she? Does she live nearby? asks Ellinor. I promised you coffee. Would you like some? asks Anna. Oh, yes please, says Ellinor. She's almost forgotten the smell of coffee, but now she senses it anew and realizes it's been there the whole time. Anna Guttormsen goes into what must be the kitchen. Her steps are as light as those of a young girl, but she limps slightly.

The coffee is served in blue and white china cups. Russian, says Anna Guttormsen, from the time of Pomor merchants trading around the coast. The coffee is strong and black, better than coffee at Ellinor's favorite coffee bar in St. Hanshaugen. Is your foot okay? asks Ellinor. Yes, not too bad, answers Anna Guttormsen.

Call me Anna, she says, when they are halfway through their cups of coffee, and Ellinor does so. She talks about the project. Anna listens and nods, says she understands that Ellinor has a thoroughly theoretical background and that's not to be scoffed at. Ellinor says she would like to learn. Anna smiles and takes a sip of coffee. Shall we look at these questionnaires? asks Ellinor uncertainly. Anna doesn't answer, but moves her coffee cup.

Anna answers all the questions she's asked. Efficiently. Correctly. Informatively. After a while the answers grow longer, the tone more confiding. You know, she says, there was never any doubt about the ranking. *People first, then Lapps,* went the saying. Norwegians were best, then Kvens, then Sami. And of the Sami, the Sea Sami were completely at the bottom. A coastal Sami wasn't a Norwegian, but wasn't a real Sami either. My grandmother was called a bastard. Her name was Ravna, and she never learned Norwegian, and she had days when she was angry about that and blamed herself. Then she met my grandfather. Grandfather was strong as a wolverine and proud as a reindeer ox. She had decided she wouldn't have more children after her son Juhán died, but Grandfather managed to convince her otherwise. And Ravna stopped blaming herself. If she hadn't done that, we wouldn't be sitting here.

No, I don't believe that so many people lied, that they directly rejected their background. I only think they didn't say certain things. As long as no one asked, nothing was said either.

Yes, the forced evacuation increased Norwegianization. Many people think that. The Germans united the Kvens, Sami, and Norwegians. And after the war as well, when a large part of the country had to be rebuilt.

Anna is quiet, pouring more coffee for Ellinor. Ellinor's self-confidence has increased while Anna has been speaking, and after the questionnaire has been filled out she asks tentatively about the relationship between the Guttormsen and Rist families. She glances timidly up into Anna's face, prepared for it to harden, for her lips to tighten again. But what Ellinor gets is the same fleeting glimpse in Anna's eyes as earlier. Ironic, expectant? Ellinor doesn't know, but she knows it's not anger. Perhaps Anna was waiting for her visit, and perhaps she was waiting now for just this question.

"As you know," Anna begins, "there are no longer many Sami families here, at any rate not many who speak Sami. For me, it's been what you might call, to put it boldly, my life's mission to do everything I can to preserve the Sami language and culture in this place."

Ellinor nods. So far Anna hasn't said anything Ellinor didn't already know about the Rist family.

"But some people always want to wreck things. Some have told the local newspaper that support for education in Sami is *not of interest and completely irrelevant.*"

"But Sami is taught, isn't it?"

"Yes, *now* it is. But regardless, the Rist family betrayed us a long time ago."

"What do you mean?"

"They haven't spoken Sami for two generations. Now it's too late."

"But there is more?"

"Of course."

"Kåre once mentioned something about a teaching position he didn't get. He thought it was because of the Guttormsen family."

"How's it going with you and Kåre? Do you see each other?"

Ellinor shrugs her shoulders, doesn't answer.

"Kåre applied for but didn't get the teaching position," says Anna curtly. "Applicants with a command of Sami were preferred."

"I see."

"The part about Sami was in the job description. He had no reason to be so surprised," continues Anna.

"But there is something else too?"

"Yes. And one day I'll tell you the story of Ravna and Juhán. One day you'll understand, but not yet. I've certainly not thanked you properly for giving me your lamb steak. That was kind of you. More coffee?"

Ellinor smiles, glances down at her still-brimming cup and shakes her head. She has no choice; she must just wait.

31

Ravna was born in a *gamme,* as the seventh child but the first daughter. When Ravna is six months old, she sees the sun for the first time and she smiles for the first time. If her mother had been asked to describe what Ravna was like as a little girl, her mother would have answered perhaps *lavlú,* which can best be translated as *singing.* When Ravna was three years old, she could sing all the words to the lullaby:

> *Unna mánná niehku*
> *lea viegadit go muohta.*
> *Biegga dutnje lávlesta*
> *duoddaris.*

> The dream of a little child
> is whiter than snow.
> The wind over the mountain plateau
> begins to sing for you.

Ravna has known Benedikt her whole life. He is a couple of years older, redheaded, and broad shouldered, and able to say just the things that will make her think of him for many days after. Benedikt works as a hired man for a Norwegian family living on the other side of the fjord. But when the water is calm, he comes rowing over to see his mother, who needs whatever help she can get, and to talk with Ravna, to joke with her. To make her jaw drop, as he's begun to say. No one knows as many myths and legends, fairy tales, and joiks as Benedikt. And no one can tell stories like him. Ravna often gets chilled all the way down her throat because she forgets herself, sitting with an open mouth, listening to him. Benedikt laughs at her. Close your mouth! he says.

Benedikt is different from everyone she knows. When they were small and sat close together when the teacher came to give lessons, he followed along better than all of them. Benedikt sat ready with his slate, slate pencil, and hare's foot for an eraser. He hushed those who couldn't sit still, fought with one of the worst troublemakers—and got his ears boxed by the teacher, who didn't understand he was hitting the boy who wanted peace and quiet. During lunch, the teacher put a heavy kettle on the fire, and Benedikt made sure that no one touched the piece of meat marked with blue wool thread, for that was Ravna's.

Benedikt was patient, sitting in the smoky, drafty room; he learned to read and write in both Sami and Norwegian, even though Sami was supposed to be only a helping language for those who didn't speak Norwegian. Ravna never learned Norwegian properly, and the little she learned disappeared quickly again. What would she do with it?

She spelled her way through the catechism without understanding what she read, but was confirmed. She didn't need more.

Ravna was curious about the Norwegian family Benedikt worked for. They came from the south, from Western Norway. She asked. Benedikt told her. Their daily life wasn't much different from hers, but she liked to hear about it, asked repeatedly about clothes and food, animal care and table prayers. Their house, situated far down by the rocky coastline, was large and white. And in the barn were both pigs and cows.

They haven't seen each other for a long time, each living their own life. Ravna has received a marriage proposal from someone much older; she hasn't accepted but believes she will say yes. He has many reindeer and a larger house than most. One day in late summer Ravna and Benedikt meet by a mountain lake. They have both been sent out to cut sennegrass to stuff into boots and shoes. Benedikt is collecting it both for his mother and for the Norwegian family. Are you still there? asks Ravna. No reason not to be there, he answers. They pay well. One day I'll have enough money to buy my own place, and then I'll leave. Do they also wear Sami shoes? asks Ravna. *Skaller* in winter and *komager* in summer, says Benedikt. The shoes they brought from Western Norway won't do. Look, interrupts Ravna, and she bends over. *Heavdni!* You should never kill a spider, says Benedikt. No, says Ravna. There is a drop of dew on the spider's web. We owe a debt of gratitude to the spiders, he continues. Ravna wonders if she should drop her jaw so he can tease her, but this is a tale she has known from childhood. She doesn't listen, just looks at him as he speaks. When he comes to the end she opens her mouth a little.

He kisses her. It's always been the two of us, he says afterward, and pulls up his trousers. One day, not long from now, I'll come and fetch you. When you have earned enough money, she says. Yes, he says.

Frost has appeared in the mornings when she realizes she is with child. She says no to the man with many reindeer and a larger house. She hasn't seen Benedikt since that August day.

She is used to waiting. She sings and waits, carries out her daily tasks. He has promised they will wed. There is no hurry. She doesn't need a paper saying she and Benedikt belong together. The sea isn't safe now when the autumn storms are raging. One day she hears news about the family he serves: the man of the house has drowned. That must make it more difficult to get away. But one day he will come to her. One day not too long from now. She knows that.

32

Tomorrow Ingolv and I are traveling to Hammerfest. We'll meet my contact list Relative, who now has a name, Randi. She'll take us out to Sørøya and show us the place where Grandfather grew up. At the moment, we're in Tuscany. I sit at a glass table outside the apartment we've rented. The sun is going down, and the warm darkness falls around the table, the chair, my body. There's not enough light to write by, and the crickets sound unusually loud to a northerner. But I sit here with a cup of water, my notebook, and pen.

We've traveled around two thousand kilometers south from Oslo. Tomorrow we'll fly home, and then we'll travel around two thousand kilometers north from Oslo. When my elementary school teacher once in the 1970s talked about what a long country Norway was, she said that if you cut Norway out of the map of Europe, put a thumbtack into Eastern Norway and let go, then Finnmark would hang down into Italy. She didn't actually do that, but that's what I see before me now, this warm August evening when crickets rub their legs like mad and the cypresses stand like powerful silhouettes against a sky that is almost as dark as they are: the teacher with the natty seventies-style dress in front of a rolled-down map and with a heavy pair of scissors in her right hand. A shiny thumbtack in the middle of Oslo. She cuts first along the Swedish border. That goes quickly. Then she takes on the coast, the Oslo Fjord, Southern Norway. Into the narrow fjords of Western Norway, where a large number of my mother's relatives come from and also, strangely enough, my great-grandmother on Sørøya, the mother of Nicolai. The teacher cuts and cuts, turning and twisting the glittering scissors. It takes time. Norway has the world's second longest coastline, beaten only by Canada. The teacher is precise, no dillydallying here, and then she's finished and lets go. My country hangs upside down over Europe, long fjord fissures, villages with white and red wooden houses, mountain lakes with trout; north becomes south, east becomes west. At first after it falls, it swings widely; eventually there are only small oscillations before it completely stops. Yes, it's true. Finnmark reaches down to Tuscany.

Hammerfest's coat of arms is red with a white polar bear. The inhabitants continue to call Hammerfest the world's most northerly city, as they have done since 1789, even though Honningsvåg received city status in 1996 and thus won the record. And it is as I thought: Hammerfest got electric street-lights in 1891, the first city in Norway to do so, and one of the first in Europe. In 1945 the city was forcibly evacuated, burned, and bombed to pieces. I read that the only build-ing left standing after the war, and thus the oldest building in the city, is the cemetery chapel from 1937—that is the year Grandfather died. It must be strange to belong to a city where all the buildings, all the objects, all the physical memories once disappeared.

I don't know if Ellinor, Kåre, and Anna live in Hammerfest. I believe I know where they live, but prefer that they live in a nameless place. It's enough that Anna has photographs of the Hammerfest artist Kåre Kivijärvi on the walls and that the novel's Kåre is named after the Kåre of real life. I am the one who has named Kåre after the photographer, but perhaps he was also named for Kivijärvi by his own parents. Perhaps his parents admired Kivijärvi's photographs and called their son Kåre to honor the photographer. Kåre Kivijärvi was the first photographer to have his work shown at the Autumn Exhibition. That was in 1971, around the time that Kåre Os was born. For all I know, his sister could have been called Frida, after Frida Kahlo, by the same culturally aware parents. That's how it should be. Kåre and Frida.

Sørøya is Norway's fourth largest island. There is no road connection between the southwest and northeast sections. Ferries, express boats, and even planes go to the west. Today about a thousand people live here. Grandfather was from the northeastern part. One boat a day goes there, and fewer than a hundred people are inhabitants. We'll travel Tuesday morning, spend the night, and be back in Hammerfest on Wednesday.

Sørøya lies at seventy degrees north, and the midnight sun lasted there up to August 1. The night is still completely light. Tomorrow, August 6, we'll be there.

In 1890 Johannes Kvalsvig came to Sørøya. He and his brothers emigrated from Vanylven in Sunnmøre. Finnmark in those days was the land of possibility. The Russian Pomor trade had its heyday toward the end of the century, and Finnmark was a place where clever, adventure-hungry people could set themselves up in trading and fishing. The Kvalsvig brothers had likely imagined heading a little farther north, but then Johannes found Bismervik in Akkarfjord. The place lay sheltered under a south slope, with steep, green hills around it. Johannes went ashore here and settled down. It's said.

He sent a message to Oline, a girl he'd had his eye on in Vanylven. Perhaps they were already engaged when Johannes traveled north? Oline came. She and Johannes married and continued to live in Bismervik. At the farm there was also a hired hand. He was Ole Nilsen and was my great-grandfather.

On January 24, 1894, Oline stands on the steps of her house, looking out over the Akkarfjord. The shore is like a black band between the sea and the snow. A sea eagle crosses over the mountain behind her. To the right Melkøya rears up, the outer sea is straight ahead. Between Oline and the outer sea is the boat, far out. Johannes and two other men are line fishing. Oline has small children, a cow, perhaps some pigs, and most certainly plenty to keep her busy. She milks and shovels manure in the barn. She makes food, cleans, takes care of the children. She weaves, mends, and sews. She has no time to stand on the doorstep, staring out. But the wind has come up, and maybe that's why Oline has gone out. Now she places a hand on her stomach, sends a prayer on behalf of herself, her children, and the unborn baby that Johannes and the others may return safely to land. The wind grows stronger, the waves increase in size. The boat looks ever smaller out there, disappearing between the wave crests, popping up again, disappearing. Her son Johan comes out and holds his mother's apron strings. While they stand there, praying and hoping, the boat is lost, and the three men aboard drown. Johannes Kvalsvig set off. That wasn't the verb she used, my great-grandmother, Oline. There he went, said Oline. It's said.

Her son Johan, he who stood clutching his mother's apron, later said that was the only time he had seen his mother cry. Six days later Oline gave birth to a daughter. Oline calls her Johanna, after her father.

Now there are three fatherless children in Bismervik. Johannes's brothers don't think that Oline should live there alone with the children. They maintain she can't manage it. They want to take the children from her. Oline refuses. The children are the dearest things she has. No one, except God, will take them from her.

On October 27, 1895, in Hammerfest, Oline marries Ole Nilsen, my great-grandfather. What made Oline marry Ole? Was it because he was a solution to the hopeless situation she found herself in? A practical arrangement? Or were they in love with each other? Deeply and sincerely in love? Love. Love looks different perhaps when you live in a drafty house, when it's many degrees below zero outside, when you have children to take care of, when someone wants to take your children;

but I don't know anything. And those who once knew whatever feelings there were between Ole and Oline are dead. So I choose love. I decide that Ole and Oline are burning with love and that they choose each other in spite of everything. In the same omnipotent way that I rule over Ellinor and Kåre, over Ravna and Benedikt, I now rule over Oline and Ole. If I want I can decorate the night sky with reindeer eyes.

It was necessary, you see, says my relative. Oline had no choice. But I don't want to listen to her. In the census I discover Oline's first husband had a middle name: he was Johannes Nicolai. When Ole and Oline's first child was born—my grandfather—he was given the name Johannes Nicolai. Is that not a declaration of love from Ole to Oline, or at any rate a recognition from Ole's side of Oline's sorrow and loss? I take it as support for my story, that it was not *just* a practical arrangement.

Oline looks severe in the pictures I'm allowed to see during our visit to Sørøya, her hair combed tightly back from her face, high cheekbones, large mouth. It's impossible to judge whether she's beautiful or not. It's not important. Ellinor isn't beautiful either, but she has a lazy power of attraction, something catlike and relaxed. It's easier to get a handle on Ole Nilsen's face. It's easier to say that he is a good-looking man. Long, narrow nose—the Nilsen nose—beard and moustache, light haired. In my story they fall in love, in spite of the sorrow of Johannes who departed, crying children, daily life, toil, milking, fish, sleet, and the winter dark. And they have two summers together after Johannes is dead and before they marry. Two summers where the sun never goes down over Sørøya, two short summers with gold and red cloudberry bogs, warm rocks on the shore, and blooming wild roses. In my story they fall in love, they gather sennegrass, they don't care what people say. He wants her. She wants him. In spite of people's gossip and judgments.

When Oline married, she was pregnant. Ole Nilsen is a hired hand in Bismervik. He is six years younger than she is. And he is Sami. Was it scandalous that the widow at Bismervik had gone and gotten pregnant with her Sami servant? Did they keep it hidden? A little more than five months after the wedding, in any case, Grandfather was born, April 2, 1896. For me Nicolai is a love child.

From 1898 Ole Nilsen is the one written up in the tax rolls for Bismervik. Things go well for him. He has hired hands, and in the house is a servant girl. In the local history book it is written: "Ole was for a generation one of the luckiest of the active fishermen on Sørøya Sound." He was also a skilled hunter; in particular, he could earn a lot of money hunting otters. He pays down the mortgage faster than the contract requires, and he and Oline decide they will build a new farmhouse in Bismervik.

The new house is finished sometime just after 1900. I have a copy of the fire insurance papers from 1939 and can see that the main house is 10.78 meters long and 6.25 meters wide, two floors. On the first floor there are five rooms and on the second, six. In addition, Ole Nilsen insures a second house, two dairy barns, a hay barn, a farm shed, and a boathouse—in all, seven buildings in Bismervik. The houses were, just like all the buildings in Finnmark, burned by the Germans in the winter of 1944–45. But I was able to see the pictures when I was there. Grandfather didn't live in a turf hut. He lived in a rather large, white-painted house, with many gleaming windows, with two gables in front, and with a fine outside entrance with steps coming up from both sides.

I am on Sørøya. I am in Bismervik, where my great-grandparents Oline and Ole lived until they died and where Grandfather was born and grew up. I must have met at least seven relatives. Second cousins, second cousins once removed, a cousin of someone's parents. When we have run into someone new who is also a relative, I'm introduced as Nicolai's granddaughter. I can see you are a Nilsen, someone says and then looks me in the face. It's impossible it can be the nose. Mama pokes me in the back: No, *that* you have from me, she says.

For the first time in my life I wish I were named Nilsen. I dropped it when I was seventeen, preferring my middle name, Mama's maiden name, as a last name. Was Papa hurt by that? That he didn't protest means nothing, in any case. Why didn't I want to be called Nilsen? Vanity? A wish to be different, better, more original than having a quite ordinary last name? Certainly. Mama didn't like being named Nilsen, and she didn't hide it. She was, until the end, pleased that Uri was attached to Nilsen. She was definitely not Nilsen but Uri Nilsen. She didn't avoid mentioning, half-irritated, half-resigned, that when she and Papa married, she had suggested Papa change his name to the place his father came from, that is, Bismervik. It was her repetitive irritation that made me, that day in January, remember Bismervik and find Grandfather in the census.

We take a walk with two of my second cousins. The sky is high and blue and Norwegian. We have gone to Mefjord, a small bay on the other side of the island where Nicolai attended school before he left for the district boarding school in Alta. We've seen sea eagles, reindeer, hares. We are overwhelmed. We have slept in the house that was rebuilt in Bismervik after the war. We've had the special North Norwegian dish *seimølje,* made with pollock and fish liver and roe, cloudberries for dessert, thin *lefse* for tea. I know much more now. I've seen papers and photographs, leafed through albums, listened to stories, repeatedly asked questions.

I'm balancing on the coastal rocks along the fjord, out toward the outer sea. I know he has walked here, jumping from rock to rock, watching to make sure he doesn't slip on the seaweed, fall, and trap his leg between two rocks. I know he has stopped and turned his face toward the sea, as I do now. Breathed the sea air into his lungs, which at the time were healthy and pink with no trace of stone dust. I know he's seen the sea eagles, perhaps the ancestors of those we've seen flying above today. He's seen the salmon jump, the otters dive; he's heard the minke whales breathe, seen the porpoises play. Here he's sat and thought about how, just off this shore, Johannes Kvalsvig drowned.

Grandfather and Johanna, who was born only a few days after the accident, are half-siblings. There are only two years between them, and they're close. They talk often together. Johanna's father drowned, and if he hadn't died, Nicolai wouldn't have been born. It might be something they talk about, this too, or it might be something that Nicolai thinks about when he is alone.

Sometimes the fjord is gray and clear, sometimes it's opaque and dark green, other times black and foaming. Across the fjord he sees Melkøya, Muolkkut in Sami. Maybe his father, Ole Nilsen, used that name. Muolkkut.

They raised pigs on Melkøya when Grandfather was a boy. Now Melkøya is a receiving terminal for natural gas from the Snøhvit gas field. It's industrial buildings, pipes, and tankers that *I* see. And I see the gas flame that burns brightly as an obtrusive but not unlovely symbol for the oil and gas industry that in past decades has transformed Norway. A hundred years ago it was the smelting factories. Now we have oil and gas.

I don't know what Grandfather thought when he sat where I am now sitting. But I'm certain he sat here. Here, exactly. It's Grandfather's secret place. I allow myself to sit, childishly disappointed that there isn't a bottle with a message from him to me between the rocks out on the point. A letter that could have lain sealed in a glinting green bottle with barnacles and algae, written from Nicolai to the grandchild who would be born almost thirty years after he died, a letter that gave me answers to everything I don't yet know.

She had eleven children, my great-grandmother—two of them died young. Five children with Johannes and six children with Ole. We're not talking about a rich man's home, but they had the means to help Nicolai get an education. Nicolai left Finnmark at quite a young age. His little brother Astrup, born in 1898, next in the flock of children, became a teacher and moved later to Stavanger, but that was only in the 1950s when he was a grown man. The others stayed. Why did Nicolai leave? Did he have a strong wanderlust? Was he thinking about getting far away when he sat on a rock and looked out at the sea?

Yes, it's true that Nicolai was given the support to study

elsewhere, say my relatives. But otherwise they don't know much about him. When did he go to America? What did he study? Was his plan the whole time to return to Norway? Was it by chance he ended up in Southern Norway? He was back on Sørøya in 1920. That I know. I was allowed to see a photograph of him with his parents and brothers and sisters. At that time he was twenty-five—must have been finished with his engineering studies, perhaps he was already engaged. He married the following year, in any case. His parents were not at the wedding. The trip in 1920 was probably the last time Nicolai and his parents saw each other. They were not at their son's funeral either, I'm told.

People read a lot in Bismervik, say my relatives, and they bring out a photograph of Oline, who is washing dishes while a little boy, one of Grandfather's younger brothers, sits bent over a book. Perhaps he's reading aloud for his mother. War reparation records show that the Nilsen family received five hundred kroner to replace lost books. That's quite a large sum compared with the other items. One krone for a pitcher, sixty-five øre for a ladle.

Now I know the date of Grandfather's death: July 6, 1937. I have a picture at home of Papa that must have been taken around that time. When I was small I got an ache in my stomach when I looked at that picture for a long time. His hair is parted on the side and slicked down with water; he has serious eyes and a sensitive lower lip. I always thought he looked sad. His eyes were sad, and I felt I could see right into his thoughts, while at the same time I had no idea what he was thinking.

It was an interest in genealogy that prompted Randi to call me that day in January. She and her sisters have gone back and found the forefathers and foremothers of Oline Amundsdatter in Sunnmøre and of Ole Nilsen in Finnmark. I now know that Ole Nilsen was born on Sørøya, but that his ancestors came from, among other places, Karasjok. In the census of 1910 where he is listed as a settled Lapp, it's recorded that his language is Norwegian. Naturally enough, he spoke Norwegian with his wife from Sunnmøre. But I also know that he could speak Sami, for among the relatives some could remember how Ole Nilsen sat speaking Sami with his brothers, telling stories, laughing and cracking jokes.

Could Grandfather speak Sami? Could he understand it? Or was Ole unwilling to let Nicolai, whom I've turned into a love child, learn Sami? Did his father close that door, not allowing Nicolai into that room with laughter, legends, good hunting stories, and joiking? Folktales about *stallo*s, the evil giants; about *ulda*s, tempting females with beautiful dresses and long hair; about the bloodthirsty Chudes, legendary bandits. I believe Ole and Nicolai had this secret room that Nicolai was invited to enter, and that the mother from Western Norway was excluded from. A room that Nicolai himself closed when he left Finnmark, married, and settled down in Eastern Norway, but that he now and then opened a crack. He whispered a few words of Sami to himself, thought about one of his father's tall tales—about the magical white reindeer cow—and smiled to himself. What are you thinking about? asked Astrid softly. She lay on her half of the mahogany bed. Kjell, her firstborn, slept in the cradle alongside. Nothing, answered Nicolai. It must be something? said Astrid. Just something from when I was a boy, Nicolai answered. He turned his back to her, a blue-and-white-striped-pajamas back.

I see the cousins on my mother's side frequently. I have a good sense of them, but I don't have a full grasp of those on my father's side, and they are the ones I need now. Have they known Great-grandfather was Sami? Do they know more about Grandfather? Do they know where he studied? How he and Grandmother met?

To be called Nilsen is no advantage in this case. My female cousins changed their names when they married, didn't they? I haven't found my male cousin, even though I know his date of birth and know he's an engineer. I've searched on the Internet and in tax records. I've called up strangers with the same name, who are definitely not my cousin, when I hesitantly introduce myself and my mission.

I ask Randi. Perhaps she's had contact with him in connection with her genealogical research? Randi answers: he was here last week. I shake my head; it's easy to get mixed up with all these unknown relatives who keep popping up, and who we've been incessantly discussing the past twenty-four hours. No, I explain patiently, *my* male cousin. He's the son of the middle boy in Papa's family; he grew up in Western Norway, has studied in Trondheim at NTH. Exactly, says Randi. He lives in Hammerfest now and was out on Sørøya just a few days ago.

It turns out my cousin is the manager of Snøhvit. He is, quite simply, the one controlling the gas flame on Melkøya. When he sits in his office, he looks right across to Bismervik. He has the same long Nilsen nose he had when we last saw each other at Grandmother's funeral in fall of 1996. We talk a long time. My cousin knows things I don't know. I know things he doesn't. We work on putting together the jigsaw puzzle, finding piece after piece, we eat carrot cake, and, for some reason, both Ingolv and I drink several cups of coffee.

I know that Great-grandfather was Sami. My cousin had never heard that. What, is that true? he says. Yes, I nod. For his part he knows how Grandmother and Grandfather met: they both worked as newly trained engineers at Fiskaa Factory in Kristiansand. A piece falls into place.

"By the way, I've seen a photograph from that time, of Grandmother together with Søderberg himself!" says my cousin. He gives me no reason to doubt that what he's saying is big, almost sensational.

"Hjalmar Söderberg?" I ask. Hesitantly.

"Who's that?"

"A Swedish author. *Doktor Glas?*"

"No. Wilhelm Søderberg," says my cousin kindly, as if I'm mentally deficient. "Of the Søderberg electrode. The self-baking continuous electrode. Grandmother is in the same picture as Søderberg!"

I understand this is big and smile, impressed.

I tell him that our part of the family has a chest known as *the seaman's chest,* and that I believe it comes from Grandfather's home in Bismervik. In that case it's the only thing from there. My cousin doesn't know anything about the chest, has never heard a word about such a chest. He says that in his family there's nothing from the relatives on Sørøya that he knows about. Apart from one thing. When my cousin was small he got a carefully constructed sailboat that Grandfather had made as a toy for his sons when they were children. My cousin got the boat because he was the only boy among the grandchildren. The boat. Grandfather must have found a suitable piece of wood in the shed, hacked out the rough shape of a hull, and whittled it into a finely detailed sailboat. He made the mast, with a boom and a stay for the staysail. Perhaps he came to a standstill at times, thinking about the boats his family had when he was growing up. Perhaps his father made him a wonderful sailboat, for Nicolai the love child. Perhaps Grandfather thought about the secret place there in the coastal rocks, about all the hours he had spent at sea. He longed a moment for his parents, for his brothers and sisters, for Johanna, whom he'd always talked with so often. He hears her high voice, remembers some of the words she always used, the nickname only she called him. He sits on the chopping block. He is a grown father of a family now. The boat lies in his lap. He should sand the hull smooth, but he sits there without doing anything. Perhaps he's thinking he should write to them up there. Or ask Astrid to do it. Then three white-blond boys peek in on their father. No, it's probably an earlier time. There's only Papa and the next eldest who have been born. And the next eldest is still little. The boat is for Papa. And Papa stands in the door of the woodshed. He has short trousers and grass stains on his knees, canvas sneakers, and knee socks. Father? He is impatient but doesn't want to nag. He respects his father, doesn't see much of him. Engineer Nicolai Nilsen works six days a week. He's really home only on Sundays; when he returns after work he has to rest. Maybe he's already sick; he breathes heavily and is easily tired.

Ingolv says we have to get into the car; it's not long before our flight leaves. We stand in the entryway and say our goodbyes. I tell my cousin I think he resembles Grandfather, Grandmother, my uncle, and Papa. He laughs. I try to hide how moved I am by what I just said. We'll see each other again, we reassure each other. I back out of the door. I have a pile of letters from my cousin. One of my sisters tried to discover a few things, he explains to me. There are many who are curious, I say. It's not a sure thing you'll get a lot out of them, he says. But you can definitely look at them when you have time, he calls after me. Before we've landed in Oslo, I've read them all.

Johanna, the child that Oline was pregnant with when her husband drowned, and Nicolai, the first child in the next group of children, were very close. It's said. What does that mean? That Johanna and Nicolai confided in each other? That it was to Nicolai Johanna said she missed the father she had never seen? That it was to Johanna Nicolai said that he dreamed of going away? Johanna's father was Norwegian. Nicolai's father was Sami. Did they speak of that?

The evening the sailboat was finally finished, when it was painted in the correct style and Astrid had sewed a sail for it, Nicolai sat down at his desk and wrote a long letter to Johanna. He wrote about his son, my father, who would receive the boat the next day. He wrote about the mild winter in the South, about how much he missed a real Finnmark storm. He asked her to greet his parents and younger siblings. Perhaps Grandfather wrote such a letter, perhaps he didn't. Perhaps Johanna and Nicolai wrote to each other when he went to America, or after he settled down in Notodden, or while he was sick and lived in the sanatorium. I don't know. None of these letters are to be found. What I know is that Astrid, my grandmother, exchanged letters for many, many years with Olaug, the daughter of Johanna. Some of the letters were saved, and I sit with copies in front of me. Blue ink in cursive script and old-fashioned orthography. Olaug describes her apartment in Hammerfest, she complains about the weather, the long winter, and the darkness. She writes about a nasty flu that has plagued her. She writes about nieces and nephews who sing in the choir, go to school, celebrate Christmas, about old uncles in feeble health. There are lots of people with names I don't recognize or can't place. Occasionally I find sentences about my great-grandparents, Oline and Ole, who are Olaug's grandmother and step-grandfather. I don't learn much from the letters, I don't end up finding out anything new about my grandfather. All the same, reading the letters makes an impression on me. I've read them many times since I read them for the first time on the flight south. I don't know why they move me. Is my throat choked with tears only because I know that she, who once wrote these letters, is related to Grandfather, to Papa, to me, to my children?

The pile also contains letters from Olaug to one of my cousins. From the letters I understand that my cousin contacted Olaug precisely to know more about the relatives in the North. "I could write a whole novel about those relatives," writes Olaug.

Olaug was present at Oline's deathbed in 1949. She describes it several times. And twice it concerns a particular episode. Toward the end, Oline asked constantly if letters had come, but no letters came. Oline lay in bed, waiting to die, and asked for letters. Every day Olaug had to shake her head and say that today no new letters had come. But then, on what would be the last day of her life, three letters lay in the mailbox. Three letters on the same day. Two of them were from Oline's sisters in Sunnmøre. The third was from her daughter-in-law Astrid, my grandmother. In her ink-blue, cursive script Olaug says that she read aloud the letters to Oline, and that her grandmother followed along and was happy about them. Then comes the sentence I've read many times. I want to continue the letter, but my eyes seek out the sentence again and again: "She was so fond of the boys in Notodden," Olaug writes in the letter. I'm surprised anew that this transfixes me, that I won't let it go. The boys in Notodden—that's Papa and his brothers. Olaug writes that her grandmother was so fond of them. And I know she never met them. Ole and Oline never met Nicolai's sons. All the same she was fond of them, it's asserted. Perhaps that's just a phrase. But perhaps she really was. Naturally Oline was happy that her son got an education; she was proud he found good positions in the smelting industry in Southern Norway. She was pleased that he and Astrid had three sons. She mourned that Nicolai contracted silicosis and later died. She felt sorry for Astrid losing her husband and for the boys losing their father. But could she be fond of three boys she'd never met? They were her relatives, her grandchildren. She could. It's possible. And I can be touched by reading what a woman I never met writes about another woman I never met either. It's also clearly possible.

That night, the afternoon after Olaug had read aloud the three letters for her, Oline died. My great-grandmother. Nicolai's mother, who must have tousled his hair, reprimanded him, and taken care of him.

Olaug writes that Ole Nilsen was "a handsome man, dependable, a hard worker," and that his relatives were "clever people, quick to learn." She writes this to my cousin, who has expressed a wish to learn more about the family. Olaug never, with a single word, mentions that Ole Nilsen is Sami. Perhaps she feels it's irrelevant, perhaps she believes it's not something you talk about. None of us knew it, none of his great-grandchildren, the descendants of "the boys from Notodden."

In a letter from Grandmother to my cousin, dated 1994, when Grandmother was ninety-seven, she admits that she can't understand who the various people are whom Olaug describes in her letters. She writes that many of them are probably "born after Nicolai's death." And even when he was alive, he didn't say much about his family. No, he probably didn't. Perhaps he was also a man of few words. Perhaps he believed there was every reason to keep quiet.

37

I don't know any longer if I see the distinction. What I remember from childhood, what might be something I read in a
book. As if it wasn't about me, but about another light-haired
young girl with braids. My mother ironed the hair ribbons
before she tied bows. At night the girl also had braids, but then
she had rubber bands, ordinary, thin, brown rubber bands,
which her big sister had wrapped so that the rubber bands
wouldn't chafe the ends of her hair. Sometimes the girl lay in
bed and was scared to death because her parents were fighting.

I don't see clearly. I don't distinguish. The last Christmas
Eve with Mama. She sits in a chair at the dining table, but she
will also sit there in years to come. Grandfather who sanded
the boat for Papa. I see it as clearly, as unclearly, as I see the
frightened girl on the bed, as I see Mama on the chair wearing
her holiday outfit. As I see Clyde in *An American Tragedy*. The
princesses in the book of fairy tales, with a fox on the cover.
The Chudes of Sami folklore. Mama and Papa as students in
Trondheim. Ellinor who can't get off the sofa, who eats sliced
tongue right out of the plastic package. I see her. I know what
things are like for her. I've eaten sliced tongue right out of the
package. I've read David Crystal. I've eaten sushi at the same
restaurant as Ellinor. I've even met her there. But I've never at
any time chewed on a ballpoint pen so its tip splinters.

~~~

The others have gone to bed. It's quiet in the apartment, it's quiet in the streets. If I put my ear to the cat, I hear she's purring. The computer also whirrs a little, whirrs and works for me. I've pulled out the picture where Grandmother is posing with Søderberg. A helpful librarian at the National Library has hunted it down and sent it to me. "Main researchers gathered at Fiskaa Factory, August 17, 1919, in honor of a visit by an international expert group to investigate the significance of the Søderberg electrode." Eleven people are in the photograph: eight men, three women. The women are young, wearing light-colored dresses that fall far below their knees. The men wear summer suits; one has a jacket and white trousers, all wear ties. Their names and titles are listed in the photo caption. The great Søderberg himself stands modestly in the background, third from the left. Among the men are engineers, a professor, a doctor. There are two "Misses" and one "Mrs." Judging from her name, the Mrs. is married to one of the engineers in the picture. The blonde is *Miss Søderberg;* perhaps she is Wilhelm Søderberg's daughter? The last Miss is Miss Nilsen. That's Grandmother. In truth, that's not her name. She was Miss Jacobsen until she married and became Mrs. Nilsen. But it's her. The narrow, sloping shoulders. Her hair appears to be dark blond and wavy. Her dress is white with inset lace. Her shoes are small and white with rosettes. Around her neck she wears a medallion. Around her waist is a loosely hung, thin chain. One of her hands is clenched, as if she's nervous or excited. Two weeks before the picture was taken she turned twenty-one. Astrid Jacobsen has attended Kristiania Technical School. And she is probably in the picture on her own account, not because she's anyone's daughter or wife. Perhaps she's been part of some measuring or analyzing work on Søderberg's electrode.

201

I zoom in on her face. Does she appear to be in love? Does the right fist conceal an engagement ring? Was it the summer of 1919 she met Nicolai? Or don't they know each other yet? I continue to zoom in until her face dissolves into dark brown and white squares.

The cat must have gone away. For a quick moment Mama sits in the chair where the cat usually lies. Didn't you understand it was death I wanted to talk about when I said I was afraid? She simply establishes that without a hint of complaint. Then the chair is empty.

The Oslo night has become even quieter. I've searched out the digitized church registries, those that cover the early 1920s in the area around Kristiansand. These registers are scanned, and I can't search by name but must scroll through the screen, hunting. Finally I discover them, Nicolai and Astrid, and I am disproportionately happy, stand up, look for the cat, clutch her, and tell her I've found them. I have found them! As if I needed proof that they really had been alive. They married in Oddernes Church, outside Kristiansand. Nicolai Nilsen, chemist, Fiskaa Factory, and Astrid Jacobsen, chemist, Svelgen. Nicolai is the son of fisherman Ole Nilsen; Astrid is the daughter of postmaster Abraham Jacobsen. The witnesses are engineer Jens Kjølberg, Svelgen, and the engineer Einar Lund, Fiskaa Factory. Einar Lund, that's the man in the light summer trousers who stands right beside Grandmother in the picture with Søderberg. I click on the picture again, look searchingly at the man who, on a warm August day almost a hundred years ago, stood a few centimeters away from the young woman who would become my grandmother.

Papa's baptism in Kristiansand Cathedral on July 22, 1923, is entered in a later church register. In addition to his father's father, Ole Nilsen, and his mother's mother, Marie Jacobsen, he has Jens Kjølberg as godfather. *Svelgen* and *Jens Kjølberg* awaken something in me, and I know instantaneously that I've heard both names before, that they are meaningful. I whisper the words to myself. The cat pricks up her ears. Svelgen. Bremanger. Nordfjord. Jens Kjølberg. I don't connect them at all with the long Sunday dinners at Grandmother's in Notodden, Mama, Papa, and Grandmother talking. I leaf through a book perhaps, half-listening, bored. I am a restless child on a visit to a well-meaning grandmother smelling of carnations, who doesn't even have a TV. Would you like to play with the puzzle cross again? Ferrosilicon, zinc, energy production, turbines. Mutton-and-cabbage stew or fricassee. Rosehip extract. The Venetian paperweight. The china egg dish in the shape of a hen with crocheted light-yellow innards. Coffee in the living room afterward. Cookies on a silver platter. Marble clock striking every half hour. The silent conch on the mantel.

The August night is impenetrable and dark, the streetlights are on. Two young men with loud voices stagger in the middle of the street on their way from one pub to the next. A barelegged girl pads a few meters behind them; she's wearing shoes with sky-high heels and talking on her cell phone. When I search the Internet I get many matches for Jens Kjølberg. I read: Jens Kjølberg came to Svelgen in 1919 and discovered new and more effective methods of producing zinc, received patents for this, but the times were uncertain and there was no significant investment. Later he worked for Bremanger smelting works. Svelgen was a tiny little place far up the arm of a western fjord: there were forty inhabitants in 1900. But it had the fjord and a waterfall, and they were the two ingredients that were needed: a trade route over the sea, power from the waterfall. Some ten years later it was an industrial town, and by the 1980s, fifteen hundred people lived there. A small piece of Norwegian industrial history. But it doesn't explain why his name has such a strong resonance for me.

Only when I search in the censuses do I see the connection. I find out that Jens Kjølberg was married to Grandmother's sister Margit. Uncle Jens! That's what Papa called him. Uncle Jens, yes, how many times I heard that! He was some years older than Grandmother, and perhaps he's the one who got Astrid Jacobsen to choose engineering studies. They obviously had a good relationship, Jens and Astrid. She definitely looked up to him, showed interest in his work. On his side, he saw Astrid as hungry for knowledge, good at science and math, curious about the new industry springing up in Norway in the years after the turn of the century. Grandmother as I knew her was a quiet and modest woman. No doubt she destroyed her bladder function because she worked for so many years in a male-dominated environment where there was no toilet she could use without bumping into men on the same mission. I hear the echo of more or less unsuitable witticisms and jokes about this (All men out! She's coming! Miss Jacobsen/Mrs. Nilsen needs a pee!), and I have no problem understanding that Grandmother squeezed and waited as long as possible. She was certainly no bulldozer as a young woman, but all the same she had to have possessed courage and will when she went to the capital and became the first female student at Kristiania Technical School, the same school her brother-in-law had attended years earlier.

38

Ellinor is strong willed, with a tenacious determination that is not always well articulated. Her strong will is such a natural part of her that it tricks her into believing she doesn't have one. Ellinor chose linguistics, but strictly speaking it was more a non-choice than a choice. It *had* to be language; she didn't consider anything else. She had grown up with her father's expectation that she also would be an architect. No, that's not correct. Ellinor grew up imagining that her father expected she too would design buildings and take over his architectural firm, which he himself had inherited from his father. When she chose the language curriculum in high school, she postponed telling her father until the day she mentioned it so casually over dinner that it was impossible to understand this was something she'd been reluctant to say. I've always known, said her father, that you would work with language and words. Have you? asked Ellinor. Yes, said her father, and it's a good choice. Let's toast to it! What about the firm? asked Ellinor, leaving her water glass on the table. I'll sell it all in good time, said her father. *Skål!*

Life isn't really too bad right now, she finds herself thinking one morning, for no particular reason. She sits on the sofa with her laptop, a cup of coffee and the half-full French press on the table. She has ragg-wool socks on her feet, one of them with a hole, so her big toe sticks out. She wiggles it and decides it's a toe without fault, a well-shaped toe. She's finished all the interviews, filled out the forms, and begun on a rudimentary statistical treatment. There are so few informants that it's nothing but a research aid, but she's always liked mathematics and numbers. In addition, she's come a long way on what will turn into a popular scientific article about Anna Guttormsen. Outside it's dripping from the roof eaves. The days have become noticeably longer. The world still looks like an old black-and-white picture, but some promising nuances in brown and light gray have appeared.

She meets Kåre regularly. He lights a fire in the soapstone fireplace, and she settles into the crook of his arm. She has told him about her father. She's complained about Tom, talked about her colleagues at Blindern. Kåre has also been over to her place, in the ochre-yellow house. He's spent the night in the bedroom with the sloped ceiling and shivered at the bathroom's cold floor, more in sympathy with her than in true discomfort. He often lives in a tent, and he says that if he shivers when he stands on an unheated bathroom floor it will destroy his image. They laugh about it. Most of the time they spend together is at his house.

He hasn't said anything about the night she left him in anger. She hasn't either. She has reconciled herself to the fact they don't talk well together. Ellinor has met his sister. Her name is Frida, and she lives 120 kilometers away. Practically near enough to be considered a neighbor, says Kåre. Frida has a limp on the right side; she's almost speechless after a stroke a few years earlier. Her smile is crooked but beautiful. Is Frida named after someone? asked Ellinor in the car on the way home, and her question hangs in the air a few seconds before Kåre answers. A strange question to ask, not quite appropriate for Ellinor to ask in fact, but after a short pause Kåre answers the way I've planned he should: Frida is named after an aunt who worked at the fish-processing plant. Kåre himself got his name because his parents liked the sound of it.

She's seen photos of his children, albums from when they were small. Kåre and his ex-wife and the two children. In a couple of weeks his son is coming for a visit.

"He's the one who's studying medicine in Tromsø?" asks Ellinor.

"Yes," says Kåre. "You know, my grandfather was a doctor."

Ellinor smiles at him. "Yes, you mentioned it."

"His parents wanted only the best for him. So they raised him in poor Norwegian."

"And your parents?"

"My father never bothered much about it. My mother was against romanticizing indigenous people in the way she believed some did."

"Anna."

"For example. But my children have definitely become interested in their Sami heritage."

"You were young when you became a father," Ellinor notes.

"That's just how it was," says Kåre. "How about you?"

"I think I've been too afraid," answers Ellinor. Why did she say that? She knows the answer, hears her father's voice teasing: Because you didn't think beforehand, but recognized it afterward.

"Anyway, there's something or other wrong with my uterus, an inhospitable climate, I don't know," she says.

"It's not strange you're afraid. You lost your mother," says Kåre.

"It's something physical," says Ellinor.

Ellinor and Kåre eat dinner and breakfast several times a week. They take walks along the fjord. Sometimes Kåre has a flask of homemade cloudberry liqueur in his pocket. They toast and kiss. We do have a good time, don't we? says Kåre occasionally. We don't talk well together, Ellinor says then. But we're good in bed together, answers Kåre.

One day when Ellinor is about to flick off a spider that's on its way up the sleeve of her anorak, he stops her. You shouldn't kill spiders, he says, we owe them a debt of gratitude. Ellinor looks questioningly at him, her mouth half open. A spider once saved human lives, Kåre tells her. Two Sami fleeing from the bandits, or Chudes, hid themselves in a cave. The spider spun a web across the opening, and the bandits ran past. Ellinor allows the spider, a microscopic mite of its species, to creep farther up her arm.

He has taken her up to the plateau, where the snow still lies on the yellow hillside. He has pointed at herds of reindeer on their way through the mountains, has passed her the binoculars. He's lit a fire, boiled coffee in a blackened kettle, and she's promised him she'll bring a pan and make him some backcountry pancakes. Maybe in the summer, says Ellinor. Won't you have left by then? says Kåre. Yes, says Ellinor, of course I will have.

One evening Ellinor has a long phone conversation with one of her friends in Oslo. How's it going with your Sami lover? giggles her friend. With Kåre? says Ellinor. Fine, it's going just fine with Kåre.

Ellinor flips through the calendar of the Society for the Blind. She smiles at a Labrador puppy that's being trained as a guide dog, counts the weeks, and longs for the gym and espresso bars, small cafés and French pastry shops. Now it's spring in

Oslo. Spring in Oslo! Obscenely red rhubarb shoots sprouting up all around in gardens. The chestnut trees. The pitiful, exhaust-damaged trees on Bygdøy Allé that still bloom earnestly with white clusters. Far too expensive ice cream on a bench in Studenterlunden. Strolls in Frogner Park, tourists among the Vigeland statues, voices speaking Japanese, German, and American. Just-baked currant buns at Ullevålseter. A half liter of beer at Herregårdskroa. Just a few weeks now, then she'll be there. She shoves away the thought of how she'll earn money when she comes home. It will probably have to be copyediting. Instead she checks the web to see what the National Theater is putting on. Then she finds her way to the Opera's program, thinks she's never been to the new Opera House, except during the book festival, and that it's really time. *Figaro* premiers in August. It will be good to come home.

Ellinor sees Anna almost as often as she sees Kåre. On the first visits Anna is reserved, she needs time to warm up, but she invites Ellinor in with a smile that Ellinor doesn't yet know how to interpret. The last two evenings that Ellinor has been with her, Anna is already beaming as soon as she's opened the door. The only thing that makes Anna press her lips together is when Ellinor says something about Kåre. One day Anna shows her a child's shirt with embroidery on the cuffs and along the collar. It's made of linen, fragile with age. Anna has pulled out a drawer behind another drawer in the secretaire; there lay the garment, nicely folded. Ellinor has a strong feeling that the infant garment has something to do with the unfriendliness toward Kåre. But Anna says nothing, only praises the handiwork and invites her to look closely at the small stitches. In the evening Ellinor asks Kåre about it, but he only shrugs his shoulders. He's never heard talk of any embroidered child's shirt. She lies against his arm, and suddenly he begins to hum:

Biegga dutnje lávlesta duoddaris. I don't remember it all, he apologizes, and there are some lines I don't understand. It's pretty, says Ellinor.

~~~

The wine in the bottle has gone down far enough that Ellinor admits without embarrassment that *boknafisk,* salted, winddried cod that is soaked and boiled, will never figure on her list of favorite recipes. Anna merely smiles and says that Ellinor could get used to it, in time. When you've lived here several years, you'll come to love *boknafisk!*

For dessert, Anna serves an airy, pale-yellow foam she calls syllabub. Ellinor suspects it's a traditional Sea Sami recipe made from reindeer milk and mysterious ingredients from the shoreline. She's about to ask when Anna informs her that syllabub is an old English dessert with cream, honey, white wine, and muscatel.

"You probably thought it was something endangered and ethnic?"

"No, I . . ."

"Just admit it!"

"You're right."

"I'm always right. It is ethnic."

Over by the sofa all the tea lights are lit; they flicker and glow and spread an aura of mystery and coziness around the room. On the table is a knife. The handle is bone or antler, with etched brown figures. The fittings are brass. The steel blade is shiny, long, and looks razor sharp. For some reason or other, Ellinor gets a twinge in her stomach when she sees the knife on the table. Anna is in the kitchen, preparing the coffee. Ellinor stretches out her hand, but pulls it quickly back when she hears Anna coming with the cups and coffee pot.

"*Duodji*," says Anna, nodding at the knife.

How did she know that Ellinor had been looking at just that object?

"Knife?"

"No, *duodji* just means handicraft. It was my grandmother who made it."

"Ravna?"

"Yes, Ravna. She was a strong woman. She fought the *stallo*s in herself. She forgave and moved on."

As Anna says this, Ellinor sees how old she is. Ellinor seldom thinks about Anna being at least thirty-five years older than she is. Naturally her hair is completely white, but it's thick and healthy; her eyes are so quick, her skin smooth. But now it's as if the whole woman falls apart, and her age emerges, years accrete on her face and body before they slip away again and become invisible. Anna straightens up, places the coffee tray on the table, and picks up the knife.

"This is antler," she says, stroking the handle. "And here, up on the handle, it's brass. Brass protects the owner of the knife against evil powers. It's said."

Ellinor nods. "Does it work?"

Anna smiles, places the knife on the table's surface, and allows her index finger to twirl it around as if she's playing spin the bottle. Both women follow the knife with their eyes. The knife rotates more and more slowly. It looks like it's going to stop with its blade tip directed toward the blue-gray sky outside the window, but then the knife finds new energy, pulls itself together, whirls one last half round, and comes to rest with the blade tip pointing directly at Anna. A few seconds go by. Neither says anything before Anna pours coffee for both of them and clears her throat.

"How is it going between you and Kåre?"

"Fine," answers Ellinor, surprised.

"Just 'fine'?"

"Yes."

"You're good for each other."

"I thought you didn't like Kåre."

"I don't know him. But I see you are a changed person when you come from his house. You become different when you think of him."

"There's so much that's difficult between us. Are your earrings jade?"

"Yes. Chinese jade. What is difficult?"

"Oh, many things."

"Like . . . ?"

"It's very difficult for us to talk."

"Is that so?"

"I just think we're too different."

"Is similarity a condition for talking? Are *we* similar?"

"No, but . . . ," says Ellinor. "He doesn't listen."

"Doesn't he?"

"He doesn't understand me."

"There you're wrong."

Ellinor doesn't answer immediately; she takes a breath to explain what she means.

"*Enough talk, Ellinor, feel it instead*," says Anna.

Ellinor jumps, looks confused, a child caught red-handed, rebuked by her father. She grips the coffee cup, feels its warmth spread through her hands, like the warmth from Mama's hand. Her index finger and middle finger are around the cup handle, which clamps them fast, won't let them go. She wriggles her fingers, wants to get free—from the grip, from the warmth. The cup falls. The remaining coffee runs out over the table.

Anna looks at her gently, shakes her head. One of her long

drop-shaped earrings brushes her shoulder. Around her neck she has an amulet on a narrow black leather band, a bone-white tetrahedron, which looks like the tooth of a beast of prey.

It's when she's sitting on the sofa at home, after dinner with Anna, with a toe sticking out of her ragg-wool sock and with a nighttime invitation from Kåre to look forward to, that she gets the news. She jumps when the phone rings, but smiles to herself, certain it's Kåre. Then she sees the number. She recognizes it at once. It's from her father's hospital, not from his floor, which she has saved, but the first six numbers are identical. When she answers, her voice is almost inaudible. Yes? She must come as soon as possible. It is critical.

39

Ravna finally decides to go to Benedikt and show him the baby. Soon they must also have the boy christened. He will be called Juhán. Unless Benedikt wants another name. She borrows a boat from a neighbor. She waits for a clear, still day, puts the boy in the bow and rows across, pulling the boat up on shore. The house is large, painted white, and built almost down to the rocky shoreline. Ravna lifts the boy up on her shoulder and walks quietly up to the house. It has a prosperous look. Several rows of fish-drying racks. A small flock of sheep. An unpainted barn that houses a cow or two perhaps. The main house has a steep set of stairs leading up to the front door. She stands there, uncertain. Juhán moves restlessly against her body, kicks her in the side; his face turns red, crumpling with anger and impatience. Should she go up the steps? She doesn't move.

When he comes around the corner of the house, she can't help smiling: *Buorre iðit!* Benedikt greets her in return. *Bures.* But he doesn't smile. He doesn't want to kiss her. He doesn't want her in the house. He doesn't want to look at Juhán. He's about to walk away from them when the widow appears. She is dressed in black with homemade Sami shoes. Her wrists are narrow and blue with cold. She has an upturned mouth with small, even teeth. She says something in Norwegian. Ravna can only shake her head. The widow straightens her head scarf and gestures for her to come into the house. Benedikt says Ravna should leave, but Ravna follows the woman inside. They're about to eat. Five big-eyed children sit around the table, the youngest, who can't be many months older than Juhán, wriggles on the lap of the oldest girl. A maid stands at the stove, stirring a kettle. The widow makes a sign to Ravna to sit down. She perches on the edge of the bench. Benedikt acts as though he is the man of the house, reprimanding the children, being served first—as if he weren't the hired hand but the husband. Ravna wants the widow to understand that Juhán is Benedikt's son. She asks Benedikt to tell her that. Benedikt says something in Norwegian; she doesn't recognize any of the words, doesn't understand the meaning. The widow looks over at her, smiles in a friendly way with the small teeth. Ravna points at her child, at Benedikt, at herself. Saying again and again: This is his child. *Dat lea su mánná. Dat lea su mánná!* The widow nods again, and she is no longer smiling. Finally Ravna gets up and goes. Benedikt doesn't look up.

Sometime during the spring she hears rumors that the widow is with child. A few months later she hears that they are married. She, the widow from Sunnmøre, has married Benedikt, who until recently had been a hired hand on the farm. Ravna can manage alone. She's always done that. She sings to Juhán. She buys embroidery thread and a far too expensive length of linen from the local merchant. The shirt will have beautifully embroidered magical figures and flowering stems on the cuffs and around the collar. Her boy should have the best.

When a novel is finished, it no longer belongs to the author, but to the readers. When a person is dead, it is those who are left behind who take charge of him or her with their memories and experiences or with their wishes and descriptions. I've become accustomed to my readers taking charge of my novels. I've met many of them, I've received emails and letters where they tell me what the book means to them. In the beginning I didn't like it; I felt the need to correct them, to set them straight about their opinions. But gradually I learned to value what they were saying. I was happy about it, in fact. Nothing should please an author more than to know that readers find their own stories in hers.

I have greater problems with Mama. There are others who want to have a say in the matter. On the one hand, my ears prick up when anyone says something about Mama, but on the other hand, I myself want to control the story about her. Well, that isn't the complete story, I want to say. Yes, but I think she meant that a little differently, I want to interrupt. *Those* weren't the words she always used. But of course I don't do that. I let them speak.

It's September. Ingolv and I take long hikes in the forests around Oslo. I put my foot in a puddle between two stones in the path; the water splashes up over one of my jogging shoes. *Svupp* it says every time I take a step. Just as when I was a child squishing through water, hiking on Sundays with my parents in these same forests. Her apartment is finally going to be cleared out, emptied, and sold. I've looked forward to that, in the same way I looked forward to the funeral, as a milestone, something to put behind me, one step further on the road to normality.

We let ourselves in. We haven't been here since the previous summer. The smell is overwhelmingly Mama. I'd forgotten that, at least I didn't think about it until now, even though olfactory memories have always preoccupied me. I feel a certain connection to the carnation smell of my grandmother and her possessions. I miss the smells of the family farm, the distinct smells of its yard, of its rooms, of its pantry. I grieved when the smell that was lodged for a long time in Papa's sweater disappeared. I lack the vocabulary and conceptual apparatus to capture smells in words, but I'm sure I would have been able to recognize them all. Mama's favorite perfume clung to my wrists when we let ourselves into the apartment, and it is on my wrists as I write this. I have the scent, but now it is part of me and not of her.

I stand in the entryway and am surrounded by the smell, and I know there is no way to preserve it. It disappears, evaporates, disperses. I can twist off the top of the shampoo bottle she used during her last years, and I'll see her hair before me, feel its structure in my fingertips. I can continue to buy Trésor, and I will always be able to open the flacon and be reminded of her. Or will the scent, if I continue to use it, become only mine after a while? Maybe it's best to stop using it? I can bake the caramel cake that was her specialty, or the honey cake from the old family recipe. I can inhale the fumes of the fireplace flames and burning wood. But the particular smell that is just her, that still lingers in her apartment, in the furniture, in her clothes—that will inevitably disappear.

I begin with the linen closet, setting aside tablecloths I'd like to keep in a pile and tossing the rest on the floor. The sight of Mama's tablecloths in a messy pile on the floor is more than I can stand. I'm barely finished with one shelf, nevertheless I go into the living room and sit down on one of the dark-blue sofas.

The husband of my speechless sister has already been here to take the few things he wanted. It's empty without what was called in our family the *drunkard*—a chest for brandy bottles that a great-great-grandfather, a sheriff, used on his work trips to Western Norway. The samovar always stood on top of the drunkard, a heavy little gadget in copper that originated from my grandmother's shipping family in Southern Norway, brought home perhaps from Russia sometime in the mid-1800s. But it's not the empty spaces in the well-known interior that make me huddle on the sofa and put my head down on my drawn-up knees. There's something about the tablecloths on the floor, or more likely the whole idea of starting in on what was her life, discarding what we don't want, seizing all the rest for ourselves. Erasing the traces, emptying, switching off the lights, locking up her home. Treating her things as what they are: things.

I don't have time for whims. Before I start on shelf number two, I've decided I'll nicely set the tablecloths I don't want on a chair. That helps. I'm finished with the damask tablecloths and napkins. I keep out a cloth case that holds thirty-six fabric plate dividers with tatting around their edges. On the next shelf are at least two dozen embroidered coffee-table cloths, embroidered by Mama, by grandmothers on both sides, by female relatives in an era when sewing and embroidering were as natural as covering the coffee table with a newly ironed cloth every day. I can't quite recall that we used them when I was a child, only now and then when Mama had her girl-friends over. Some have spots that clearly didn't disappear in the wash. Some have flowers and patterns I can't make myself like. I keep many. Coffee-table cloths will suit Svea. The girls will perhaps want them one day. Those I don't like I put in a pile, binding them neatly together, to be picked up by people from the thrift shop or just thrown away.

Old bed linen with openwork insertions and monograms. Terry-cloth hand towels and washcloths that I recall from my childhood. Bath towels. Tea towels. I set aside the hand towels so I can use them to pack up glasses, crystal, and crockery.

The children arrive. They're quiet and serious as they walk around in the apartment. They've been here at least once a week from the time they were very small. They don't remember their grandmother ever living elsewhere. There's the deck of cards they used to play with: *caRds* is in clumsy, childish handwriting on the box. There are all the scarves and ker-chiefs they used to dress up in. Mama had endless numbers of them because for some years she wore a neck support that she decorated with constantly new kerchiefs. Behind the writing desk is the toy box that has been there since they were small. They dig down through layers of dolls, stuffed animals, plastic blocks. The eldest finds a huge soft yellow hippopotamus; she rises and remains standing with it hanging from her hands like a loose sack. I try to find something consoling to say, but can't settle on any words I haven't already used. Then they discover the coin bank. A white and black china cow with a plastic lid in its stomach. They shake the cow up and down, remove the lid in a practiced way. One-krone coins, fifty-øre coins, a couple of fives, and even some tens pour out on the floor. Among all the coins, a slip of paper with figures. One coin rolls a long way before it falls over. Oy, I say. Grandmother saved for us, they explain. We counted it up every time we came over and wrote it here. I'm happy my children and mother had something I didn't know about, had their own secret customs, routines, ceremonies.

In the basement storage unit, in the tall chest that Mama and Papa once had in their bedroom, I find her ski sweater. Her ski sweater! The one I thought had disappeared many, many years ago. That she herself made when she was able to knit and that she always wore when she was still able to ski. Gray with a red and white pattern. It's the sweater I had Ellinor remember a few chapters ago. I stick my nose down into the stiff stitches. The next time I go hiking in the forest, I'll wear it.

Her clothes. For the most part they'll be given away. The sweaters, flowered dresses, striped shirts. Unfashionable, unfashionable, unfashionable. Deep in the closet hangs a blue-checked silk dress. Heavy, smooth, expensive silk. Made in Switzerland, from the label. It appears she bought it at the end of the 1950s; it fits with that style. It doesn't smell like Mama; she certainly never wore it during the past forty years. This one I want. I'll put on the dress, cinch the belt around my waist, spin around on my heels, and think about her when she was a young mother in Geneva, when she held my sister by the hand. She was talkative then: *elle bavarde trop* was written on her report card.

Farthest back in the closet are worn-out shoes, bearing witness in black and brown leather to the various phases of rheumatism. Modest jogging shoes. Comfort sandals. Wide, orthopedic shoes. Specially made shoes. And slippers. The last years she wore only slippers, even outdoors when she was helped over snow and slush from the front door to a waiting car. The years they lived in Geneva she always wore Bally shoes, elegant, high-heeled pumps.

We write down what we're going to take. Some large things. The heavy, carved writing desk that was once in the home of my mother's parents in Ullevål Hageby. A sofa covered in blue-gray velvet from Grandmother's family. The teak dining room table, designed by Hans Wegner in the slender aesthetic of the 1960s, which Mama and Papa bought when they lived in Stockholm. And the black-painted seaman's chest. That, most of all. I may have been mistaken, but nevertheless it's been important to me in the course of these months. The movers carry everything into a rented van. Some things are going home with us, some will go to Svea.

Ingolv will use the writing desk for work; we've already removed the IKEA desk at home. I put the black seaman's chest in the living room, next to the fireplace. The seaman's chest has been with Mama and Papa as long as I can remember. Some months ago it occurred to me it had belonged to Grandfather. I sit on its lid, and right at the moment my backside touches the round lid I feel in my whole body that I've sat on this chest many, many times. With dangling legs. Now my legs are sharply angled. I decide it's from Grandfather, that it was once in the house on Sørøya, that he packed up clothing, books, and other necessities before he traveled to the United States. Or did people really travel with such chests at that time? Didn't they use suitcases? I urge myself to be quiet. This *is* my grandfather's chest.

Ingolv carries the boxes with the Rosenthal china service up the stairs, into the apartment, one after the next. There are three full boxes. Twenty-four large plates, twenty-four soup

221

bowls, just as many dessert plates, twelve dessert bowls. Tureens in various sizes, square dishes, rectangular dishes; one for rolls, another for sauces, small saucers Mama said were for pickled cucumber slices. Mama inherited the service from her mother's unmarried sister, a dentist. I feel an intense flash of happiness, happiness that it is now ours. I pause, wondering if I can allow myself to be happy, decide that of course I can. Put them in the bedroom, I say to Ingolv. I don't know where we're going to put all this. Later, I'm alone. The cat lies on the floor, between the boxes, on her back, exposing a stomach with white fur and small teats that have never been used. I open the first box. All the china is wrapped in Mama's tea towels and small hand towels. I packed it myself only a short time ago, but all the same I'm not prepared for the smell of Mama that remains in the towels and that flows toward me now.

The boxes of books are placed in the office. An unstable tower of brown cardboard. More than anything I wanted to have Papa's books, but I have so many books already. Even though the shelves extend all the way to the ceiling, they are almost full.

At home, growing up, we always kept Scandinavian literature and foreign literature on different shelves. Naturally I've done that as well. Papa's books were alphabetized. Naturally mine are as well. Now I must reorganize and move a whole shelf of travel books into the bedroom, piling the J authors vertically so they take up less space.

In the first box are the Scandinavian titles, still practically in alphabetical order: As, Bs. Bendow, Boye, Brøgger. Sigurd Christiansen. Evensmo. I've picked out some fine examples of Falkberget. Papa had many books by Fønhus. He read Fønhus aloud to me when I was small. *Beveren bygger ved Svarttjern. Enøre.* One of them looks ancient: *Under the Polar Sky,* 1922. That's the year after my grandparents married, the year

Papa was born. It's clearly well read, with stains and scratches. Nilsen is written inside, Nilsen with a fountain pen, the ink lines a little too thick in the last letters. But it is not Grandmother's hand. It seems that the letters look more masculine. My heart starts to race, and I dash through the girls' room into the kitchen, where I keep the cookbooks. I search for Grandmother's copy of Schønberg Erken as quickly as I can, find a sheet with her recognizable handwriting, a recipe for onions in butter and lemon. I compare the letters with the name in the Fønhus book. The letters are sadly enough the same, coarser, larger, but undoubtedly like Grandmother's. At least Grandfather would have read *Under the Polar Sky,* wouldn't he? I pad back to the unpacked books.

Heyerdahl, of course. An early TV memory is the *Ra II* expedition, with a correspondingly large production of drawings of *Ra.* I must have drawn many every day: a yellow reed boat with a white sail and red circle, dark-blue sea, light-blue sky with a yellow sun. Bright yellow. Bright red. Bright blue. But the TV experience stays with me only in black and white. Richard Herrmann, Sigurd Hoel. Two thin novels by Mette Hansen from the late seventies, bought because she was our neighbor in Ullevål Hageby, and Papa believed you should be supportive if a neighbor published any literature. I remember that now, hear his voice as I put them on the shelf. A good principle, Papa! Then some books by Lars Hansen. I've never heard of him but take the time to open one up, and then I find out he was a Northern Norwegian writer who often wrote stories about the sea. That fits. Can they also possibly be Grandfather's? Nothing is written in them. Disappointed, I put them in place. I've long given up trying to understand why this is so important to me. Ingstad. I already have Alexander Kielland's collected works, but these were so fine that the youngest wanted them for her room. Five or six titles by

Axel Kielland, the grandson of the great writer. Laxness, Max Manus. *Petter Moen's Diary*. This has a dedication on the title page: *Dear Kjell, Accept suffering, live through it, and see what you can learn from it and get out of it—don't avoid it—your Ragnhild.* A good friend? A sweetheart? Someone who knew my father's friend Juster? I don't know and put it in place. Moberg in Swedish. There's not much room in the Rs and Ss, but squeeze them in, I will. Ring, Scott, Strindberg. Now there are more empty boxes than full ones.

Next box. The books are more helter-skelter in here. Dostoyevsky. Balzac. Lots of American and British. Pearl S. Buck. Louis Bromfield. Howard Spring. Caldwell. Cronin. Dorothy Parker. Negley Farson. Edna Ferber. A meter's worth of Nevil Shute. Forester. Remarque. Kirst. Grass. Half a shelf of Theodore Dreiser. I sit on my heels and leaf through *An American Tragedy*. Clyde who comes from a poor background, with such a strong drive to rise socially that it overwhelms everything else. His lover Roberta, from the same social class, becomes pregnant. In Clyde's life plan, marriage with Roberta would bring him to a standstill instead of propel him upward, since Clyde has finally succeeded in winning Sondra, the rich man's daughter. I close the book. I know well enough how it ends.

And then there's *Anthony Adverse*. Papa's favorite novel. At least we used to tease him about that. My sister would get ten øre per page if she read the whole thing—that was when she could read. He raised it to twenty-five øre for me. I put it on my desk, thinking I'll have to read it at some point. It's twelve hundred pages, thin pages with cramped print. Papa read it about once every other year. It grew so worn that he got his students to rebind it in cognac-brown leather. His name is written on the title page, in blue fountain pen. Mama always said Papa had really nice handwriting; when I was a child I felt that his script was even more difficult to make out than that of other grown-ups. Now I think it's attractive. Of course I think that. If I had been a fictional person in the novel, it would not have suited the character traits I'd given myself if I had *not* admired the beauty of Papa's handwriting. I leaf through a bit more of the novel, read the beginning, a paragraph here, a line there. "The peasants working on the corvée of M. de Besance had just completed filling the hole in the causeway and were gathering their tools to depart for a well-earned night's rest, when the sound of galloping hoofs once more fell upon their ears." It sounds like a true picaresque novel, and from what I read on the Internet, it appears that I'm quite right. In 1933 it was the best-selling book in the world.

Over the next weeks I read only Papa's books. But *Anthony Adverse* I leave temporarily in peace. I read the books I once read at home. I read the ones he read aloud to me. I page through *An American Tragedy,* drink tea, and ponder whether Clyde is just a cunning betrayer; I pour a fresh cup and wonder what Papa thought of him. I have piles of this fall's books that should be read. I have a book that should be written, but I can't manage to leave Papa's books alone.

I bought and received a ton of new children's books for the girls when they were small. I also wrote some myself. But many of their books were old, from when I was a child, from when my sister was a child, from when Mama was a child. And the fairy tales were from then, too. Asbjørnsen and Moe in two large volumes, published in 1911. Light-blue cloth binding with a fox imprinted in yellow on one book, a bear on the other. On the title page of each is written: *To Helene from Grandmother, May 1972.* My favorites are "Three Lemons" and "The Twelve Wild Ducks," with the princesses who were thrown into the snake pit, and for that reason they were the ones I read often to the girls. I liked Mama's stories from her student days in Trondheim, stories of when *her* mother was small; I liked stories about the war. Cream made with skim milk and potato flour. Dancing parties. The often-mended dress that finally ended up as curtains in the mountain cabin. She related some of them to the grandchildren. Papa and the boys in the woods, shooting moose. I've told the girls about my father, who shot moose during the war. I've told them about Juster. Reidar the grouse with the red eyebrows is something I never told them, I don't know why.

Some of the stories they'll remember when the time comes. Some they will remember part of, remember differently from what they were. The stories are no longer mine, but theirs.

When Grandfather was a boy and saw the northern lights flickering over Sørøya, perhaps his father told him about the giant swans that flew farther and farther north. They flew so far north that they froze fast in the ice. Each time the poor swans flapped their wings, struggling to free themselves, the northern lights danced across the sky. The stories of the evil *stallo*s and the beautiful *ulda*s. The age-old story of the spider who saved two people from the bandits. All that, my great-grandfather told my grandfather. But Grandfather never told the stories to any of his three sons, so Papa couldn't pass them on to me.

What was it like for my great-grandparents Oline and Ole to return to Bismervik after the war? What was it like to see a burned-out lot where the old house once stood? To know that all they owned and had was gone, burned? Books they loved. The rose-painted coffee service. The sooty kettle they'd had so many years, with a dent in its side because it once fell on the floor. The birch-bark basket, the books, the embroidered

226

kofte that Ole's mother had sewn. The painstakingly crafted sailboat Ole created when his firstborn Nicolai turned four. Or perhaps they had quite different things. They lost them, regardless.

You can't take it with you when you go, said Grandmother. Leather-bound books with names printed inside. A carved writing desk, lobster forks and dessert spoons, tablecloths, a paperweight, a puzzle cross. A black-painted seaman's chest. I am astonished at myself. For the moment my life seems to be all about objects. I hold them, smell them, think about them, write about them.

In a painful way I allow myself to be touched by them. I feel sorry for Mama's tablecloths, which will probably become landfill. I speak consolingly to the ceramic pig that has now moved in with us, this unglazed ceramic pig with white stripes on its back, standing so lonely in our apartment. I have a crazy thought that I should move the pig closer to the pewter candleholders, so it can be in the vicinity of something familiar.

I know objects have played a role in the lives of my mother, father, and the people no longer here. I know that Mama lit the candles in the pewter holders, for I saw that. I saw Papa reading *Anthony Adverse*. I believe that Grandmother held the conch shell up against her ear. That Grandfather packed the seaman's chest. And I know that my great-grandparents must have set the table for Sunday dinner with their monogrammed silver: the Jacobsen family in Sarpsborg, the Østbye family in Gjøvik, the Uri family in Ålesund.

There's so much I don't know, and so I cling to the only tangibles left. I make the objects bigger, more meaningful. For me, who owns them now, for those who used to own them.

Things are like words. A single word has a clear function; it's not without significance. A word can be beautiful and melodious. Or it can have disgusting connotations. But it's only when the word is placed in relation to other words that it can expand, bursting with meaning. I set a fluted glass bowl on the kitchen table, take a step back, tilt my head to one side, act as if I'm being observed, as if I'm part of a novel. The eldest comes in. Look, I say enthusiastically. Isn't the bowl wonderful? Sure, says the eldest, but it's just a bowl, isn't it? To myself I say, My girl, that's exactly what it is not. It's not a bowl that can be exchanged with other bowls. I have the urge to draw two axes for her: the paradigmatic is vertical and along it you'll find thousands of bowls: a blue plastic bowl, an IKEA bowl, a ceramic bowl, a chipped, flowered, china bowl. Horizontally, across the page like a crisp stroke, runs the syntagmatic axis, and here we find all the situations the bowl has been in: the houses and apartments, the dinners we ate, Papa's hands around it when he passed it across the table to me.

I feel the urge to tell her that this bowl, this glass bowl produced by Hadeland Glassverk in the fifties or sixties, in the Siri line, in transparent pressed glass, can't be substituted by a blue plastic bowl or by an IKEA bowl. As far as I'm concerned, the paradigmatic axis can be removed. It's not relevant here. I have enough bowls in my cupboards; it's not the function I need. This is the bowl we used for grated carrots. This is the bowl that Mama and Papa packed up in tea towels and took with them from place to place, from city to city, probably in three different countries. This is the bowl that just a few weeks ago I carefully took out of Mama's kitchen cupboard and moved here.

11

Some things are too real for my liking. Some things I'd rather have forgotten. When I was small, all children had coin banks, at least all the children I knew. I had one too. Not the unglazed ceramic pig that Mama had made, because that was in the living room; of course it had a slot in its back for the coins, but to get the money out again you would have had to smash the pig. My coin bank was a plastic yellow man with striped trousers. Under his feet was a metal plate that could be flipped open if you had the little key for it. When my grandparents were visiting, they always put coins into the little man. Occasionally, other guests did too. Birthday money went there, and I slipped in some of my weekly allowance. A couple of times a year Mama put the bank into her mesh shopping bag, and then she and I went downtown to the bank. Adult and child to downtown, thanks, said Mama to the bus driver.

In the middle of the bank's main hall was a miniature landscape with green hills, with trees, a river with a bridge over it, small houses, and people. And in the landscape, train tracks had been constructed, and a model train drove around and around, over the bridge, through the tunnels, to the station where the stationmaster stood with a flag. We could hardly believe it.

We stood a long time looking at the train. There were always other children and mothers there, also staring. All the children were nicely brushed and combed, large eyed and solemn. The space echoed as in a church, and people automatically spoke in muted tones, almost whispering. Mama took the savings-bank man out of her mesh bag and gave him to me. We got in line, and finally I could go up to the counter, with the coin bank clutched to my chest and Mama right behind me. I gave him to the man or woman behind the counter, who in a serious manner unlocked him under his feet and emptied out the coins, swiftly sorting them into piles. Copper-brown one øre, two øre, and the large five øre with the moose. Shiny krone coins and fifty øre. The ten øre had a picture of a bee; the twenty-five øre had a picture of a bird. Once or twice there was a yellow bill. The sum was written in ink into my savings book. My savings book. Once in a while the serious person behind the counter said I was a good saver. The sum grew each time. It was for my education, said Mama and Papa.

One time, when Mama and I were going to the bank to empty the coin bank, my savings book had disappeared. Mama said it would all work out, we would apologize for having lost the savings book and ask nicely for a new one. Adult and child to downtown. We stood a long time looking at the train, which ran around and around, stopping at the station and starting off again. Then we waited our turn. Mama and the lady behind the counter spoke gravely and earnestly. Maybe I couldn't get a new savings book? Maybe the lady was angry because my savings book was gone? But my coin bank man smiled in his normal way, and I let him walk noiselessly on top of the counter. Mama took me carefully by the arm and said I must give the lady the coin bank. She emptied it, counted the money. We got the empty man back along with a new savings book. I don't know if Mama said it, or if I understood it from what she and the lady behind the counter said: Papa had been to the bank a few days before and had taken out all my savings. In the new book all that was written was the sum that had been in the coin bank this time.

42

Snobbish!

Ingolv and I are visiting my aunt in Western Norway. She
is not my blood aunt, but she was married to Papa's middle
brother. The three brothers—the boys from Notodden—are
dead. Only my aunt is left of the three married couples. She's
over ninety, spry as a young girl, and she's set out a wonderful table of cakes and cookies for us. I've told her I'm trying
to find out more about Grandfather. She says she doesn't
know much. I ask her what Grandmother was like and she
answers: Snobbish! With at least one exclamation mark. Do
you mean that? I ask; one doesn't dig down too deeply before
all our illusions vanish. She laughs, looks as though she has
a guilty conscience, and adds a list of positive qualities that
her mother-in-law *also* possessed. But she *was* snobbish, she
repeats. How? I ask. She was very preoccupied with her fine
family in Southern Norway, answers my aunt. And she was
preoccupied with other people's families, what the fathers did
for work, what their family names were, where they came
from. For her middle son, the one who married the aunt we're
drinking coffee with, Grandmother had picked out a suitable
wife, the daughter of a dentist. Grandmother was almost in-
sulted when her son fell in love with and married someone

other than the woman who had been chosen for him. It's said. Says the woman he married.

I've found out that Nicolai's father was Sami, I say. She nods, having heard it from her son—my cousin I met up with in Hammerfest. You didn't know anything? I ask. No, she never heard anything along those lines.

Yes, Grandmother was certainly snobbish. Now that I've been confronted by the allegation, I admit it's correct. Perhaps she was aware of having married the son of a Sea Sami and attempted to compensate for that by talking far more about her relatives, the shipowners. Or had she always been preoccupied by her background and family, and had Nicolai for just that reason kept his upbringing quiet? Or perhaps she knew, didn't worry about it, but was still proud of her Southern Norwegian relations?

I ask if my aunt knows where in the United States Grandfather went to school. She shakes her head, but knows something I haven't. She knows that once, just after my father was born, Grandfather traveled to the United States. The plan was that my grandmother and the child would follow. It didn't happen. Nicolai came home, and the family remained in Norway.

It's strange to walk through the rooms of her house and see objects from Grandmother's apartment. Objects I've seen earlier that belonged to a place I've been and that were taken from it. The toddy set in silver. A large painting by a rather well known artist. The christening cup belonging to Marie, my grandmother's mother. The table that looks like a tray; I remember it as different, much larger.

13

I dream that I'm walking through large, almost empty rooms. It's dim. A cold spring sun makes rectangles of light on the wooden floors. I call out a quiet hello. My voice frightens me. I look for something recognizable, something I can connect with something else, but I notice nothing I've seen before. I sit down on the floor, next to the wall, let my index finger trace the crack between the two floorboards. I get ash on my hand. I'm in the house at Bismervik. Not the house that Ingolv and I slept in, not the one that was built again after the war, but in the old house. Grandfather's childhood home. A few simple shelves hang on the walls, but the shelves are empty: no books, no vases or coffee cups. There's no furniture in any of the rooms. No black-painted seaman's chest. The kitchen has neither an oven nor pots and pans. No clothes hang on the porch. No tall rubber boots or Sami shoes stand along the wall. Dead flies lie on the windowsill. The windowpanes are made of wavy glass that distorts everything I see outside. The rocky shoreline, the fjord, Melkøya.

Ellinor has left in a hurry and has no idea whether she has with her what she needs. She doesn't know either how long she will have to stay in Oslo. She registers this but has no energy to be irritated about it, far less to be worried. She's forgotten things she should remember, she hasn't sent a message to the institute that she'll soon be in Oslo. Kåre knows. It makes her feel secure that he knows; that strikes her as irrational, irrelevant, but she's not able to think more about it, far less to be worried. Luckily, she's managed the first change of planes. She's so tired, heavy limbed, light headed. She falls asleep while they're still on the ground, isn't aware of anything before the flight attendant asks if she'd like coffee. She shakes her head, sleeps again, has no one in the seat next to her, then wakes with a start and the conviction that something significant has just happened. She shivers with cold, is hot the next instant, so hot that she has to grab the neck of her sweater and pull it away from her body. She has the feeling something has slipped away without her knowing what it is. She takes out the flight magazine from the seat pocket, leafs through it but can't force herself to concentrate on what is inside. Closes her eyes again, drifts back into sleep, awakens as the wheels bump the runway at Gardermoen.

She begins to walk to the right, toward the airport trains, but changes her mind and jogs out to the taxis. Ullevål Hospital, she says. Only now does she take out her cell phone from her purse, turn it on, wait. There are no messages. She calls her father's floor, stares at the driver's neck as she listens to it ring one, two, three times, then she hangs up. There's no reason to bother them; the nursing staff always has too much to do. Her calling will only be seen as unreasonable and bothersome, something that breaks up their workday unnecessarily.

She's not aware how quickly she's been moving until she arrives at the corridor where her father's room is and notices how breathless she is. She reduces her speed and walks slowly the last few steps to his room. Two white-clad people stand bent over his bed. A wave of relief washes over her, from her stomach up through her chest, and she takes a breath, fills her lungs, and lets the air and relief leak out of her nose. But then they turn, and she sees their expressions. He died at half past three, says one of them. He didn't regain consciousness, says the other. Does he say that to console Ellinor, or is it just information? Half past three. She quickly calculates where she was then: it was right when she experienced the strange feeling.

When Ellinor was a child, she had a clear picture of what a soul looked like. The soul was located in the stomach, in the region under the ribs and above the navel. The soul was a rounded little clump, about the size of a Victoria plum. Beautiful, round, smooth, rosy. The soul was a light flesh color, surrounded by a transparent membrane. She was probably influenced by the appearance of the lamb kidneys that her unmarried aunt sometimes served them for dinner. Ellinor had thought a lot about souls when her mother died. She had clearly seen for herself that her mother went to heaven, even though her father made it obvious that he didn't believe in anything of the sort. But he had been generous enough and compassionate enough to emphasize that Ellinor could, of course, be right and she was the one who must find out what she believed. She remembers that she asked her father where her mother's soul was if it wasn't in heaven. Where is Mama? He stroked her cheek, didn't want to answer. Tell me, Papa! No place, he answered, and she couldn't accept that.

She bends over and strokes her father along his cheekbone up toward his forehead. When she feels that he's warm at the top of his face but already cool on his cheeks, it occurs to her that what she sensed on the plane was her father's soul on the way to heaven. And it is a kind of consolation that she was so near him, so high up, so near both him and Mama. It is a sign. Inside her head the nonsense words from the refrain of Mama's song are buzzing: *ai, ai, ai, ai, ai, boff.* She takes his hand, squeezes it. The song reprises, she can't stop it. When the troll mother had put her eleven little trolls to bed. She closes her eyes and tries to absorb the fact that he will never again squeeze her fingers back, that this is the very last time she will touch him.

She leaves the floor, goes down the stairs to the exit. She hasn't arranged anything with anyone, knows she can call her girlfriend but also knows she doesn't have the energy to talk with anyone. Not now. Should she sleep in her father's apartment? Could she handle it? Papa's lifeless hand in hers. Mama's song. Who will *she* sing that to?

A person gets up as she comes through the door. There's something familiar about the man who quietly comes toward her. Oddly enough, it takes a moment before she manages to place him. It's Tom.

Tom is here. She moves into his open arms. He is unexpectedly tall and thin. For a moment it's foreign. Then it's just familiar. These are the arms she's had around her in good times and bad. Do you want to talk? She nods into his throat. Shall we find ourselves a place to sit down and have some coffee? She nods. He releases himself from the embrace, takes her by the shoulders and looks into her face. She opens her eyes. He has a wrinkle across the tip of his nose, she'd forgotten that. In spite of the many times she'd teased him about it (How is it possible to get a wrinkle right over your nose, so far down? If you push it up, can you make your nose into a pig snout?). I came as quickly as I could, says Tom. He was called by the hospital. Her cell was off during the flight, and Tom's number was written under hers in the record, under the heading *closest next of kin,* like a forgotten fragment of what was. Imagine, that she could forget the wrinkle. He used to answer her in the same way (Well, you'd better watch out for your own nose!), and afterward he'd kissed her. Now he says something. I think your favorite coffee bar is open. She nods. The lullaby continues to buzz in her head, blending with Tom's words, making them unintelligible. Or shall we drive back to my place? She nods again, allows herself to be led to Tom's car, the same old car, sits as if paralyzed, merely raises her arm so he can fasten her seatbelt. Tied them fast to her tail.

In 2005 the second to last speaker of Yahgan died. Now only Christina Calderón, born in 1928, is left. She has not become accustomed to the sight of her hands. They are so crooked and dry, like the branches on the tree outside the house where she grew up, in Navarino. The years lie on the back of her hands like a lattice of roots. Now and then her fingers drum in time with the lullaby in her head; the one her mother used to sing to her when Christina was going to sleep or when she needed consolation for other reasons. The song buzzes in her head, but she has no one to sing it to, for no one understands the words any longer.

Chesten Marchant died in 1676. He was the last monolingual speaker of Cornish. John Mann, born in the 1830s, was the last to have Cornish as a mother tongue. Walter Sutherland, who died around 1850, was the last to speak Norn. Norn stems from Norrønt and was spoken on the Shetland and Orkney Islands. With Tuone Udaina's death in 1898, Dalmatian was extinguished. Watt Sam and Nancy Raven, both of whom died toward the end of the 1930s, were the last two fluent in Natchez. Mary Yee (1897–1965) was the last native speaker of Barbareno. Ned Maddrell (1877–1974) was the last speaker of Manx. When Tevfik Esenc died in 1992, no one was left who had Ubykh as a mother tongue. Rød Tordensky, who died in 1996, sixty-seven years old, was the last person to know Catawba. In 1997 Vyie, the last native speaker of Sirenik, an Inuit language, died. The last person to speak Livonic, a language in Lithuania, was Viktors Bertholds. He was born in 1921 and died in 2009. Doris McLemore, born in 1927, is still living, but with her will die Wichita. When Edwin Benson, born in 1931, dies, Mandan will disappear.

46

She doesn't know if her legs will carry her all the way up there, if her voice will hold out. One minute she thinks she can manage it, the next she is convinced she can't handle either walking or speaking.

She sits in the first row. There are just a few meters between her and the casket. By her side sits Tom. He is freshly shaven, in a white shirt, black suit, and black tie. Kåre asked if he should come; he didn't ask just once, but several times. She has said it wasn't necessary. You never even met him. I would like to be there for your sake, he says, not for your father's.

Behind her, the church is full of people. They must be colleagues, friends, neighbors. She doesn't know. She nodded to some familiar faces but now she doesn't recall whom she's greeted. Her father would have liked that so many came. She tries to figure out whether it means something to her, and it does. The church is filled with hacking and coughing, shaky breathing. Restless feet on the floor. Someone blows his nose; it sounds like a trumpet blast.

She notices she's staring at the coffin and quickly looks down, at her own white hands. The pastor comes over to where she's sitting on the bench. He has on a golden, full-length chasuble. He wears orthopedic shoes with one of the laces untied. She half rises. Her white hand in his; it's shaken up and down a couple of times. The pastor wears a heavy sports watch. She stares a moment at the watch, then her eyes follow her own hand as if it's owned by someone else. He lets go, the watch disappears in his sleeve, and her hand remains in the air a moment. Now he greets Tom; a sliver of the watch is exposed again. And at that, without her understanding why or how, she senses that there's something that doesn't add up. She doesn't understand why she didn't see it long ago. Her father didn't die when she was up in the airplane; he died before she took off from the airport in Finnmark, while she dozed in her seat, with her belt on and her cell off. The feeling she got on the plane, it was merely . . . nothing. Imagination. Tiredness. Stress. Stomach gas. It wasn't a sign of anything in particular.

The pastor begins his talk. She doesn't listen, looks at her hands; she gathers he's saying something about the Resurrection. Resurrection. What is that? What does that have to do with her father? Now it's her turn. She has the prepared words in her purse. She's told Tom she doesn't believe she'll be able to give a talk, and even as she walks the few steps up to the rostrum, right past the casket, up to the pulpit, she doesn't know if she has the strength.

Ellinor goes up two steps to the pulpit. The white papers glow against the black dress. She sets the pages down in front of her, looks out over the dark-clad gathering, and swallows. The worst that can happen, she thinks, is that I'll begin to cry, that my voice will betray me, that I can't finish. It's better to give up beforehand. There's nothing more to do for him, but I can give a speech. I've worked many years at Blindern. I've given countless lectures. I have the words in front of me. I'll manage this. And she does. She manages it.

For Ellinor, standing behind the pulpit in a black dress and coming to the end of the eulogy for her father, the last two sentences are more important and more truthful than anything else. I'm glad I had a father who was so painful to lose. Dear Papa, thank you for being just who you were. Tears overcome her only as she reads the last words, as if she had held back the tears so long that they simply must come now; they can't handle staying in the tear ducts one second longer. She goes back down and sits next to Tom. His eyes are shiny, the whites are the same color as the inside of a conch shell. Like the inside of a cowrie. The pastor stands with bowed head and folded hands. Our Father who art in heaven. The congregation falls in with him, mumbling. Lovely talk, whispers Tom, gripping her hand. Forgive us our trespasses as we forgive those who trespass against us. Lovely. That must be wrong. Her talk was not lovely. She wanted it to be true, not lovely. She opens her mouth to ask. Tom squeezes her hand much too hard.

The pastor strides over to the wreaths and bouquets, reads all the messages on the ribbons. Thanks for the happy memories. Thanks for everything. He reads the name of one of the neighbors with the wrong pronunciation, and momentarily it's as if the name belongs to someone else, as if the presenter of the wreath is a stranger. And everything feels wrong.

Then it's over. They get up. Tom, two neighbors, a second cousin, and two of her father's colleagues bear the casket, three men on each side. For a second, she's confused before she sees the plan is for her to follow right behind the casket. She starts to walk, placing one foot in front of the next. She doesn't raise her eyes. The flower arrangement someone has put in her hands is so tall she can't see anything anyway. She didn't suspect that the middle aisle of the church was so long. Then she's outside. The daylight burns her eyes. The casket is already in the hearse with an open back door. Papa. A dark-clad man from the funeral parlor takes the flowers from her, puts them in the hearse together with the casket. Tom is at her side, putting an arm around her shoulders. The hearse drives off. Definitely over. Nevermore.

The sunlight is sharp, and in the flowerbeds alongside the church crocuses have sprung up—stubborn, brightly colored explosions. It should have been pissing down with rain.

For a few long moments she's alone. Tom's sleeve is being pulled discreetly by someone from the funeral parlor, who needs to have an answer to something or other. Those who've been in the church stand in an awkward, dark bunch ten or twelve meters from her. A hum of sniffling, of hawking, of lowered voices. The sound is distant and distorted, as if she hears it through a wall of water. Muffled, unintelligible. An unfamiliar language. That's how it must be when everyone else understands, everyone else is speaking, but your language is different. Milk-white, blurry faces blending into each other. Anna's face turns up among them, only to dissolve and vanish. The hearse disappears down the hill. A forgotten memory comes up; she's standing behind a fence, perhaps it's the first day of kindergarten, and she sees Papa's car drive away. She doesn't know anyone, doesn't know whom she should play with, what she should say. She is alone. She is the last. She is over forty, but she not only *is*—that is incontestable fact—she also *feels* parentless. Without protection, without a shell, without the possibility of creeping into the safety of parental arms, of holding a parent's hand that in spite of its frailty doesn't leave any doubt that she is loved, admired, protected. Parents who can speak her language, explain to her what is going on, tell her stories. Ellinor will never be a child again. Her right hand grips the left, finds the index finger and middle finger, and squeezes them together.

Then the group disperses; a couple of people in black break away, crowd around her. The words they use are meaningless:

Condolences. It's very sad. Lovely talk. He was a great fellow. At the same moment Tom comes over and stands next to her again. He speaks the same language they do. Thank you. Yes, it is sad. Yes, Jørgen was a fine fellow. A beautiful service. A really lovely talk. She is silent, shakes their hands, smiles, thanks them. She hugs one of her father's college friends, someone she knows from when she was a girl. Beige marks remain on the shoulder of his suit, from her face powder. It looks like a Chinese ideogram.

At the memorial gathering in the parish hall there are a crushing number of people. Almost all the people from the church have made their way over here. Ellinor is in high spirits. She's touched that all these people cared enough, pleased that architect Jørgen Smidt meant something to so many people.

Speech returns. It works again. She organizes, gives unnecessary orders to the servers, goes into the kitchen to see that the slices of pastry are nicely arranged on the platters. Fiddles just a little with the flower arrangements. A place for everything, everything in its place.

Tom is a sort of toastmaster, welcoming everyone, saying that he and Ellinor are honored that so many have come, *each and every one of you*. He says a few words about how he always admired Jørgen. Then he turns it over to the first speaker: the second cousin who talks about childhood memories, summer vacations, swimming and paddling. Several people jump in. One man was a fellow student of Jørgen's in architecture at NTH. Jørgen was active in Uka, NTH's cultural festival, as a songwriter, something Ellinor didn't know. One of his colleagues gives a speech. After that, a woman friend of her mother's, who came for a visit every year before Christmas and who brought lamb steak for Easter.

Ellinor listens to the speeches; she's disappointed there

aren't more, but also lightened. She appreciates seeing new sides of the father she has always known, now that it is too late to ask him. The pastry tray is almost empty, the slices of cake eaten up. People begin to leave. She doesn't want them to leave, doesn't want things to be over already. Doesn't want what will come next. But she doesn't know what to say, which magical words to use to stop the stream of sober people coming up to her, thanking her, and mumbling something about Jørgen being a fine person, a lovely talk, and yes, well, it happens to us all.

She sits down. The last dark-clad man turns in the doorway and raises his hand in a half wave. She's nauseous. Her piece of cake is covered in marzipan and sprinkled with powdered cocoa; her fork slides out of it at an angle. She runs to the restroom, supports herself against the white-tiled wall, and throws up. Tom knocks on the door and says her name. Ellinor? Ellinor, are you okay?

She is back home in Finnmark. *Home?* Back. She's back in Finnmark. Kåre meets her at the airport. She walks right into his open arms. He is stockier and shorter than she remembered. He's the one to end the embrace, holding her by the shoulders at arms' length and smiling at her. But she is the one to say no thank you to dinner and sleeping over. She briefly answers that she's tired. She can allow herself some whims at the moment; she knows he can't protest, she's in mourning and therefore untouchable. She gets out of the car, says she needs a break, she needs to think. That's fine, says Kåre. She should have known he wouldn't say more. All the same she remains standing on the steps, uneasy and disappointed, looking after the car like a little girl on the first day of kindergarten.

When she comes inside she's almost happy to see the linoleum floor, the tomato-red dial phone on the telephone table, and the stove with its two defective burners. Then she begins to cry because she didn't take the ceramic pig with her from Oslo. You're hysterical, she thinks, followed by: coffee. That solves most things. She puts the French press and mug on the coffee table next to the laptop, which has been open and untouched since she got the phone call from the hospital. She moves the mouse, taps in the password, and the document she was working on, the popular-science article about Anna and bilingualism, comes up. She was interrupted mid-sentence, it seems. "The greater linguistic self-confidence a society has, the less risk that . . ." She reads the beginning of the sentence once more, bites the pen that was lying at an angle near the laptop, and begins to type, still with the pen in her mouth. And she doesn't stop, doesn't look up for a long time. It's as if it was analysis, reflection, and writing she's missed during her stay in Oslo, as if it was exactly this work she needed now, because she writes until the coffee is long cold, until her shoulders are stiff and her eyes hurt. She drags herself upstairs, barely stops by the bathroom, and falls asleep immediately, wakes in fine fettle the next morning and throws herself into writing again. She continues in this way. She writes, barely taking breaks to go to the store, to make dinner, for necessary trips to the bathroom. The draft of the article is done in four days. She knows she's done a good job, and she sends the document off to the project manager, accompanied by a cheery email, even though she is very aware that the jokey, optimistic tone will be met with a shrug. Now and then her father appears before her: his face, his body. She sees details of his features—the pores on his nose, the long single hair in his old man's eyebrows, the one crooked front tooth—but she shoves him away, says to him and to herself that she has no time for grieving, not just now. She has other things to think about.

Kåre calls. Tom calls. She speaks to both of them without enthusiasm or a sense of being present. She's curt, saying nearly the same thing to both of them: that she appreciates their calls and that things are going better and that she's working a lot and would rather not be disturbed. Lying on her back in bed, her muscles and head aching after a long day's work, it strikes her that she doesn't have room for a hint of triumph. Nor does she have the need for it. Yet she allows herself, now and then, to acknowledge that both Kåre and Tom have called her a number of times. They have. A number of times. Even Tom. He's now finished being angry with her. They were in despair, both of them, and his despair turned into accusing anger: You should have listened to me. We should have started trying right away. You were the one who absolutely had to wait until after your PhD defense. She pushes the old thoughts away—as mentioned, she has other things to think about—and goes to sleep. Her dreams betray her, take control, surge into every crevice and crack in her body. In her dreams Kåre, Tom, and her father appear. She smiles in her sleep from a memory, she writhes in pleasure, she sits up for a moment after turning on her stomach. She rubs her face in the pillow, yawning. But after a few intense hours she wakes, unsuspecting, her brain washed clean, all traces of the night's guests removed, and her head filled anew with linguistic terms, with academic literature, with the article nearing its conclusion.

The nights and days are light, the transition between them is almost erased. Ellinor doesn't need more than a few hours of sleep. She's gotten the article back from the project manager with some comments that she immediately incorporates. She has now embarked on a weighty academic article she hopes to have accepted in an English-language journal. She must also finish her project report. But that goes slowly; she is out of the flow, out of her trance. Now she often feels like pulling her hair out; occasionally everything comes to a stop. A word on the screen, a movement outside, a familiar but unexpected sound. Almost imperceptible stimuli set off a memory, and then she sits there, frozen, with a scene or an image in her mind. She and her father at the movies, the time he lied about her age and got her into a film for sixteen and above. One of her father's regular sayings, a reply he gave once. A cup he used to drink from. One of Mama's items of clothing, the ski sweater, the old blue-checked silk dress. The portrait of her mother packed away in Oslo. She's unprepared for the grief over her mother to be renewed, to grow stronger and different. Her father, who just a few weeks ago was someone she could stroke on the cheek, hold by the hand, hear breathing, races away from her at high speed to become a collection of memories. Memories she can caress and strengthen, retouch and beautify, ignore and betray, until he becomes the way she—without consciously willing it—wishes. Her mother grows less transparent, more solid, coming closer until she and her father stand next to each other, hand in hand, as in a photograph. And after a while *that* becomes the mental image she imagines when she's sitting idly in front of the screen, or when she walks at a fast pace to the store for groceries, or when she puts on her jogging clothes in the evening. Mama and Papa, together as in a wedding picture, but different all the same. Her father looks like he did before he died, only his eyes are younger, quicker. Her mother has become an older woman, gray haired, with a soft, loose chin. Ellinor can't see her features clearly, but she knows it's her mother.

She visits Anna, knocking on the door unannounced, like the first time. She needs some factual information on language shifts, identity, and attitudes. You're the expert, after all, says Ellinor. She hasn't found what she wanted on the web, but she knows Anna has the article she needs. Anna nods. But most of all Ellinor has missed sitting in the living room, hearing her voice, drinking her coffee. She says that, too. Anna gives her a hug.

"I've thought of you every day since you lost your father," she says.

"Thank you," Ellinor says.

Today Anna is wearing a miniskirt and short jacket in blue, a green sweater, and red leggings. Like the Sami flag, thinks Ellinor. Around her neck Anna wears the amulet she had on the evening her father got sick and she and Ellinor ate *boknafisk*.

"What is that amulet, actually?" asks Ellinor. "Is it a wolf's tooth?"

Anna laughs.

"Did it belong to Ravna?"

"No, it's some expensive French thing. I bought it at Galeries Lafayette a few years ago. Made of plastic, but by a designer, which caused it to cost more than I could have ever imagined. Sit down, I'll grab the coffee and the papers."

Anna opens one of the small drawers in the desk and returns with a couple of stapled sheets. "In 1930 in the district of Sørøysund 30.2 percent of the population said they were Sami. In 1950, only 1.8 percent did. You see, people ceased to define themselves as Sami; they had become Norwegian. After the war a questionnaire was sent out to investigate whether it was realistic to offer classes in Sami in the districts. Many coastal districts in Finnmark didn't even answer, even though it was obvious from the census of 1930 that hundreds of Sami lived there—it was no longer of interest."

Anna's coffee is as good and strong as usual. She serves thin *lefse* spread with butter, sugar, and cinnamon.

"How was the funeral?" asks Anna.

"The worst thing was clearing out his apartment," says Ellinor. "Everything became so concrete, so real."

"Only bad?"

"No," answers Ellinor softly. "Good as well. Order. I needed that."

"Did you have to do it alone?" Anna wants to know.

Ellinor tells her about Tom, that he supported her through everything. The funeral, the emptying of the apartment. Anna's forehead wrinkles. I see, is all she says.

"Now the rest of Papa's life is in storage in Oslo. The dining room table he liked so much. The sofa he inherited from his father. The books. The pictures. Monogrammed silverware."

"And the apartment?"

"As soon as summer vacation is over, it will be put up for sale."

Anna stretches out a hand and pats Ellinor on the arm.

"I found a letter in the drawer of his night table," says Ellinor, and that's when her voice cracks, when it gets to be too much for her.

Anna lets her cry and merely continues to stroke her arm. And finally Ellinor is able to talk again.

"He must have written it sometime during the last days before he went into the hospital. It wasn't legible. I recognized a word or two, but long passages were unreadable. He wrote how much he loved me. He had obviously meant to gather information about the family, both his own and Mama's. Many names were there, some dates. Mama's and Papa's years of birth, the year they married. My birth date. Mama's name and his own, with some lines connecting me below. And from my name a line down to the name Regine. His brain was full of holes, his thoughts didn't hold together, but the hope he'd kept quiet about his last years, out of concern for me, found a way out. But he hadn't managed to spell my name. Elinor, he'd written, with one *l*. And that was the worst thing. I don't

know why the sight of my own misspelled name was so un-
bearably sad, but it was."

"Do you know this?" asks Ellinor a little later that evening,
and she hums the lullaby Kåre sang for her. She even remembers a couple of the words: *Biegga dutnje lávlesta.*
    "Did Kåre Os know that?" asks Anna. Ellinor hears she's
surprised. "I always sang that to my daughter."
    "Tell me about your daughter," says Ellinor.
    "Not yet," says Anna. "But one day I will. And you'll tell
me about yours."
    Ellinor looks at her, and for some reason she is quite calm
and knows that one day she'll tell Anna about the child she lost
and that she's always thought was a daughter.

Tom continues to call every day. In the beginning she's happy
to see his name lighting up the screen. She imagines the wrinkle over his nose and answers with a smile in her voice. Then
she grows irritated, answers briefly, eventually can't manage to
speak to him in a friendly way. One afternoon she asks him
not to call anymore. I only want you to know I'm here for
you, he says. Yes, she says, and her voice is thick with tears.
Just give me a little time. As she hangs up, she's filled to the
brim with gratitude. She's touched by Tom's sympathy. They
belong together, she and Tom, they have for so long. Her father with his arm around Tom's tuxedo-clad shoulder shouts
into his ear: Now she's *your* job! Now *you* are going to take
responsibility for her! Tom knew Jørgen. There's no one else
she can talk to about her father, not in that way. She could say,
Do you remember when he got so angry about that news report? And Tom could have shaken his head about Jørgen Smidt
along with her. Can you remember the time he couldn't stop

laughing? When was that? Tom might have answered. And then she would have reminded him about it, and they could have laughed together, remembering her father's neighing laughter. Her father had loved Tom from the start, and she'd teased him about loving Tom from the moment he found out that Tom had attended NTH. In her enameled jewelry box is her wedding ring. *Your Tom.* All the times in the hospital corridors, in the waiting rooms. His hand in hers. It will be fine. This time it will be fine. To wake up from the dream, but with Tom's warm, safe body right next to her. Tom's family, his big, noisy, irritating family. She would miss them.

One evening Kåre knocks on her door. She's just on her way to bed, is wearing the striped terrycloth bathrobe and the ragg-wool socks where one big toe sticks out. He says nothing, just smiles, and holds out the rounded flask of cloudberry liqueur. She's about to protest, but then she opens her bathrobe and lets him slip inside. Feel instead of think. His back is as furry as the leaves on the African violet. I've missed you, he whispers in her ear.

One day when Ellinor is visiting, Anna says she has something to tell her. Outside, in pale but convincing sunlight, a flock of seagulls fight over something edible. Anna has made reindeer-and-vegetable stew, *bidos,* and she and Ellinor sit, each with a spoon and bowl on the table in front of them.

"Well?" says Ellinor. "Now I'm excited."

Anna smiles knowingly, like an expectant child who will soon see her mother open the gift she's wrapped.

"You have reason to be. But first I must say something else. Something about the Rist family."

"Kåre," begins Ellinor.

Finally she'll get the story.

"Kåre's grandfather. What happened, happened almost a hundred years ago."

"Yes?"

"No, there's nothing more than that. A long time has passed by now. At some point you have to stop getting caught up in what is already over."

"But what actually happened?"

"Thoughts are like *stallo*s. They can grow gigantic, destroying everything in their paths. But you can outsmart them. I'm finished with that story."

Ellinor looks out the window, at the seagulls that elegantly plunge down into the waves. She draws a breath to say something, to ask more, but Anna beats her to the punch. Radiant with joy, she explains: "But what I wanted to tell you was that there's an open position at the high school here!"

Ellinor laughs. Mostly because she's surprised and doesn't know what she should say. Either about what Anna said—or didn't say—about the ill will between the families or about a job she would never dream of applying for.

"If there's one thing I'm *not* going to do, it's to be a teacher again," she says finally.

"I would have thought you'd be an extremely good teacher," says Anna calmly. "Would you like another ladleful of *bidos*?"

"Gladly," answers Ellinor, holding out her bowl.

"You know I'm a *noaidi*."

"I've heard rumors of it."

"Tonight I'll take out my runic drum. I'll steer you in the direction *I* want."

Ellinor laughs. Anna smiles. They toast with their water

glasses, clinking them together. I must hold on to her, thinks Ellinor.

"I'm always going to hold on to you," says Anna. Ellinor looks at her.

"Yes," she says after a minute. "And I to you. No matter how many miles are between us," she adds.

"The miles are shorter than you think," says Anna.

Ravna's son grows strong. He has red hair like his father; in fact, he completely resembles him. All the same, Ravna still thinks he's good-looking. He's strong and brave. Curious and stubborn. Ravna is happy to have him. She's kept to herself since Juhán was born. She doesn't want more children.

Over four years have gone by since she cut sennegrass with Benedikt. The dark time of the year has come, and Juhán begins to cough. In the beginning, Ravna believes it's just the smoke in the turf hut. But it doesn't pass. He grows weak. He refuses food. He doesn't even want *bidos*. One day Ravna knows she must take action and find a doctor as quickly as she can. She attaches her skis, wraps him up, stuffs him down in the boat-shaped sled with an extra reindeer pelt for protection around his head, goes as fast as she can to her Aunt Rakel, and leaves the child with her. Then she sets out for the town.

The streets of the town are quiet and almost empty. She doesn't recognize anything, even though she has been here a few times before. It's hard to orient herself quickly. The houses cast a shadow. The streetlamps confuse her. She goes up one street and down another and doesn't grow any wiser. She puts her skis on her shoulder, looks around, chooses a street leading up from the green-painted house. Wasn't she here once? It looks different, or is it the same white house? At the end of the street a small group of people are standing. She runs toward them; the man on the left looks Sami, at least at a distance. But the moment she opens her mouth, she knows she's made a mistake. He shakes his head, turns away. A woman in a long coat, decorated with bobbin lace and muttonchop sleeves, says something and spits at her.

Finally, on a side street, Ravna meets someone who can tell her where the doctor's house is. He points out the direction, and Ravna thanks him breathlessly and runs as fast as she can. The skis gnaw at her neck through her scarf. When she gets there, she sees a light on the second floor. She bangs on the door. A maid in a black dress and white apron opens it. Ravna asks for the doctor. The maid surveys her up and down, doesn't understand or doesn't want to understand what Ravna says. Doctor, says Ravna in Norwegian. The girl looks at her, closes the door, and makes her wait outside. After a while the doctor comes. Ravna knows who he is. Both his parents are Sami, but they had decided their son should move up in the world, and they refused to speak Sami with him. He was brought up in poor Norwegian. He studied down south, had just returned home as the district doctor. He wishes he could understand what the desperate woman in front of him is saying, but he can't. All the same, she continues to tell him about Juhán. What else can she do? She sees he doesn't understand. Ravna takes him by the arm, wants to pull him with her. He shakes his head. He gets her to understand that he must fetch someone. She sits down in the hall to wait. She sits on a high-backed chair and looks directly at her image in a narrow, rectangular mirror that reaches almost to the ceiling. After a long time the doctor returns with a man in a *kofte*. An interpreter. Ravna's words about Juhán have meaning at last, finally they're understood by someone. They pour out of her until she has no more. She's empty. The doctor nods quickly, says something. Then he gets out his skis and is ready to go with her. The doctor says it will be fine, translates the interpreter. But Ravna has no further words. She can't even manage to say *giitu,* thank you.

When they get there, her aunt is sitting next to Juhán's body. She is stroking him over his forehead and eyes. Again and again.

The trees along the Randsfjord are white. This Christmas is snowier than last year. Ingolv stretches out his hand and strokes my arm. Are you dreading it? The car is full of presents; sheaves of wheat tied with a ribbon in a bundle for the birds; grocery bags of cold cuts, a red cabbage, fingerling potatoes, nuts, dates, paper towels, dishwashing soap. In a rectangular box lie pork ribs, rubbed with pepper and salt. They need to marinate thirty-six hours before they're roasted, and it's already the day before Christmas Eve. The cat sits in a plastic cage, meowing. In the luggage space, wrapped in several layers of newspaper, is a package of frozen, thin *lefse*, already buttered. I've been up to Hammerfest again, seen more pictures, talked with more relatives, and these are the *lefse* Randi baked. Last Christmas I barely knew where Grandfather came from; this year we're eating *lefse* baked by a newly discovered relative. The girls bicker in the backseat. For a long stretch the birch trees are snow free but shiny and glazed with ice from the dampness of the fjord. We've hardly made any Christmas cookies this year. It's been limited to coconut macaroons and lemon bars. Ingolv's hand still strokes me, one hand on the wheel, the other on my arm. His hand feels heavier, soon he'll grasp my arm, he will ask me again if I'm dreading it. No, I answer briefly, let's not talk. The trees shine from the headlights.

The cat meows more loudly. Perhaps I'll have time to bake this evening? We have to cut down the Christmas tree. I must iron the tablecloth and napkins. We still don't have a gift for the eldest. We'll have to get that tomorrow morning. Do we have enough bed linen? Clean hand towels? We'll have guests both Christmas Eve and the day after Christmas.

On Christmas Eve Mama sits in the chair by the dining room table. Her eyes follow me. Watch me set the table: white tablecloth, white napkins, the old earthenware plates from Stavangerflint, red candleholders, white candles, white flowers, a cluster of elves in the middle of the table. She nods in recognition as the little elves are put in place. A few were acquired in the last years, but most of them I remember from when I was a child. I wasn't supposed to play with them, but I did anyway. Three of them are from when Mama was small, two little china elves and a beat-up elf made of crepe paper with a sack in front of him that holds a mustard jar. Mama laughs at Ingolv, who's cursing that the tree remains crooked no matter what he does. She watches us eat pork ribs at exactly five o'clock, just as we did in my childhood home. I don't know when Christmas dinner began at Papa's, but I know Grandmother served cod. We clear off the table, set out a tiered stand with the poor little Christmas cookies, cut up the *lefse* baked by my relative and put the slices on a platter. We walk around the tree, singing with our high-pitched false voices. Mama hums along, in her equally unmusical voice. She hears me swallow tears but also accompanies me through the last verses of "Oh Joyful Christmas."

The Christmas songs, the same selection we sang when I was small. Mama, Papa, my sister, and me. I had white stockings, patent leather shoes, and a plaid dress. Bangs and freshly ironed ribbons in my braids. We say the same things that are said each year. This year the pork was crackling crisp. It's so cozy when there's snow at Christmas. Thanks so much, just what I wanted!

Language is a collection of practices. On one level, it's nothing else: phonetic conventions that the members of a language group agree on. *Cat* is the sign for a furry animal with paws and a muzzle. *Woman* is an adult of the female gender. A *paperweight,* for example, can be a glass ball with internal blue, red, and yellow canes that end in flowers. And when I describe a ceramic pig, other speakers can recognize words I use and can more or less visualize it. Common linguistic practices are a prerequisite for communication. But languages are customs in another way, customs inherited by a family. Like the choice of Christmas songs and the order they're sung in. Names of baby toes. Rules and exceptions. Lullabies. Good-night songs that one generation sings to another. When Mama was small, her mother sang a lullaby to her, "Dear God, I'm Thankful," and I sang it to my children. Routines at bedtime. I lie in my bed in my room. My pajamas have countless small dogs printed on them; I try to see how many different ones I can find, but I always get mixed up. On the closet door I have a picture of Bambi. Soon Mama or Papa will come in to sing to me, tuck the comforter around me, give me a last hug before sleep. Before I know how it happened, I'm the one sitting on the side of the bed singing to two girls with pajamas with a different pattern, and soon I'll probably be sitting and singing a lullaby to one grandchild or another.

Inherited words and phrases. Where do they come from? For how many generations have they been told? The little brandy chest, the "drunkard." It belonged to Great-great-grandfather, the district sheriff. Did he call it the drunkard? The pedestal created in flame birch. The seaman's chest. Was that Grandfather's term? Papa never said that dinner was ready; he just whistled or sang "Now there's food to eat, now there's food to eat, bring your knife, spoon, and fork." Who taught him that? Isn't it possible that men in the military were called to meals like this, with the aid of the bugle? Could Grandfather have whistled or sung the same thing? How do family sayings arise? Stupid, half-funny phrases one uses within the family. Some are carried on. Some disappear.

I belong to a card-playing family. Whether Grandfather liked cards, I have no idea. My three other grandparents all played cards. Bridge above all, but also card games. As early as 1910 my great-grandmother in Gjøvik was a member of a bridge club with eight ladies. Mama told me that. Evenings of cards, afternoons of bridge. Easter break, summer vacations, weekends at the cabin, always with a couple of decks of cards on hand. The etiquette was important. *Card play* was a phrase I learned early. You dealt out, clockwise of course, one single card to all, except for casino, where you dealt two at a time. It's strongly forbidden to pick up the cards before all are dealt out. If you're playing bridge, you have two packs, and one is already shuffled, so the partner only has to take one off the top before dealing. You lay the tricks out nicely in a pattern. To do it any other way is unthinkable and bad card play. *Make a game, grand slam, rubber.* You clear your hand, you're sitting with a single king of spades, or with the fourth queen in reserve. These are common vocabulary words for all card players. I say the words aloud, the cat pricks up her ears. The sound of the words, the feeling they leave afterward in my mouth, the sight of them on the computer screen bring up the image of a table, the folding card table, its surface covered in green baize, the marvel of such a surface, the feeling of stroking the baize. And on the table: the pads of bridge paper, the small pens used only to add up the game results. The clinking of glasses, the triumph in Mama's voice when she and her partner carried out a boldly played rubber.

Some of the expressions I've heard from the time I was tiny are still probably used only within the family. When someone plays a nine, one of us always comments, "Nine pulls the ace," meaning that when someone plays a rather high card like a nine, then it's followed often by an ace on the table. I know that my mother's mother said this, in her meticulous, old-fashioned way of speaking Norwegian with the clear, rolling r from Sunnmøre. I know that my parents said it. I say it. If Ingolv and the girls don't beat me to it. If an ace, a two, a three, and a four all appear on the table, everyone breaks out with *"Skål!"* And my father often said, as a friendly reminder to me as a less skilled bridge player than he was, "Remember the poor children in London!" That is, the poor children in London had to go hungry to bed because their fathers had forgotten to take the trump from their opponents. Where did that come from? Are we the only ones who say that? Is it an allusion to a Dickens novel? I have no idea.

Chicky and troll baby, Mama's pet names for my sister and me, for the grandchildren. Maybe Mama was called that when she herself was small? Sayings and adages she fell back on: Don't let the sun go down on your anger. The lazy man would rather carry something so heavy that he falls down dead from the weight rather than make two trips. *Qui vivra verra.*

I've maintained that Grandmother used to say that you can't take it with you. It's not true she said that. I've heard the phrase many times but can't recall if Grandmother said it. She could well have said it; it fit with who she was or in any case with what she has become in my mind—but I don't believe she did. But I allow her to say it. And I allow her to be right about it. Of course she's right. That's probably the point of the meaning of things, my possession of them. The dead take with them their voices, thoughts, hands. Their smile. The smell of a warm body, the sound of shuffling steps on a parquet floor. After they go, there's nothing left but inherited objects and passed-down words to cling to. The rest you have to make up.

We're having guests. The carpets must be vacuumed, the ingredients bought, the meal made, the table set. After many years of marriage the division of most tasks is a given. Others are negotiated each time. Who's going to the store? Him? Me? Both of us? It's ice cold even if it's March; the sidewalks are slippery, snow is in the air. I don't feel like going out. I don't want to go out. Suddenly it's the most important thing at this moment. *I don't want to go out.* Ingolv vacuums the carpet and along the baseboards. I set the table. The Rosenthal china. White napkins, triangles underneath the silverware. Tangen glasses. An old-fashioned table. A table Mama could have set. A table set for guests when I was small. Will *you* go to the store? I shake my head, get out the candles. Shall we go together? he asks. I shake my head and hope he'll just resign himself and go out. One of my fingers strokes the edge of a Tangen glass. A delicate tone is barely audible. Are you sad? Ingolv asks. I shake my head: can't he go? I've made the grocery list and everything. Are you thinking about your mother? Ingolv asks. I look at him. I've been thinking of her and noticing that the table I just set could have been set by her. But I'm not sad in the way he means, not in the way I have been. All the same, I nod. And of course Ingolv goes off alone and shops for what we need.

266

Grief is like a daughter. In the beginning it was with me all the time, clinging to me, never letting me go, not for a second. It craved my body, my attention. Then grief was like a little girl, who left me in peace for several hours at a time while she went off elsewhere. Now the grief is like a teenage daughter. Someone always there, whom I never forget about but who lives another life and lets me live, and who occasionally makes the most unreasonable demands.

So you got out of it for now, says Mama. I've found the serving spoons. Outside the snow comes down more thickly. She laughs. She laughed often. Just don't make a habit of it, she says.

Finished! The manuscript is written. Now comes the best part. Revising, reading sentences aloud, letting the words vibrate unfamiliarly out into the room, through my eardrums. The cat shakes her head and pricks up her triangular ears. She listens. I listen. Sniff, taste, substitute one adjective for another, cross out a word, a whole paragraph. Clean up the tenses. Much will continue to happen; the text will open up in places, call for more or something different. In other places, the text will close itself off, avoiding my gaze. What once was important can now be a matter of indifference. And something I imagined was an insignificant detail swells both in volume and meaning. But the foundation of the story is in place. I know that, and it's a relief.

It's a Friday in March. I sit in a bar, along with a few writer colleagues. We've been at a meeting. Now we're drinking Calvados, dry white wine, gin and tonics. We didn't do it, but it wouldn't be unlikely if we'd toasted my almost completed manuscript. We could well have done that. At the very least I'm certain that my thoughts, in pure joy, swept through the manuscript in the course of the evening. Writerly conversation, mild intoxication. People spoke of their editors, of the smell of a newly published book, of a book review that took itself too seriously, of e-books. We toasted.

A vague unease about the children comes over me, a maternal restlessness. I dig out my cell phone from my purse to make sure that no child has called or texted. They haven't, but I have a voice message from a number I don't recognize. At the same moment a text arrives from my male cousin. I take a sip of Calvados before I open it, imagining it to be a pleasant greeting, wishing me a good weekend, and therefore I have to read what he's written twice before I manage to understand it. "You'll have to write a new chapter of your novel! Our fathers had a half brother in Nordmøre."

There's been a gap in Nicolai's life from 1910, when he was fourteen and a student at the district school in Alta, until he married Astrid in the fall of 1921. I haven't discovered anything other than that in the course of those years he educated himself, probably in the United States. The need to know more about Grandfather has gradually faded away. It's not that I'm no longer curious, but I feel I know enough. I know what I need.

Nicolai Nilsen. My mysterious grandfather who, up until I began this book, was only an attractive man in his single photograph, who had only appeared in some vague stories as a father who took his sons on fishing trips. My almost boundless ignorance, my half-conscious desire to shape the past so it fit me, my reverent fantasies, my naivete turned him into a hero who fought to get the education he wanted, who found love, who died a sacrificial death caused by his job. The story became this: Nicolai, the ambitious man from the North, met a young woman with the same education but a completely different background. They fell in love, my grandfather and grandmother. The summer they were engaged, he held her hand tightly; perhaps he brushed a crumb lovingly but

269

quite unnecessarily from her cheek. They married, had three sons. The firstborn was my father. My, what a lump of fat, exclaimed Grandmother's mother the first time she saw her grandchild. It's said. Later, Nicolai made a sailboat for his son, which sometime in the 1960s was passed on to my cousin, the only male descendant after Nicolai. "The three boys from Notodden," my great-grandmother Oline called them. She was proud of them. It's said. Olaug writes that in one of her letters. I write that. Nicolai dies, leaving behind three sons. I've understood how difficult it must have been to be them, to grow up without a father. I've missed him on their behalf. On their behalf I've raged at the injustice and powerlessness they must have felt, the three fatherless boys.

But now there are not three but four. And one of them has been fatherless his whole life. From the time he was born, November 18, 1919—three and a half years before my father. Mikal. In the church register, Nicolai Nilsen, Hammerfest, is recorded as the father, but Mikal is all the same *illegitimate*.

～～

The unanswered message from a number I didn't know is from Mikal's son. He calls back, and this time I answer.

While I squeeze the phone between my ear and shoulder, I search for photos of him on the computer. At first I think this is something that I, amazed and overwhelmed, am just imagining, but after the conversation I show the pictures to the considerably more restrained Ingolv. And he also sees it: Mikal's son resembles us. He resembles my father, he resembles my cousin. He has the Nilsen nose.

A completely new half cousin and I speak together for forty-five minutes. There hasn't been much talk about this story in his family, so he doesn't know much. Again I'm putting together a jigsaw puzzle with a male cousin.

In 1919 Nicolai lived in Trondheim. Trondheim? I say. I never heard Grandfather was in Trondheim. What was he doing there? It was probably because he was studying. Oh, I say. At NTH, the cousin believes. I don't believe that, I say decidedly. Nicolai wasn't a civil engineer, only an engineer. Of course, he could have started at NTH and dropped out, but I never heard that. I don't know, says the cousin. Apart from what he was doing in Trondheim: Nicolai meets Ingeborg, two years younger, from Nordmøre, who was a waitress in a café where Nicolai used to go. If they were in love, if they had a long-lasting relationship or if it was a brief affair, no one knows. Ingeborg became pregnant, at any rate. Whether she was the one who didn't want him, whether they agreed that it was best to part, or whether he betrayed her is also not easy to say. Nicolai saw his son once, just after he was born. He never contributed money to raising the boy. And he never contacted either Ingeborg or Mikal. Mikal never was given a toy sailboat by his father.

When Nicolai and Astrid married in 1921, Nicolai had a son already. My father wasn't Nicolai's firstborn. Did Astrid know that? Or did Nicolai keep it hidden from her? There's nothing at any rate to suggest that "the three boys from Notodden" suspected they had a half brother.

The strangest thing of all, a coincidence that seems like something from a novel: When Papa graduated from NTH, he started working at Årdal and Sunndal Factory. At the time, his half brother was working there, the almost four years older Mikal. Perhaps he and my father talked together, standing next to each other in the smelting hall. Perhaps some passerby thought for an instant that, really, the two of them looked quite alike, seen in profile, Mikal and the new engineer.

～～～

And the *tankekors*, the mysterious paradox: Nicolai, who is he now? A cunning deceiver? A fellow with such a powerful social ambition that it overrules everything else? In his plans, a relationship with a waitress is a step in place, not a step upward. Ingeborg is listed as a "servant girl" in the church register. His child is a stain on his reputation, and he moves on. Refuses to have anything to do with his son. And when he gets engaged to Miss Astrid Jacobsen, an educated woman, born the same year as Ingeborg but with a desirable background in many ways, he concealed his language, his upbringing, and his son.

It could have been completely different.

～～～

I'm visiting my two female cousins on my father's side. They both live in Trondheim. They are practical people, of course they are. True, only one of them has a degree in engineering, but on the other hand she's become a professor of chemistry. Dinner, coffee, cake. It's wonderful to see them again. The last time was Grandmother's funeral. We help each other remember. Together we recall the doves on Grandmother's roof, the gloomy backyard with weeds through the asphalt and a view of a small soda factory. And Grandfather? They don't know any more than I do, they say. We talk about the sailboat he made that their brother now owns. I tell them about the seaman's chest. They shake their heads. They have never heard a word about it. The shooting prizes Nicolai won, the silver trophy cups. We remember those. He took his sons, all three, out fishing and hunting, I say. Again, I'm touched by the thought of Papa and his younger brothers and the far too few years they had with their father. It definitely wasn't like that on their vacations, says one of the cousins. Oh, I say. No, Grandfather left his wife and children in the hotel while he went out fishing and hunting, the other cousin adds. Oh well, I say. I guess maybe times were different then.

On the wall hangs the same photograph of Grandfather that I've always known, but this is a lighter copy. His features are blurrier, the contrasts stronger.

We've been emailing the past months, these two cousins and I, and I've told them about the three objects from Grandmother's apartment that I remember best: the Venetian paperweight, the puzzle cross, and the conch. Both cousins remember the conch; both have held it up against their ear and listened to the stories inside. None of us know where the conch ended up when Grandmother's apartment was cleared out. Neither recalls the puzzle. And the paperweight: one of the cousins has brought it to dinner. Now she takes it out of her purse where it's been protected by a knit sock. For a second I visualize it, all the details, the clear colors, the small flowers at the tips of the glass canes. She gives me the wrapped paperweight. I recognize its heaviness and shape. I recognize the sense of holding it. Then I take it out of the sock. It's different from what I remember, completely different. Am I disappointed or just bewildered? I take a picture of it with my cell phone, and I'm looking at the picture now as I describe it, the day afterward, in a hotel room with a view of the river, the Nidelva. The colors and the pattern in the glass aren't what I'd remembered. There are actually no flowers inside; they are more like swirls. And I had forgotten that there was white inside—in spite of white being the dominant color. The five air bubbles I can't remember at all.

Could Grandfather have studied here in Trondheim? Yes, maybe, the cousins hesitate, then one of them wonders if she might have heard something about it once. For me, Trondheim has always been a city wrapped in myth. I grew up with stories of NTH and its many student organizations and mountain cabins for students. A northern pike named Jonathan, a new one that each year was set free in a fountain in a deserving hotel. Parties with lab-made alcohol. Papa was in charge of one of the mountain cabins. When Mama began to study at NTH, in 1949, there were so few women that they were all featured in a single photograph in the newspaper. My mother's father had gone to NTH, along with uncles, distant relations on both sides, and later cousins, male and female. I grew up hearing the songs and drinking ditties from one of the student associations, Smørekoppen. They were sung particularly on car trips. I'm now the one who owns Mama's albums from her years in Trondheim. There was something about her in the student paper, something about hoping she wouldn't fall as far down as her father did when he was taking chemistry classes in his day; apparently he had once fallen down an elevator shaft. Grandfather Nicolai has never been part of the stories from Trondheim. But perhaps it was also his city for a time.

At the city archive in Trondheim I get an answer. Nicolai Nilsen moved to Krambodgata 18 in Trondheim on February 15, 1918. He is a *machine worker*. He was a student at Trondheim's technical college from the fall of 1918 until he graduated in the spring of 1920. *Chemical engineer*. My mother's father studied chemistry at the more prestigious NTH, beginning in 1919. I allow myself, for a moment, to picture them, my two grandfathers, side by side, in a café, each with his beer and each with his glass of port—a *potion*, as this combination was called in Trondheim student jargon, according to what Mama and Papa taught me. That my mother's father and my father's father could have met and struck up a conversation is merely a fantasy, of course. The only thing I know is that Grandfather at one time or another in the course of the period he lives in Trondheim meets Ingeborg. They didn't cut sennegrass; maybe he bought her a meal, perhaps he brushed away a crumb from her cheek, maybe they went hiking together or strolled on Nordre Street. The child was born six months before Nicolai graduated. He finishes up, travels to Kristiansand, meets Grandmother there, marries her a year later.

In 1910 Nicolai was a student at the district school in Alta. That's in the census. He was probably still there in the spring of 1911. What he did in the years until he moved to Trondheim in February 1918, I don't know. Perhaps it's during this period when he traveled to the United States; perhaps he never went to school in America, perhaps it's something I made up? He did something at any rate that gave him the right to be called *machine worker* when he registered at a new address in Trondheim. Did he save money? To study for two years cost a lot. I don't know. And yet I now know enough.

Finished! Ellinor raises her hands over her head, grabs one hand with the other, and punches them straight up three times, as if she's won a sprint challenge and now is paying tribute to herself along with a packed stadium. She's embarrassed as she drops them again, placing her hands nonchalantly behind her neck, leaning her head back and looking around the room. She's finished with her project report. Now she's completed what she came to Finnmark to do. Half in defiance, half in arrogance, she creates a nice title page. She composes a restrained email and sends it, attaching her report, to the project manager. Then she goes upstairs and begins to pack. She is still chock-full of energy. She must think about getting back to Oslo. It's beginning to be urgent. This is her last month with a salary. The well-proportioned and healthy physical therapist has confirmed, quite without Ellinor asking about it, that she will be out of the apartment by the fifteenth, as promised. So there will be an end to the rental income as well. Ellinor will have to take up copyediting work again. She has come so far up the stairs that when she stops, the embroidery of the three stylized people in *kloster* stitch are at eye level. Mother, father, child. One foot is already on the way up to the next step. She stands with her weight on the foot that is planted on the lower step. She might have to sell the apartment, find a smaller one?

It's a possibility. The apartment has too many rooms, is too large and impractical. Why does she need an extra bedroom? She doesn't want to think about that room. She gets out her biggest suitcase from the closet in the hall, puts it on the bed, folds one sweater, sets it inside, and then she's completely exhausted. All the tiredness she hasn't felt during the past several weeks washes over her at once. She removes the suitcase, falls down into the bed, barely manages to pull the comforter over her before she's asleep. She has one last thought, that the door is unlocked on the first floor.

For the next twenty-four hours she mainly lies under the comforter. Kåre calls her, but she just sends him a text message that she's not quite well. *OK, see you later,* he answers. Of course he answers that. She is downstairs making coffee when the telephone rings. She jumps, thinking for just a second, before she remembers, that it's from her father's floor at the hospital. It's the project manager. Congratulations, he says, this is solid work you've turned in. Thank you, she says. He's praising her! That never happens, at least it's never happened to her. She walks around with the phone while he talks, catching a glimpse of herself in the mirror. She has an enormous smile on her face. Have you read the email from the institute's administration? No, she says, turning her back on the mirror. That smile was far too wide. Now the criticism is coming. Take a look, says the project manager, and he hangs up.

She remains sitting for a long time with the computer on her lap after having read the message. The head of the institute also congratulates her on well-done work. Ellinor has to read the next paragraph several times: she's being offered the opportunity to continue in a three-year project position at Blindern. The salary is far higher than what a humble linguist could expect. She could get back everything. Oslo. The apartment. The job. She should celebrate. Coffee. And doesn't she have a bar of chocolate in the cupboard? She should rejoice. And that is what she's doing, without a sound, when her cell rings again. It's Tom. She lets the phone ring. She can talk with him later. First, Anna must get the good news.

Ellinor awakes, her body unsettled. The bedroom is bathed in sunshine, but the clock says it's only half past three in the morning. She jumps out, runs down to the first floor, feels a strong need for coffee, boils water, fills the French press, drinks half a cup, pushes it away in disgust, as if coffee is the last thing she could imagine. She goes out into the living room, is restless without understanding why, sees how filthy the windowpanes are in the sunshine, decides to leave them as they are but to do the dishes. This is one of the very last times she'll stand in this kitchen with checked linoleum floors and crooked cabinets. It's one of the very last times she will wash up by hand, get her hands wrinkled because she still hasn't gotten it together to buy rubber gloves, look at the nasty bits of food and globs of fat floating in the dish tub. Soon she's going home to her own apartment, with a dish-washer, heated floors, and familiar, self-chosen furniture, and with a sushi restaurant around the corner. She goes over to the window, gazes out. The trees have light-green buds that seem as though they're about to burst even as she stands there looking. Her eyes fill with tears, overflow, the wetness pours down her cheeks. I'm grieving for Papa, she thinks. That is allowed. And tonight Anna is coming for dinner. I'm going to tell her what she has meant to me, say that I admire her resolve and strength, say that I want us to always be friends. We will hold fast to each other. No matter how many miles between us. And in the morning I'll meet Kåre and tell him I hope we can continue to be in touch. He can stay with me when he visits Oslo.

When Anna comes in the evening, she brings a present, wrapped in tissue paper. It appears to be one of the Greenlandic *tupilaks*.

"Thank you," says Ellinor, overwhelmed. "It's lovely."

"Lovely? Strange adjective choice."

Ellinor peers at the little figure that at first glance merely looked comical and sweet, and she almost jumps. Now she sees the distended nostrils and the gaping, evil smile.

"You see? You must bring him back here with you. He wants to be together with his brothers."

"Aha. But does Inuit magic work here in Sápmi?"

"Yeah, you know. Indigenous people. Same shit. Listen, tomorrow morning when you go to the airport, I'm going to be standing in the window with my runic drum. *That* works."

They share two bottles of Spanish red wine, smiling at each other with blue teeth. Toasting to friendship, to Sápmi, to good coffee. It's after three o'clock in the morning, in the middle of the night, when Ellinor walks her home. It's light, the sun shines like mad. People are out in their gardens, trimming hedges or grilling hot dogs. The fjord is teeming with boats. In the local paper there was an article that this year too the reindeer had enjoyed eating all the tulip bulbs. It's soon midsummer. And it's only six hours until Kåre comes for a farewell breakfast.

~~~

The suitcases are in the trunk. Her laptop case and purse are beside her in the backseat. She wonders if it's the same taxi driver who drove her to the house when she moved in almost five months ago, but she's not certain.

She had served Kåre eggs and bacon for breakfast.

"You understand, I know," Ellinor had said. "The job, the apartment, my girlfriends."

279

"Of course I understand."

"And then you can come for a visit, stay at my place," Ellinor had said.

"Thanks. And what about Tom?"

And that was when Ellinor realized she hadn't thought about Tom.

She sums it up for herself, there in the backseat of the taxi: apartment, girlfriends, job, sushi restaurants, coffee bars. But not Tom. Him, she's finished with. Oslo! How happy she'll be to come home. She decides she'll have a lager at Aker Brygge, and then take the boat out to Hovedøya. Decides to go to the Colosseum, to the theater with the biggest screen, and see a film there, no matter what it is. Ellinor smiles. The driver catches her smile, turns in his seat, and says conversationally that yes, now it's nice here, with the midnight sun.

And there I leave Ellinor. I've gotten her a job, secured her apartment. She's smiling on the way to Oslo. The city she grew up in, the city I grew up in, the city Mama grew up in, with gentle, rounded hills, well-trodden paths in Nordmarka, ski runs, and swimming beaches. Cafés, galleries. Coffee bars for Ellinor, tea houses for me. The city she loves, like I love it, like Mama loved it. I feel I've organized everything quite well for her. I've planned for so long that it will happen like this, that she will be offered a job at Blindern, that *she* is the one, and not Tom, who will choose or not choose the relationship. I count on her to choose no. Perhaps she'll take a tango class and meet a guy there. Perhaps she'll meet someone right after the film at the Colosseum?

Ellinor looks out the car window, at the low trees, at the houses—she glimpses the roof of Anna's house—at the sea, at the mountains that are snowy white far down their slopes. The taxi speeds up; in half an hour she'll perhaps be already checked in. In an hour she'll be on the plane, on the way home.

But Ellinor refuses. She defies me. Or maybe it's Anna who defies me. Ellinor asks the taxi driver, who of course is the one who drove her to the house that day after the new year, to turn around. The driver does as she asks. And I remain standing again, watching the rear lights of the car until they completely disappear around a curve.

Helene Uri is a Norwegian writer whose work has been translated into more than a dozen languages. Trained as a linguist, she is the author of more than twenty books, including *Honningtunger (Honey Tongues)* and *De beste blant oss (The Best among Us)*. She teaches creative writing and has been a board member of the Norwegian Language Council and on the jury of the Nordic Council's Literature Prize. She lives in Oslo.

Barbara Sjoholm is an award-winning translator of Norwegian and Danish, as well as the author of many books of fiction and nonfiction. Her translation of *Clearing Out* received the Nadia Christensen Prize for Translation from the American-Scandinavian Foundation.